SURRENDER

Titles by June Gray

SURRENDER

JUNE GRAY

BERKLEY BOOKS, NEW YORK

THE BERKLEY PUBLISHING GROUP
Published by the Penguin Group
Penguin Group (USA) LLC
375 Hudson Street, New York, New York 10014

USA • Canada • UK • Ireland • Australia • New Zealand • India • South Africa • China

penguin.com

A Penguin Random House Company

This book is an original publication of The Berkley Publishing Group.

SURRENDER

Berkley trade paperback ISBN: 978-0-425-27214-5

An application to register this book for cataloging has been submitted to the Library of Congress.

PUBLISHING HISTORY
Berkley trade paperback edition / November 2014

PRINTED IN THE UNITED STATES OF AMERICA

10 9 8 7 6 5 4 3 2 1

Cover photos: "Couple": Rolfo / Getty Images; "Birds": Melinda Fawver / Shutterstock.
Cover design by Lesley Worrell.

To my fellow writers.

Keep writing, my friends. Keep trying.

ACKNOWLEDGMENTS

To my husband, Mark, for your never-ending support and epic bookkeeping. I appreciate all that you do so that I may be able to focus on writing.

To my daughters, Amelia and Abigail. Thank you for your patience, hugs, and kisses. If there's one thing I want you to learn from me, it's this: Your dreams can come true through a lot of hard work and a bit of luck. So work hard and dream big.

To my beta readers: Lara, Gillian, Shannon, Kerry, Liza, Victoria, and Beth. It's been quite the journey, ladies! Thank you for all you've done.

To my mom—aka "Boon"—who once again came out to stay with us while I wrote this book.

To bro-in-law Matthew, for putting up with my incessant texts asking about your time in Bagram. Thank you for going above and beyond, you Crazy American!

To my agent, Kim Whalen, for your guidance and expertise, and to my editor, Cindy Hwang, for this great partnership. Thank you, ladies, for believing in me. To Tara, Kristine, and Nina: thank you for all the help!

And once again, a huge thanks to the readers. Thank you for sticking by me when I wrote about Elsie and Henry, and thank you for coming back for Julie and Will. I hope you've enjoyed reading this series as much as I have writing it! This book marks the end of the Disarm series, but it is by no means the last you'll hear from me.

For more information on future releases, visit my blog at authorjunegray.com.

Once you have tasted flight,
you will forever walk the earth
with your eyes turned skyward,
for there you have been,
and there you will always long to return.

—Leonardo da Vinci

PART ONE

ASCEND

Over Five Years Ago . . .

"I don't think that kind of love—the kind you read in romance novels—actually exists."

Jason Sherman, my boyfriend, fixed me with a skeptical stare. "You don't?"

"You do?"

"I've seen it. It exists," he said in a tone that brooked no argument. "Three words: Henry and Elsie. Those two are so in love with each other but are too dumb to figure it out."

"You said they weren't even dating."

"No, they're not. I should just knock their heads together to give them a clue. Everyone else knows but them." Jason slid his arm under my head and gathered me close. "Anyway, that's the kind of love I was talking about. Sometimes you just love someone without even knowing."

I studied his handsome face, jaw scruffy from not having shaved for a few days. I liked him, more than anyone I'd ever known in my life, but did I love him the way his sister felt about his best friend?

Was the fact that I was questioning my feelings a sign that I already did?

"Do you, um, want that with me?" I asked, afraid to meet his eyes.

Jason touched my chin and tipped my head up. "I want everything with you."

"What if I can't love you like that?" I asked. "My parents' marriage was pretty screwed up. I don't know if I even know how to be a good girlfriend."

"You're doing fine so far."

"Fine?"

He laughed, the sound rumbling in his chest. "You're a great girlfriend, Julie Keaton," he said, cupping my face and kissing me tenderly. "And that's why I was talking about the kind of love that burns so bright it lights you up from the inside—because that's how I feel about you."

A lump caught in my throat and it took a few minutes to figure out how to breathe around it. "What if I can't love you the same way?"

"Stop questioning yourself, Jules," Jason said, kissing my forehead. "It will happen naturally."

"Okay," I said. "I'll try."

I settled onto his chest, my muscles finally starting to unwind. Talk of love and of the future had always unnerved me. I could lay all the blame on my parents for the way I am with men, but deep down, I knew that my actions were my own. The fact that I was inept at love and relationships was my own doing, but maybe, just maybe, I'd finally found the right person to trust with my heart.

"Will you write me romantic war letters while you're deployed?" I asked after some time, toying with the trail of hair below his navel.

"E-mail is faster," he said with a grin. "And I'll call whenever I can."

I slid my hand down and took hold of his already swollen shaft, pressing my lips to his Adam's apple. "Will you dream about me?"

He groaned, his hips arching up to my hand. "Every fucking night." Then he flipped over and crouched over me, his eyes raking over my naked body. "I'll remember you just like this."

"Unshowered and smelly from hours of sex?"

He dipped his head and pressed his face to my chest, nuzzling my breast with his bristly cheek as he inhaled deeply. "You smell perfect—like sex and sweat and me."

"Jason," I said, grabbing what I could of his short hair and lifting his face to mine. "I do care about you a lot. You know that, right?"

His eyes pierced mine, so blue and bright. "Then show me."

I gripped his shaft and guided him to my entrance, taking all of him into me, loving him the only way I knew how. I gasped as he withdrew then slid all the way back home, opening my legs to allow him farther inside.

"I love you, Julie. When I get back, I'm going to take you back to Oklahoma City with me."

I stilled, my legs wrapped around his back. "You will?"

"Just try and stop me," he ground out before thrusting back into me. "Nothing's going to keep me from you anymore."

1

The lonely seagull caught my eye as I jogged, and I followed it along the water's edge, picking up speed to keep up. Eventually the bird turned toward the horizon, its silhouette dark against the brilliant orange and blue Monterey sunrise. I stopped to catch my breath, the view of the ocean before me stealing the air from my lungs.

I closed my eyes and lifted my face to the wind, tasting the ocean breeze on my tongue. I gazed back out at the sea and saw a lone figure out on the water, sitting on his surfboard and biding his time. When a large wave rolled by, he caught it and leapt onto his board effortlessly, crouching down as the ocean carried him along. He took a few rapid steps to the front of his board, looking as if he were just floating above the waves, then cantered back to the center of the board. He rode the wave to the shore, standing tall until his board finally sank under the water.

He paddled back out again to wait for another wave, traversing the ocean as if it were nothing but air. I watched him, mesmerized, as he caught another wave and flawlessly sailed back to the shore.

"Morning," he called out. It was only after he said it again that I realized he was talking to me.

"Oh, hi," I said, watching as he tucked the board under his arm and ambled closer. It was only when he was a few feet away that I noticed he towered over my five-foot-ten frame. I took in his full-body wetsuit, appreciating how it accented his slim hips that flared up to wide shoulders.

"A little early for a morning run, isn't it?" he asked with a smile in his eyes.

"A little cold for surfing, isn't it?" I countered, raising an eyebrow as I sent a teasing look down to his crotch.

He grinned, and if I thought the sunrise took my breath away, his smile inflated me with a strange buoyant feeling. I smiled back, unable to help myself. "Not going to lie, it's pretty cold," he said. "There's definitely some shrinkage going on."

I burst out laughing, taken aback by his crude kind of charm, the kind I liked best. "Well, your board is plenty long enough to make up for it."

His eyes widened, and suddenly he was laughing along with me. "You know what they say about men with longboards," he said, standing his surfboard upright beside him.

"No, what?"

"That we have plenty of wood to wax."

I let myself go as we dissolved into a fit of laughter. It felt good, trading jokes with this stranger. It was the first time in a long time that I actually felt light and without care.

He held out a hand, his dark brown eyes trained on me. "I'm Neal."

"Julie," I said, surprised to find his hand warm. I took a moment to look him over, to his wavy light brown hair tinged with gold, his straight and narrow nose, and the boyish smile that curled up at the ends. "Have you been surfing all your life?" I asked, hoping to keep him talking for a little while longer.

"Yeah, for the most part. I grew up by the ocean, actually. You can say salt water runs through my veins." He ran his fingers through his wet hair, slicking it back.

"I understand. I love it here."

"Do you live nearby?"

"I'm actually from out of town. Dallas."

He grinned. "I'm just visiting for a few days myself. Born in San Diego but have lived all over."

It was only then that I noticed the sun had already risen. I glanced down at my watch and gasped. I'd been at the beach for almost two hours. "I have to go."

"It was nice meeting you, Julie," he said, flashing me that smile that was making me wish I didn't have anywhere else to be.

"I'll be back tomorrow for another run," I called over my shoulder.

"I'll be back tomorrow to surf," he said, shooting me a look that warmed me from the inside. "Maybe I'll see you again."

I made it back to the Shermans' house in ten minutes and parked the rental car in their driveway. My son, Will, and I were in town for Elsie and Henry's wedding and were staying with the Shermans the entire weekend, the couple whose son I'd promised to marry before he'd been killed in Afghanistan. I'd offered to get a hotel but they wouldn't hear of it, telling me that I was family even if my son was the only one technically related to them.

I sometimes still wondered what would have been if Jason hadn't died and we'd gotten married. Would I be a different woman today if I'd had Elodie Sherman, and her daughter, in my life for the past several years?

I would have been a lot less lonely, that's for sure.

Inside the house, I found Elodie in the kitchen, pouring pancake batter onto a griddle. "Good run?" she asked, turning her attention to the scrambled eggs.

"Kind of chilly, but good," I said, walking around the island counter. "Do you need some help?"

"I think I've got everything under control," she said, and handed me a mug that had an Air Force logo on it. "Help yourself to some coffee."

"Oh, me, too, please." Elsie came around the corner wearing jeans and a top, her hair in a messy bun. She grabbed a mug from the cabinet and playfully hip-checked me out of the way.

"And where have you been, young lady?" I asked with a wink. "Sneaking out to see a boy?"

Her mother sighed. "You and Henry live together and are getting married tomorrow. You couldn't even go a few hours without seeing him?"

Elsie laughed, her cheeks taking on a pink tint. "I just went to say hi," she said, hiding her face behind the mug.

"I'll go wake up Will," Elodie said, shaking her head at her daughter. "You two set the table."

When we were alone, I turned to Elsie and said, "He's not going anywhere. You *know* that, right?"

She cocked her head, the easy smile gone. "I know, but I just had to make sure," she said, taking the stack of plates to the table. "I woke up this morning and for one second, I thought he was back in Korea and we were broken up. I had a bit of a panic attack." She laughed nervously, trying to ease the tension in the room.

I hadn't known Elsie for long, but I'd immediately felt a bond with her from the moment we met. Even after his death, Jason had somehow managed to bring this beautiful, flawed, wonderful woman into my life. And for that, I was grateful. "I hear it's perfectly normal to freak out right before the wedding."

"Did you?"

I thought back to my own wedding to Kyle—the man who had stepped up after Jason died and offered me a life of security—to those final seconds before I walked around the corner to face the entire church. I'd known even then that I didn't love him, at least not the way he loved me, but I'd hoped at least to grow fond of him. "No. I didn't freak out. But that's because I'd already accepted I was making a mistake."

She nodded distractedly, pinching at her lip. "But even if Henry and I were already married, it's not like a ring on his finger will keep him from leavi—"

"Elsie," I said, cutting her off. I grabbed her by the shoulders and peered in her face. "Henry is not going anywhere, I promise you. That man regretted every day that he was without you."

She took a deep breath and nodded. "I know. You're right."

"You two are going to live happily ever after. I just know it."

"I hope so." A moment later, her eyes narrowed and the smile on her face transformed to something more calculating. "Henry told me there'd be a few eligible bachelors at the wedding . . ."

I backed away. "Oh, no, you are *not* going to fix me up."

"Why not?"

"Because."

"When was the last time you even had a date?"

"A while, but it doesn't matter. I don't want to be fixed up." When she opened her mouth to argue, I cut her off. "I've already met someone, anyway."

"What? Who? Where?"

Though I hadn't been thinking of him specifically, the guy on the beach came to mind. "I met someone at the beach. You wouldn't know him."

"Bring him to the wedding."

"No, thanks."

"Why not?"

"He's from out of town. If anything were to happen between us, I want no strings attached."

"You're not going to find love if you never give the guy your phone number."

"I'm not looking for love. All I want is a quick scr—"

I stopped in time as Elodie came back in the kitchen with my sleepy-looking son in tow. "This kid sleeps like the dead," she announced.

"Just like his dad," Elsie and I said in unison. A second later, our eyes met in horror after realizing we'd just made a dead joke about someone who was, well, dead.

"I have lots of things in common with Dad, huh?" Will asked, breaking the awkward tension in the room with his excitement.

"Yeah, you do," I said, ruffling his hair. "Let's go sit down and see if you eat like him, too."

After spending the day running errands and making decorations for the wedding, we all walked down the street to have the rehearsal dinner at the Logans' house.

During our e-mails while he was in Korea, Henry had talked only briefly about his childhood, but even though he said very little about his parents, it was clear he didn't think much of them.

Still, I found his parents pleasant enough, if a little aloof. They were the complete opposite of my own parents, who had loved each other with a destructive fire, fighting and making up, then fighting some more, until it destroyed them both.

I'd figured out long ago, as they lowered my father into the ground, that I didn't need that kind of passion in my life, that I would be perfectly happy as long as I kept my heart guarded.

I suppose I owed my parents some gratitude because that lesson was the reason I was able to survive the death of Jason at all.

2

I made my way down to the sand in my running gear and searched the length of the dark beach, a little disappointed to find that I was completely alone.

I walked along the water's edge, avoiding the silent roll of the waves, taking in the orange glow emanating from the horizon as the sun greeted the day. Out here, along this long stretch of beach, I felt like the only person in the world.

A strong breeze blew by and wound around me, circling me, covering me in an invisible gauze. I fixed my eyes on a point on the horizon and lifted my arms, extending them out to the sides, a bird in flight.

I imagined flying far from shore, directly out over open waters to leave my past behind. I soared for miles, beating my wings against the harsh winds and the storms gathering in the distance. Nothing mattered in that little pocket of time but the open, endless sky and me.

When I finally opened my eyes, the sun was higher, infusing the dark blue sky with golden colors. I found Neal standing beside me, not in a wetsuit but in running attire, watching me with eyebrows furrowed.

I felt the smile tugging at my lips and didn't bother trying to contain it. "I thought you weren't coming."

"And miss seeing the first light of the day on your face?" He studied me, hardly blinking. The corners of his mouth curled up as he shook his head. "I wondered yesterday if you were some sort of siren," he confessed. "I mean, there I was, minding my own business, when this impossibly beautiful woman just showed up by the edge of the water. If you'd asked me to swim down to the bottom of the ocean with you, I probably wouldn't have been able to say no."

I laughed at the corny line and the realization that it was actually working on me. "You're cute. But I'm not of the sea."

He nodded. "I see that now. You're something else, a creature of the air."

I turned toward the ocean, slightly embarrassed that he'd seen me at a moment of pure honesty. Neal followed suit, not saying anything more. We remained like that, standing together in comfortable silence, for long minutes.

"What's on your mind?" he asked after some time.

"That sunrise is my favorite part of the day," I said, which was only partially true. "You?"

He reached out, tangling his long, warm fingers through my own. "I was thinking of doing that. And this," he said, touching his lips to the back of my hand.

My skin was tingling when he pulled away, the memory of the kiss still lingering. "That's all?" I asked, unable to help myself. I hadn't been entirely serious when I'd told Elsie about wanting a one-night stand, but now I was beginning to think the idea had real merit.

Neal raised an intrigued eyebrow, making me wonder if he could read my thoughts. "What else would you like? This?" He lifted the sleeve of my sweatshirt and kissed the inside of my wrist, pausing a few seconds to feel my pulse against his lips.

The thrill of desire tore up my arm and crashed into my racing heart. I wanted more, wanted him to rip off my shirt and kiss every inch of my skin, but was too hesitant to express it. Once upon a time I'd been good at this—had been able to bring a man to his knees with just one look—but the years after my failed marriage had made it so that I no longer had confidence in myself.

But then again, in our short time together, my ex-husband, Kyle, had never incited the kind of lust that was currently pulsing through my veins. Kyle had been the safe choice, the man I thought would give me the life that Jason had promised. And Kyle had tried to do just that, but our marriage was a sham and we both knew it.

"Julie?"

I came back to the present to find Neal had pressed my hand against his chest.

"Where did you fly off to again?"

"Doesn't matter," I said, intent on focusing on the present so that this moment wouldn't pass me by. "I'm back now."

I tilted my head back and studied his face. In the glow of the morning light, I could see that he had a nice golden tan, that his brown hair was tinged with blond, his eyes were not brown but actually the kind of hazel that changed depending on the light. Right then it was a mossy green as he stared down at me with furrowed brows.

His gaze flicked down to my lips then back up to my eyes. I held my breath and, tired of waiting, grabbed the back of his head to bring his mouth to mine. Our lips parted on impact, our tongues ebbing and flowing. He tilted his head and deepened the kiss, wrapping his arms around my back and almost lifting me off my feet.

I was light-headed when we pulled away, and I felt a trembling beginning low in my stomach. When I looked up at him, his eyebrows were drawn together, his eyes flying across my face.

I hesitated, wondering if I'd read him wrong. "I thought you—"

He took hold of my face and kissed me again, deeper this time, his tongue dipping deep inside my mouth to tangle with mine. He pulled away, surprise on his face. "This isn't why I came here this morning," he said, brushing hair away from my cheek.

I smiled up at him, my entire body still tingling. "I did."

He let out a surprised laugh. "You are something else, Julie. No beating around the bush with you."

"I don't know. Beating around the bush is definitely encouraged."

"I walked right into that," he said with a warm smile.

"So let's do what you came here to do." I turned on a heel and raced off down the beach. He ran after me, his laughter and heavy breathing right at my back. I lengthened my strides, opening my body up to the run, willing him to follow.

He kept up, comfortable at the blistering pace I had set. He didn't say anything as he slowly caught up to me, his longer legs eating up more space.

"Doing okay?" he asked through short gusts of breaths.

I sped up even more. "I'm good. Why, you getting tired?"

He pulled ahead a little, flashing me a meaningful look. "I'm fine. I can go for hours."

"So could I," I said, pumping my arms to go even faster.

We raced each other along the shore for a time, leaving two sets of footprints on the sand behind us, until we slowed and eventually came to a stop. I tried to catch my breath, holding my arms above my head, happy to see that he, too, was winded. I turned to face the ocean, and all of a sudden he was in front of me, blocking the view with his solid body.

"Got you," he said breathlessly, hooking his hands on my waist and pulling me close.

I leaned into him, feeling his firm body against mine. "You've definitely got me," I said, not wanting any misconceptions about our time together. "But just for today."

His expression darkened as his eyes blazed across my face. Without another word, he walked around me so that my back pressed against his front. He gripped my wrists and lifted them back up to my head. "Keep them here," he said in a voice deep with authority.

He unzipped my sweatshirt slowly, peeling the material away from my chest to reveal my purple sports bra.

"This is a public beach," I managed to say despite the tightness in my throat.

His warm hands traveled up my damp skin and cupped my breasts. "There's nobody here. We're completely alone," he said, rubbing my nipples to hardness with his nails.

Emboldened by that revelation, I moved my hands to the back of his head and craned my neck around, bringing his lips down to mine. He kissed me, his tongue twisting around as his fingers toyed with my pebbled nipples.

"I'm going to make you come right here, right now," he rasped against my lips.

I froze, his words making my heart skip a beat. Then a hand slid down the sweat-slick skin of my stomach and stole into the waistband of my running capris, and my poor heart just about gave out.

"If you want me to stop, you have to say so because I have no plans of being a gentleman right now," he said in a low, sexy tone. Gone was the affable guy; this man behind me was taking charge, his voice dripping with promise.

I didn't say a word; I couldn't. I simply watched him work his way deeper into my pants, his hand's outline clear under the stretchy gray material. He gasped when his fingers made contact with the bare skin of my mound. "Fuck," he whispered against my ear. "You are full of surprises."

I was about to say that waxing down there was no longer so strange when his middle finger slid down and caressed the sensitive area between my folds.

My body responded to Neal's touch, wanting more, *needing* more. The cold wind felt good against my overheating skin, intensifying the pulses of pleasure traveling through me.

"I want to fill you up like this," he said and crooked a long finger into me. I closed my eyes and groaned. "You're so ready for me." Another one joined the first, stroking me deep within, reaching that tender spot with the pads of his fingers as they slid in and out slowly.

I held on to his neck for support as my legs quivered. He wrapped his arm around my chest to hold me up, grasping my breast almost savagely as his fingers continued their delicious slide. Then he twisted his thumb so that it was rubbing directly on my clit and the pleasure tripled, quadrupled.

"Neal," I cried out. "Faster."

"No," he said in a gruff voice and continued the unhurried assault. "I plan on drawing this out."

"Just do it." I squeezed harder, focusing all my energy on that one area of my body. "Make me come or I'll do it myself."

He chuckled and his hand stilled. Then he began short strokes on my G-spot, wriggling his thumb, the new sensation building me up. I crested just as he bit my earlobe, and I threw my head back onto his shoulder, moaning long and high as the sensations washed over me in waves.

He kissed the heated skin on my neck as he gave me one last stroke before pulling his hand out. "Next time I'll be inside you when I make you come," he growled.

I took a few moments to recover, for my entire body to stop throbbing from the release, then turned in his arms. But before I could return the favor, a dog barked in the distance and its owner's voice called out to him a second later.

Neal pulled me against him and kissed my hair tenderly, a move that took me aback. Somehow it felt more intimate than what we'd just done a few minutes before. "Come back to my hotel room," he said against my hair, his voice husky with promise.

I studied his face, lust tingeing his handsome features. "I want to say yes . . ."

"Then say it." He gripped my ass and clutched me against his hard length. "Let me finish what I started."

In that moment, I was almost convinced that a bridesmaid wasn't really necessary in the wedding. It wasn't like I was maid of honor. "I can't," I said with a sigh. "But for what it's worth, I really want to."

He bent his head into my neck, releasing a noise between a sigh and a chuckle. "Damn. I wanted to spend the whole day with you."

I nuzzled his cheek. "Tomorrow?"

He lifted his head, his eyebrows high. "You're giving me another day?"

Right then, as my insides throbbed with need, I would have given him a whole month. "I'll try my best."

He grabbed the back of my neck and tilted my head back, kissing me slowly, a promise of things to come. "Beautiful Julie," he said against my lips. "After tomorrow you're going to be begging me for another day."

"Cocky," I said, pulling away and immediately missing his warmth.

He grinned. "You have no idea." When I was farther up the beach, he called out, "Wait! How do I get ahold of you?"

I called out my cell phone number and he recited it back. "Don't forget it," I warned before turning and running back to my car.

3

"Julie, where have you been?" Elodie asked as soon as I stepped in the door.

"I'm sorry. I lost track of the time."

Elodie was already wearing the signs of stress on her face. "Your son's already eaten breakfast and he needs a bath. We need someone to collect all the decorations and help set up at the beach. Then we need—"

I held the older woman by the shoulders. "Deep breaths," I instructed like I sometimes do when Will has a tantrum. "It'll get done. Try not to stress about it, please. I'm sorry I was late. I'll get right on it, promise."

Elodie gave a short nod and wandered back down the hallway to Elsie's room. I followed her, entering the room next door, where I found Will sitting cross-legged on his dad's childhood bed, playing with several die-cast airplanes.

His face lit up when he saw me. "Mom! Mom! Did you know these were my dad's old toys?"

I nodded, trying to ward away the sadness that threatened to overwhelm me every time I entered this room. My eyes remained glued to my blue-eyed son—the spitting image of his father—too afraid to look around lest it bring back old memories.

"Come on, kiddo," I said, ruffling his blond hair. "Let's get ready for Aunt Elsie's wedding."

After I dressed and did my makeup, I found mother and daughter in the kitchen, placing decorations in a box on the counter. I gently pried the shells from Elsie's hands, taking over the job. "I'll get these down to the beach," I said. "You still need to get ready, Els."

"What about Will?" Elodie asked, her hair only half-styled, making her look a little like one of the ladies on *Ab Fab*.

"I'm all ready!" Will announced beside us. My chest felt tight at the sight of my son looking so much older in his tan suit. It didn't seem all that long ago that he was a tiny, chubby thing taking his first steps.

I bent down and wrapped him in my arms, fighting the urge to get all gooey and teary eyed. The truth was, I was one of *those* moms, the one who cried when she dropped off her kid on the first day of school, the one who kept her baby's first onesie and took it out from time to time to sniff. To see my son getting so big was both a joy and an ache.

Before leaving with the decorations, I stopped in Elsie's room as she was fixing her hair in front of the closet door mirror. She looked up at me and I recognized the sadness in her eyes. But it wasn't from reservations about the guy she was going to marry; rather, it was the sorrow of a sister who wished her brother was alive to attend her wedding to his best friend.

I sat on the bed behind her, wishing I knew the right words to ease her pain. But then again, if I did, I would have told myself long ago. "I have something for you," I told her reflection. "A 'something borrowed.'"

She turned around and looked at me expectantly. "Something of Jason's?"

I nodded and pulled out the medal. "Jason's Purple Heart," I said, handing it to her.

Her eyes misted over as she touched it gently. "How do you have it?"

"Your dad gave it to me for safekeeping during their first visit in Dallas. He asked that I hold on to it until Will was old enough to understand." I had stared at that medal for hours that night, unable to sleep.

Elsie nodded, taking deep breaths.

"I'm sorry. I should have given it to you before you applied your makeup."

She let out a short laugh. "Probably so." She stood up and gave me a warm embrace. "Thank you, Julie. This really means a lot to me."

During the ceremony, as I stood to the side with the bridesmaids, watching Elsie bind herself to the man she'd loved all her life, Jason's words came back to me.

The kind of love that burns so bright it lights you up from the inside.

A person only had to take one look at the expression on Henry's face—at the way his eyes were soft around the edges, the elated smile he was fighting so hard to contain—to know that theirs was a love that spanned lifetimes.

My eyes watered at the thought that I hadn't felt that way about Jason, that even though I loved him with all I had, in the end it hadn't been enough.

I turned away from the bride and groom, blinking quickly, and looked out over the small group of guests. None—save for Elodie and John—looked familiar, but there in the back, almost a head taller than the rest of the guests, was a handsome face framed by brown hair tinged with gold.

After the wedding party's procession back down the aisle, Neal stood up and made his way toward me, rubbing a hand through the scruff on his cheek. He wore a light blue sweater and gray pants that were folded up at the hems to reveal bare feet. He, too, seemed to be considering my outfit of a dark blue sleeveless cocktail dress, my blond hair twisted up into a loose chignon. Our eyes met after the quiet appraisal and we exchanged smiles.

"What are you doing here?" I asked.

"Henry and I go way back," he said, pushing his sleeves up his tanned arms. "What about you?"

"Friends with both of them."

He took a step closer, his eyes almost a light green in the late afternoon light. "This is a nice coincidence."

I stared up at him, unable to form words, the memory of that morning flashing back in my mind.

"Don't think this means you get out of tomorrow." He reached out and took my hand, and I became all too aware of everyone around us.

I took a step back, looking around for Will. "I have to go help with the, um, food."

"Do you need a hand?"

"No." I looked down at our intertwined fingers. "But I'll need this one." I walked off, relieved to see that Will was playing with a few others kids, digging a large hole in the sand, and hadn't seen me holding hands with a stranger.

I managed to avoid Neal during the reception by staying busy, yet a part of me was also relieved that Will was old enough not to need his mother at all times. I kept glancing over at Neal, who seemed to be having a good time on his own, talking to other guests and looking relaxed in his surroundings.

After the sun set and people began to dance in the light of the candles, I found I could no longer avoid the inevitable. Or maybe I just couldn't stay away any longer. Either way, my body propelled itself in Neal's direction, with a slice of cake as my offering.

"You've been avoiding me," he said with a raised eyebrow, accepting my offering and taking a bite.

"I have," I said sheepishly. "It's like my secret world and my real world suddenly collided. I wasn't ready for that."

He grinned. "In this scenario, I'm the secret boyfriend, right?"

"I think you ought to buy me a secret dinner first before earning that title."

He set the plate down on the table behind him and leaned into me. "Would you like to take a walk along the shore?" he whispered.

To answer, I took his hand and led him away from the party.

We walked toward the water, leaving behind the soft light from the reception. Here the darkness veiled us and allowed me to shed my worries for a few moments.

He stopped and turned to me. "So tell me something about yourself, Julie."

His question caught me by surprise. I'd thought he was leading me there for a repeat of the morning. "Like what?"

"Like . . . what were you like at fourteen?"

"A bit of a deviant," I said with a chuckle. "That was the year I lost my virginity."

He laughed in surprise. "Wow. That's . . . at that age, I was still trying to get a handle on things, if you get my meaning."

I grinned, unabashed. "What can I say? I was a bit advanced for my age," I said. "Why, when did you lose your virginity?"

"I was eighteen. It was with some girl I just met."

"Ah, a one-night stand."

"I suppose, though I saw it more as a helpful Samaritan willing to help me out with a problem."

"What problem?"

"That I was eighteen and still a virgin," he said with a laugh. "Actually, up until then, I was dating a girl through most of high school, but she made me wait, saying she'd made a promise to God that she wouldn't have premarital sex."

"Let me guess—she ended up cheating on you with another guy?"

"No, not at all. After we graduated, I realized I just didn't want to be that committed yet. My whole life was ahead of me; I wanted to go to college, see the world. The last thing I wanted was to get married and tie myself down. So we broke up, our respective virginities intact." He turned to the ocean, a faraway look on his face.

"You loved her," I said softly.

He turned back to me. "I guess. At least, at the time I was sure I did. But I don't regret breaking up with her," he said. "Last I heard, she's married and now has two kids and a fulfilling career. So you see, her life wouldn't be as good as it is now if I hadn't broken up with her."

"So you did her a favor by breaking her heart?" I asked with a teasing smile.

"Not exactly. I'm just a big believer in things happening for a reason," he said, giving me a pointed look.

"Why, Neal, you're a romantic at heart," I said, affecting a Southern Belle accent, trying to steer away from the serious turn in our conversation.

He shook his head, a smile playing along his lips. "I just think there are no coincidences in life. That the universe put us in exactly the right place at the right time."

I broke away from his gaze. "I'm not so sure about that theory. What about people who die unexpectedly?"

"I'd say it was just their time to go."

"That's a heartless way of seeing things."

"It's not heartless; just realistic. You can't outrun or cheat death. When it comes for you, you can either go down with a smile on your face or go down fighting. Either way, you're going down."

"I can't believe that." I wrapped my arms around myself, but they weren't enough to keep the wind from seeping bone deep. Neal came to face me, shielding me from the wind. "I take it someone you loved died?" he asked, his face too earnest and intent for my liking.

"My fiancé." I swallowed the lump in my throat and shook my head, reminding myself that this weekend was about fun, that it was only about two people having consensual, hopefully mind-blowing sex. "We don't need to talk about it," I said, reaching out and grabbing a handful of his sweater. "Let's just keep this thing between us as uncomplicated as possible, okay? Talking is overrated."

"Okay, then." He took a step closer, all traces of gloom wiped from his face. "If we can't talk, then we're going to dance."

I hooked my hands around his neck and he wound his arms around my waist, his hands a pleasant weight on the small of my back. I craned my neck to look up at him, tracing every curve and angle of his face with my gaze, from his strong nose to his square jaw.

He bent down and whispered, "I thought about you all day." One of his palms splayed on my back and pulled me closer so that our bodies touched. I shivered at the contrasts, from the warmth at my front and the cold at my back, at the softness in his expression and the hardness of his body, at the intensity of his views on death and the easygoing attitude that quickly took its place.

I leaned my head on his shoulder. "I haven't been held like this in so long," I murmured, then realized belatedly what I'd said. I was only too glad that the darkness hid the blush that was no doubt coloring my face.

"That's a damn shame," he said, bowing his head to rest his cheek against my temple. "A woman like you should always be held like this."

I closed my eyes and breathed in his scent, soaked up his words. He smelled like the sea after a storm, clean and cool, and his words were like rolling waves that lapped at the shore, smoothing out any imperfections in the sand.

"Let's get out of here."

I tipped my head to look up at him, considering his offer. Below the surface of my skin thrummed not just lust but something far more scary and complicated: genuine affection.

I jolted out of his arms, holding a hand against his chest to keep him at bay. He said nothing, just waited patiently while I sorted through the jumble of my emotions.

I stared up at him while a war raged inside me. My brain wanted out because I was getting attached already, but my body wanted in, oh, so *in*. The memory of that morning washed over me like cold water, raising goose bumps all over my skin. There was no denying I wanted his body, but could I sleep with him and somehow not also want the man?

I let out a frustrated breath. "This never used to be an issue."

"What?"

I shook my head. "Nothing," I said, looking back toward the twinkling lights of the reception. "Let me check with Elsie first, make sure she doesn't need me anymore . . ."

I scanned the beach as we headed back, not finding Will. My heart immediately started thumping wildly while my brain went into overdrive, as it always did whenever I lost sight of my son.

Trying to stave off the panic, I walked faster, leaving Neal behind.

"I have to go." I started running, still furiously searching for my son. Henry was the first person I ran into. "Have you seen Will?" I asked, making sure Neal was not within earshot.

He motioned toward the concrete steps that led up to the street. "The colonel and Will are walking around somewhere, looking for you."

I sagged with relief.

"There you are," Elodie said, coming up to us.

"Have you seen Will?"

"Yes, he's in the car with John. He's tired so we figured we'd take him back and put him to bed. That way you can stay here and enjoy the rest of the party."

"You don't mind?"

"Not at all." She flicked a quick glance over my shoulder and smiled. "You stay and enjoy the rest of the night."

"Thank you," I said, relieved that I was free to leave with Neal yet guilty at the relief of being without my son. Being a mother is always complicated, but never more so than when another man enters the picture, battling for attention.

After Elodie left, I turned back to Neal and found him standing by the bonfire, looking so damn delicious with his hands in his pockets, his wavy hair blowing in the wind. A shiver racked my body in anticipation of what the rest of the night had in store.

He held out his hand. "You ready?"

I wrapped my arms around myself and smiled.

I sure hoped so.

4

Back in college, when I first met Jason Sherman over spring break, I hadn't been looking for a relationship. Certainly the last thing I expected when we went back to his hotel room was a friendship that spanned years, a love affair that burned bright, then extinguished, then just as quickly rekindled.

All I'd wanted was one night of pleasure from a handsome guy who seemed decent and kind, but that one night had turned into two, then three, and soon he was saying good-bye at the airport, promising to come see me in New York.

"When can I come visit?" he asked, kissing me in front of my friends, who had already entered the security line.

"Anytime you want," I said, feeling a strange sensation in my belly at the thought of having to say good-bye. "I'm going to miss you," I said, surprised to actually mean it.

"Don't worry. I'll see you soon," he said, giving me one last squeeze before letting me go. "You fly on home, little bird."

"Julie," my friend Veronica said as we watched Jason walk off down the terminal. "Be careful with him."

"What? Why?"

"He's not your usual." When I feigned ignorance, she continued, "You know, the usual kind of guy you sleep with. That guy—Jason—is different."

"How do you know?"

"Because you're already attached."

I waved her away with a laugh, pretending she wasn't right.

"If what I'm saying is not true, then when we get back to school, I dare you to call your usual booty call, Paul, and have sex with him."

"What's that got to do with Jason?"

"Nothing." She gave me a meaningful look. "Or everything."

I chewed on her words the entire plane ride, miffed that she was insinuating something bad about Jason. When we landed in New York, we headed back to our apartment and met up with other friends. I went about my life, pretending I hadn't just met the nicest guy on a sleazy beach in Florida, denying the fact that I felt his absence like a punch to the gut.

I didn't end up calling Paul, which was just as well because it wasn't long before Jason made good on his word and came to New York.

"I think we should keep this casual," I told him at the end of the three-day sexapalooza.

"I like you a lot, Julie," Jason said, scratching his head. "I thought you felt the same way."

"I do. That's why this has to end. I'd rather we end it now, on a good note, than later, when it becomes messy and bitter."

"Who said it had to be that?"

"It will. I know it," I said. "We live too far away for it to work."

He pulled me close. "I wish I could figure you out."

"You and me both."

Before he boarded his flight back home, Jason asked why I'd waited until the end of the trip to break it off with him.

"Because I'm selfish," I said ruefully, wishing we were back at my apartment so I could be selfish one last time. "I wanted to enjoy your company first."

He smiled, a sad sort of smile that still popped in my head every now and then. "Enjoy my company," he echoed with a chuckle before picking up his backpack and getting his ticket ready. "Well, you take care, Jules. Good luck with everything."

Neal opened the door from the hall in the Monterey Plaza Hotel and I stared at the beautiful room inside, my head cloudy with doubt.

I could feel his dark gaze on me, heated and intense. "You okay?"

I blinked up at him, my stomach in knots. "I think I've forgotten how to do this."

The lines around his eyes crinkled. "Then I'll have to reeducate you." He bent down and lifted me into his arms, carrying me across the threshold and into the room in one easy motion. He loosened his hold at the foot of the bed, allowing me to slide down his body before my feet touched the floor.

I turned away and took a deep breath, wishing I had my youthful fearlessness back. Funny how time makes us aware of what we have and what we stand to lose.

I sensed Neal looming behind me, felt the wall of heat he was giving off. "What's on your mind?" he asked, touching the pad of his finger to the back of my neck. Then he reached up and pulled the clip out of my hair, sending my hair tumbling loose over my shoulders.

I closed my eyes, the trembling in my stomach traveling outward. I wanted so badly to be impetuous and brave, to turn around and take this man by the belt buckle and ride him until exhaustion. "I'm . . . I guess I'm a little nervous."

"Don't be." He took hold of my wrist and lifted my arm above my head. Then slowly, he began to press lingering kisses from my wrist down my arm, pausing at length at my shoulder before moving to the other arm. He splayed both his palms on my back, his touch light, and brought them upward, sliding them up over to the sides of my neck, then to the front, where he cupped my chin and tilted my head back and to the side.

With my pulse racing, I submitted to the gentle movements as the anxiety slowly meshed with desire. He brought his lips down on the side of my neck, breathing a low rumbly sound against my skin while his hands slid down the front of my dress, tracing and molding to my curves. His fingers found the hem of my dress and stole under, caressing and exposing my thighs.

He bit my earlobe. “Lift your arms,” he said in a raspy voice.

I did as told and enjoyed the sensation of the satin fabric gliding across my skin, setting me into momentary darkness as it slipped over my head. He placed the dress over the back of a chair and returned, his fingers whisper-soft as they trailed down my spine.

“You’re not wearing a bra.”

I twisted my head and looked at him over my shoulder. “The dress wouldn’t allow for it.”

He bent down, his mouth inches from mine. “Oh, I wasn’t complaining,” he said a moment before taking my mouth in a searing kiss. His hands snaked around to my stomach and pulled me roughly against him, pressing my ass against his erection. “I’m very grateful to the designer of that dress.”

The chuckle died in my throat when his palms slid upward and cupped my breasts, which were heavy with want. I closed my eyes as he pinched my nipples between his fingers, rolling them between his thumb and forefinger until they were hard like pebbles.

I languished in the beautiful torture until I couldn’t bear it anymore. I twisted in his arms, all trace of nerves now completely gone, and grabbed the back of his head. “I want you naked. Right now.”

"So demanding," he said but stepped away, his eyes fixed on mine as he undid his belt. A confident smile played along his lips as he grasped the back of his sweater and pulled it over his head, taking his undershirt along with it. A second later, his pants pooled around his ankles, and he stepped out of them, kicking all articles of clothing aside. He stood before me with his hands on his waist, legs planted apart, looking so very pleased with himself. As he should be.

Neal was beautiful in his masculinity, with his wide, muscular chest that tapered down to slim hips with the iliac crest indentation on each side. He flexed, and his stomach muscles popped up, revealing his defined six-pack. My eyes traveled downward, to the point at which his athletic thighs met and his impressive cock stood tall and thick.

"Look at you," I breathed, congratulating myself for picking a perfect specimen with whom to have a fling.

He took a step closer, hooked a finger on the front of my thong panties, and pulled me against him, the skin-on-skin contact eliciting a moan from my lips.

"No, look at *you,*" he whispered, pushing my panties down my legs, allowing me to step out of them. "You really are a beautiful, mythical creature."

He walked me backward until we reached the wall, his eyes pinning me in place. "Open your legs," he said, urging my thighs apart with his knees. Then, without warning, he dropped down to his knees, riveted by the sight before him.

My heart thudded wildly at the sight of him, at the fact that this sexy man was kneeling before me, intending to undertake dark deeds with my body. "I haven't done this in a long time," I said, the nerves sneaking back.

"How long?" he asked, his breath tickling my thighs.

Years and years. "Too long," I breathed.

"Then I'll make it worth the wait," he said with a grin before taking hold of my ass and pulling me toward his face.

The shock of his warm tongue against my bare skin almost made my legs buckle. I leaned against the wall for support as he kissed me, his tongue darting through my folds and caressing my most sensitive spots. With his chin, he urged my legs farther apart, and he dove in once more, taking hold of my throbbing clit between his teeth before his tongue went back to work.

I squeezed my eyes shut. "Ooohhh . . ." My hips rocked of their own accord, seeking more of him. He groaned against me and slipped two fingers into my cleft, massaging that sensitive spot inside while he continued to pleasure me with his tongue.

All my inhibitions dissipated when I gripped his hair and ground into his face, the pressure building and building. "I need you inside me," I said between moans. "I want to squeeze your cock."

He sat back on his heels, his chest heaving as he licked his lips. "What else?" he asked with a ragged breath. He stood up and walked to the dresser, his back turned to me as he ripped open the condom packet and applied it. "Tell me what else you want."

"I want you to take me against this wall, make me come so loud your neighbors will wish they were getting fucked, too," I said, feeling like my old self again, that same woman who knew what she wanted and wasn't afraid to demand it.

His muscles rippled under his skin as he stalked toward me, his cock impossibly large and proud. "I love it when you talk dirty." His body slammed into me, and he grabbed my hair as he kissed me roughly. "Julie," he said between breaths, "I don't think I can be gentle right now."

I grabbed hold of his cock and squeezed, making his entire body tense. "I don't want gentle. I want you to fuck me."

He let out a strangled gasp then grabbed me by the hips and

flipped me around. He took my wrists and planted my hands on the wall above my head, then tugged my ass away from the wall. The swollen head of his shaft teased at my opening but he made no move to penetrate. "If you want it, come and get it," he ground out against my ear.

I pushed away from the wall and backed onto him, moaning as he slid partway in. I retreated, then slammed back onto his shaft, shivering as he pierced me even deeper. I pulled away one last time but before I could move, he grabbed my hips and plunged into me to the hilt.

"Fuuuck," he groaned.

I clenched involuntarily, almost climaxing from the fullness of him. Vibrators did not even compare to the feeling of this thick shaft, warm and pulsing inside me.

"Yes," he whispered as he slid out then drove back in so deep it lifted me to my toes. "You feel so amazing," he said, nipping at my shoulder.

I could only hiss out my agreement as he did it again and again, his movements unhurried yet almost savage in their intensity. I felt helpless pinned against the wall but it was a beautiful surrender, a laying down of arms. For this moment, I was without armor and it left me feeling vulnerable and powerful at once.

The pressure built and built, winding my muscles tight, until he thrust in and broke me apart. I screamed as the orgasm racked my body, filling my veins with lightning.

He crushed his mouth to my neck and came with a growl, his cock embedded firmly as he spent his seed. After several seconds, he laid his forehead against my shoulder, breathing hard, still holding me tight.

When my legs threatened to buckle under me, he pulled out then lifted me in his arms and carried me to the bed. "Hold on," he said before disappearing into the bathroom to take care of the condom. He came back a few seconds later and sat on the side of the bed, trailing his fingers along my sides, an inscrutable expression on his face.

"What are you thinking?" I asked, touching the light brown hair covering his thighs.

He shook his head. "I don't think you're ready to hear it." Then he crawled over and kissed me tenderly, aligning his naked body along mine on the bed.

"Try me."

He stopped, his eyes lit with mischief. "No."

I opened my mouth to protest but he cut me off with a deep kiss that I felt all over my body. By the time he drew away, I'd all but forgotten what we were even discussing.

We had sex again and again, filling the time between with conversation, until the sun's rays began to peek around the thick hotel curtains.

"If you could be anything, do anything, what would it be?" he asked, brushing his fingers through my hair.

"I'd be a dancer in New York," I said without hesitation. It was a dream I'd already lived, before I'd given it up for love. "Or really anywhere. I just want to dance again."

"What else?" he said, his eyes drifting shut. "Tell me something else about you, Julie."

I leaned over and kissed his eyelids. "Why don't you sleep already?"

"Because," he murmured, gathering me in his arms, "I have a sneaking suspicion you won't be here when I wake up."

"That's true. I have to get going."

He buried his face in my hair, his nose nuzzling my cheek. "Stay."

I let out a soft sigh and lay in his arms for a few moments, indulging in a fantasy where I was caught in a state of loved-up bliss. I watched him sleep peacefully and, in the quiet darkness, gave myself permission to imagine him fitting in my little family and becoming the father that Will deserved.

But, like all fantasies, this, too, would never come to life. Will and I would go back to Dallas, and Neal would go back to wherever he lived, and never would our lives intersect again. Just like I originally intended.

I slipped out of his arms a few minutes later and dressed, casting him one last regretful glance before making my way out of the hotel, the tug in my belly proof that I hadn't done enough to protect my emotions. I walked away faster from the man who had somehow already broken through my defenses, determined never to see him again.

5

I'd only had two hours of sleep when I forced my eyes open. With great difficulty, I rose out of bed and dressed, intending to spend the entire day with my son. I sneaked into his room and crawled under the covers with him. Sensing me, he turned and wrapped his little arms around my shoulders, nuzzling his head into my neck.

I kissed the top of his head, sifting my fingers through soft hair the same color as his father's. It was during quiet moments like these that the entirety of our loss hit me, how entire futures can be ripped away in the time it takes a bullet to leave the barrel of a gun and travel across a crowded street.

I wondered what life would be like if Jason had come home as planned, if we'd gotten married and raised Will together. Would Will be a different kid? Would he be more childlike instead of a kid who grew up too soon?

"I'll take care of you, Mommy," he'd always say to me. "If anyone tries to hurt you, I'll protect you."

I guess wanting to protect those we love is bone deep, an instinct we'll never be able to unlearn.

Will and I went to the movies to see the latest Pixar release. As we sat down, he once again asked why Elsie and Henry couldn't join us.

"They're busy today," I said. "They have a lot of things to take care of now that they're married."

"Like?"

"Um . . ." In lieu of a real honeymoon, the Shermans and I had chipped in to get them a suite at the Hyatt Hotel in Carmel, overlooking the Big Sur coastline. No doubt those two were very busy ignoring the ocean view at that very moment. "Husband and wife stuff."

"Are they having sex?" he asked in a stage whisper.

I choked on my drink. "What? How do you know about sex?"

He grinned. "Billy at school told everyone about it. He said that's how babies are made."

"What else did he tell you?"

"That the man kisses the woman and then he sleeps on top of her and then she gets a baby in her tummy."

"I need to have a talk with Billy's mom, then," I muttered under my breath as the movie started.

Afterward, we headed to a frozen yogurt place in Cannery Row. In the middle of choosing our toppings, my phone beeped, letting me know I'd received a voice message. I held my phone up to my ear, keeping an eye on Will to make sure he didn't get too much of the crumbled candies.

"Julie, it's Neal," said the deep, silky voice. "I was hoping to see you today. Give me a call when you get a chance."

I turned off my phone, determined to put the guy out of my

mind once and for all. It was a fling and nothing more. The fact that I had had an erotic dream about him that morning and had thought about him nonstop during the movie was irrelevant. Our time together was up.

"Mom," Will said as we sat down at a table.

"Mmm?"

"Are you going to have a wedding like yesterday?" he asked with his sweet, open face. "I think you'd be so pretty in a big white dress."

I stifled a smile, thinking that it was way too late for me to be in a white dress. Instead I said, "I don't think I'll ever get married again, sweetie."

"Why not?"

"Because I don't have anyone to marry."

He chewed for a few moments, then his face lit up. "You can marry Kyle again! You said he was a good dad when I was a baby."

"He *was* a good dad," I said, once again regretting the fact that I'd deprived Will of a father figure. But I'd tried. I'd tried to make it work for Will's sake, but the heart can't be told to acknowledge what was never there. And though Kyle was a decent man who loved us, I just never felt anything but platonic feelings toward him. "But I don't think I will marry Kyle again. He and I weren't right for each other."

"You'll find the right guy," he said, patting my hand, looking mature beyond his years. "Then you'll marry him and I'll have a dad again."

I wanted to tell him that it wasn't so easy, that men who wanted an insta-family were few and far between, but filled my mouth with frozen yogurt instead, unable to bear the thought of disappointing him with the truth. "Will, I'll make you a deal: if the right man ever comes along and he wants to be your dad, then I will marry him. But only if you promise to stop waiting around for him. Because, honestly, I don't think he exists." I swallowed hard. "Aren't you happy with just you and me?"

"I am," he said quickly. "I just want you to have a Henry."

I laughed unexpectedly. "Sweetie," I said, wiping smeared yogurt off his chin, "your dad was my Henry."

"But that means you'll never get married again."

"No. Probably not."

He stared into his empty cup, dejected.

"It's okay, Will. Really," I said, scooping him up in my arms even though he was already far too heavy. "I love you and I love our little family. Nothing can make me happier."

To cheer him up, I gave him a piggyback and we laughed all the way to the car.

Once we were back at the Shermans', I finally turned my phone back on, wincing as I waited for the messages to pile up. But there were no texts, no voice mails, no missed calls. Either Neal was an extremely patient man or seeing me was not high on his priority list.

So I called him.

"Hey," he said, the timbre in his voice doing strange and wonderful things to my insides, a reminder of the strange and wonderful things he'd done to my insides just the previous night.

"Hi. I've been out all day and just now had the chance to return your call."

He was quiet for a moment; in the background, I heard a zipper and a door closing.

"Are you busy?"

"No. Well, I'm packing," he said. "I'm flying out this afternoon."

"I thought you wanted to meet up," I blurted out then immediately smacked my forehead.

He paused. "I figured since I didn't hear from you . . ."

I didn't know why I was feeling so wretched; wasn't this what I'd wanted?

"Look," he said. "You wanted a fling. I get it. We had a nice time last night and now it's time to go our separate ways."

A nice time. Ouch. "It was more than a nice time," I said, trying not to sound wounded, though not sure I was succeeding.

"Yeah, it was." He cleared his throat. "Let me be honest: I like you, Julie. I want to get to know you. But that's not going to happen unless you can admit it's what you want, too."

I couldn't find words to speak. Was he right? Had I gone in too deep with this man? More important, did I want to wade back out?

"You were only supposed to be a one-time thing," I said, trying my best to brace the walls around my heart.

"But I'm not," he said. "You and I . . . we were meant to meet."

"For what reason?"

"I don't know yet. But I was hoping to find out." When next he spoke, his voice was different. "Come to Las Vegas with me."

"What?"

"You said you still had a few days before returning to Dallas. So come to Vegas with me and let's get to know each other."

"I can't do that."

Could I?

The idea was too crazy, too impulsive. I'd been crazy and impulsive once, but that was a long time ago. I'd forgotten what it was even like to be that girl. "I like my life the way it is. Simple and uncomplicated."

He didn't say anything for a long time. I got the feeling he was trying to rein in his frustration. I couldn't say I blamed him. "I leave at four thirty," he said. "If you'd like to do something different for a few days, then come. If not, then . . . 'bye, Julie. I enjoyed our time together."

After I hung up, I stared at the tan-colored wall in front of me, trying to make sense of my jumbled emotions. My head told me I'd made the right decision; why then were my insides in knots?

I walked down the hall, toward the living room, when I felt a strange sensation wash over me. I stopped in front of Jason's old bedroom, looking through bleary eyes at the things he'd left behind.

The years since his death had dulled the pain, but I suspected I would always feel his loss. I walked inside, my eyes landing on the three black-and-white photo booth strips arranged together inside a wooden frame.

They had been taken a few months after college, when I'd come to visit him in Texas during his Air Force training. We stumbled upon the photo booth in a mall and I pulled him inside, despite his protestations. The first set was of us looking serious, hugging and posing. In the second set we had fun—tongues out, ears covered, bunny ears, fishy faces. The last strip was my favorite: when he turned to me as if seeing me for the first time, then he kissed my cheek, then we were making out. The final image—of the two of us just looking at each other—was the image that held the most meaning.

"Can you be my boyfriend again?" I'd asked him before that final shot.

The camera snapped the picture in the nanosecond between his surprised reaction and his grinning response. "Well, yeah," was his easy reply.

"This is going to be tough for a while," he said later as we walked hand in hand in the mall. "I'll be moving again in a few months and you'll be starting work in New York."

"I don't care," I said, pulling on his hand to bring him closer, wrapping an arm around his waist. "I shouldn't have broken up with you. I know that now."

We were happy for a time, until he moved to Oklahoma and I

became too busy with an off-Broadway show, and he decided that a long-distance relationship was just too much work.

"I found those in Jason's old things and thought Will would like to see them."

I wiped my eyes with my sleeves before turning around to face Elodie, who was standing in the doorway. "I haven't seen these in years," I said.

She walked over and took the frame, smiling ruefully. "You both look so happy."

"We were."

"I'd love nothing more than to see you smiling like that again," Elodie said, looking at me like my mother never did, with warmth and kindness.

"I'm happy," I said, feeling defensive about the life I'd built with Will. "I don't know why people keep thinking I'm not."

"I'm sorry. I never meant to insinuate that you're not. It's just . . ." She looked down again at the pictures in her hand. "This is a different kind of smile you're wearing here."

"That's also a different kind of girl," I said, placing my hand over the frame. "And that smile is because she was crazy about your son."

"Well, what about the young man last night? The tall one with the nice smile?"

"What about him? He was nice, but I won't be seeing him again."

"He just seemed very smitten with you. He didn't take his eyes off you the entire ceremony."

I felt heat rise up my cheeks. "Yeah, but we live too far from each other. It would never wor—" I stopped, overcome with a sense of déjà vu. I had used the same excuse before, had wasted years pushing away the first guy I'd ever cared for out of some misguided idea that love would destroy my life. Would I have done things differently if I'd known our time would be cut short?

"I like him," I admitted softly. "But he's leaving today. He asked me to come to Las Vegas with him for a few days . . ."

"So what's the problem?"

"Will," I said, then quickly added, "Not that he's a problem. Only that Neal doesn't know that I have a son. And I can't just go gallivanting off like I have no responsibilities, like I'm single again."

"Do you want to go with him?" Elodie asked.

"No." I sighed in resignation. "Maybe. But I shouldn't."

"You can leave Will with us," she said, touching my shoulder.

I glanced up at her in surprise. "I couldn't ask you to do that. Besides, I've never even spent a full night away from him before."

"Which is all the more reason to go. You're long overdue for a vacation."

"But Will—"

"He'll be okay. He's a big kid now. He can handle it," she said gently.

A frisson of excitement wound up my spine but I refused to address it. I'd had my hopes up before and knew firsthand that what comes up will come crashing back down. That was life. Lesson learned.

"His flight leaves at four thirty," I said, looking pointedly at my watch. "And it's already three. I'd never make it anyway."

"Honey, we're only ten minutes away from the airport."

My eyes flew back and forth between my watch and Elodie, still unable to make a decision.

"What are you waiting for?" she asked, clapping her hands together. "Get packing."

6

Packing went fast, as we'd been living out of bags for the past two days. I moved decisively, leaving no room for doubt, afraid that if even a little bit crept in, I'd completely lose my nerve.

I froze when the door opened and my son came in. "Grandma said you had to go somewhere?" he said.

I crouched down and hugged him. "Yes, to Las Vegas," I said, feeling my excitement slipping away. "But I don't have to go. Not if you don't want me to."

He scratched his head. "I thought you said you always wanted to go there."

"I do."

"So you should go," he said as if it were the most obvious thing in the world. You want to do something? Then do it. Sometimes I wished adults could still live by kid logic.

"You won't miss me?" I asked.

"Yeah, I will. But I want you to have fun, too."

My sight blurred with tears, though with what emotion, I couldn't tell. I hugged him to me, holding him tighter than what was probably comfortable. He made up my entire world, and I was actually considering leaving him behind.

"Ready?" Elodie asked, coming into the room with her purse and keys in hand.

"Are you sure about this?" I asked Will one more time. "I really don't have to go."

He smiled, his big blue eyes bright as he nodded. "I'll be fine, Mom. Go."

The drive over to the airport went by in a blur, affording me no time to second-guess myself. After thanking Elodie, I went inside the tiny Monterey airport and looked around for Neal.

But he was nowhere to be found, and only then—as I stood stranded in that building—did it occur to me that he might not be waiting for me after all. I'd told him I wasn't coming, so it stood to reason that he wouldn't wait.

I went up to the ticket counter but the agent informed me there were absolutely no scheduled flights to Las Vegas departing at four thirty. I stepped out of line, swallowing down my disappointment, and stared down at my phone in hopes that a message from Neal would pop up at that very moment.

"You're here."

I spun around and found Neal beaming at me, holding a duffel bag in his hand. He bent down and gave me a kiss on the cheek. "I thought you weren't going to show."

I folded my arms across my chest. "There are no flights to Vegas."

He grinned. "Not on their planes. But Neal Airlines has one departing in thirty minutes." He took my bag and led me through the airport and out the other side of the building. We walked on the tarmac for a little while until we reached a small hangar.

"Ready?" he asked before opening the side door.

Inside was a small white plane with red and yellow stripes along its thin body, white propellers, and wheels that looked as if they belonged on a go-kart instead of a plane.

"You're going to fly *this*?" I asked incredulously as my heart thumped wildly.

"Yes." He chuckled as he walked around the plane, running his hands along its shiny body. "What did you think I meant?"

I threw my hands up. "I don't know. Maybe you were rich and had your own private jet."

"I do," he said, bending down and pulling yellow wedges from around the plane's tires. "This one. It's a Lancair IV. My dad and I built her from a kit."

All the blood rushed to my head. "You built this? From a *kit*?"

He pursed his lips, biting back a smile. "You're wondering what the hell you've gotten yourself into, right?"

"Something like that."

"Well, it's a four-seat, carbon-fiber-composite, high-performance plane and has been certified airworthy by the FAA. I've got over two hundred solo flying hours under my belt and at least a hundred with my dad." He leaned an elbow on the nose of the plane. "You'll be in capable hands."

I focused on his earnest face, anchoring my skittering thoughts to the way he'd held me in bed. In his capable arms I'd felt safe and wanted, as if after all these years of standing guard alone, someone finally had my back.

"Okay," I said, shutting out the little nagging doubts. "But I reserve the right to change my mind at any time."

He beamed and came toward me, cradling my face in his hands and planting his lips on mine. The kiss, meant to be quick, deepened as I opened my mouth and let him in. His eyes were bright with excitement when he pulled away. "You're going to love flying."

He helped me up into the cockpit, which was not all that roomy for a four-seater, and climbed into the pilot's seat, putting on a green headset.

Then he reached over and clamped a set over my ears, adjusting the mic in front of my mouth. "So we can talk over the noise."

I looked down at the piece of metal with a wooden handle sticking up between my legs, then at the identical one in his seat. "There's a joke here somewhere."

He chuckled. "That's called the stick, and it controls the roll and the pitch of the plane, while the pedals"—he pointed to both our feet—"control the yaw."

I took hold of the stick. "So can I drive the plane from my side?"

"Sure."

When he started communicating with the tower and flipping switches, I finally sat back, satisfied that he knew what he was doing. Still, as we taxied onto the runway, traveling faster and faster until the wheels lifted off the ground, I prayed quietly and fervently, asking every deity to keep me safe.

After we reached flight altitude and had been flying for a few minutes, he reached over and squeezed my thigh. "You ready to take over?" he asked, his voice clear in my headset despite the loud and constant noise around us.

I took hold of the stick with some hesitation then immediately let go. "Talk me through it first. I have no idea what I'm doing."

Neal explained about the difference between the roll, pitch, and yaw, and how each one was controlled.

"I think I got it," I said, taking hold of the stick and setting my feet on the pedals.

"I'm letting go now," he said, taking his hand off the stick and folding his arms behind his head.

"Oh, crap," I said in a moment of pure terror, until a second passed and I realized that we weren't going to crash. "I'm really doing it," I said, feeling short of breath as I looked out the windshield at the expanse of blue sky all around.

He beamed at me. "You're flying," he said with a warm gaze.

We came upon a flock of birds and flew alongside them for a few wonderful minutes, but the plane was faster and soon the birds fell behind.

"Thank you," I said after handing control of the plane back over to Neal, "for giving me the chance to fly with the birds."

He smiled over at me. "It's my pleasure," he said with naked honesty. "At this point, you could ask me for the moon and I'd do my best to steal it for you."

I believed him and his analogy, the sincerity in his voice hard to miss. And as we flew somewhere over the Sequoia National Forest, I realized that I was well beyond the point of no return.

PART TWO

FLIGHT

1

The ride up the elevator to our room in the Signature at MGM Grand was torture. I kept glancing over at Neal, my skin prickling at the thought of what was to come. Despite the fact that we weren't alone in the elevator, I fantasized about Neal hitting the emergency button in a fit of desire and pinning me against the wall, needing to have me right then and there.

The real-life Neal, on the other hand, appeared calm and composed throughout the long ride up to the thirty-eighth floor. He looked over at me a few times and gave me a bland smile, never once betraying his thoughts.

The moment the door to our room closed behind us, though, he grabbed me around the waist and hauled me against his body, his lips finding mine without preamble. He tasted of warm mint as his tongue found mine, a desperate rumbling groan coming from the back of his throat. I pushed against him, taking as much as I was giving before we ran out of breath.

"Finally," he rasped, leaning his head on mine. "I've been dying to do that since I woke up this morning."

"You've been hiding it really well."

He grinned, flicking my lower lip with his finger. "I was teasing you, keeping you guessing."

"Oh, you don't want to play this game with me," I said with a wink. "I'll test your willpower."

"You already do." One hand slid up my neck and through my hair, pulling me close as his lips found mine once again. But this kiss was sensual and soft with the promise of things to come. I wound my arms around his neck and tilted my head to the side, deepening our connection.

When we were nearing a critical point—when we needed to go further in order to keep from combusting—he pulled away. "We should freshen up before we go."

"Go?" I asked, planting kisses along his jaw. "Where?"

"Dinner."

"I'm not hungry for food," I said, nipping on the soft skin where his neck and shoulder met.

He grabbed me by the shoulders and held me at bay. "Julie, there's no hurry," he said gently, his hands continuing to slide across the bare skin of my shoulders. "I have every intention of properly seducing you, but first I'd like to get to know you."

I nodded and stepped away, even as my entire body protested. But the mischievous glint in his eyes sparked something in me, a long-dormant playful side that was aching to come out. Without warning, I reached into his pants and dragged my hand down into his underwear, my gaze holding him in place as I finally made contact with his hard cock. His jaw ticked when my fingers wrapped around the head of his shaft and squeezed. I smiled up at him, tingling with wicked mischief.

He leaned forward until our lips almost touched. "You know what this means, don't you?"

I tilted my chin up and stroked my hand up his hard length. "Oh? And what's that?"

He thrust into my hands. "This means war," he practically growled.

I pulled my hand out slowly, dragging my nails along his skin. "Bring it," I said and, with a last look over my shoulder, sauntered off to the bathroom.

Neal had changed into a gray button-down shirt, sleeves folded back, and a pair of black slacks by the time I emerged from the bathroom. I held the towel around my body, feeling Neal's eyes on me.

"You have no idea how hard it was not to jump in that shower with you."

I smirked, raising an eyebrow. "Not that *hard*."

"Julie, Julie, what am I going to do with you?" He reached out for me, but instead of giving me a warm embrace, he flipped me around and landed a swift spank on my ass that reverberated through my flesh.

"That hurt. You'd better kiss it better."

He immediately dropped to his knees and pressed a soft kiss to one cheek, the towel the only thing keeping me from being completely bare. His fingers stole under the towel, sliding up my legs, but right before they reached my aching core, I took a few steps forward and away from him.

"I'd better get dressed. Don't want to miss dinner."

He dropped his hands to his thighs, a hangdog look on his face as he watched me bending over my bag. "You are a sexy, diabolical woman."

I took my clothes to the bathroom. "You have no idea," I said at the doorway, dropping the towel a millisecond before I closed the door.

Dinner was a battle, the table between us the war zone. We tried to best each other with innuendo and flirtatious touches, waiting to see who would crack first. By then it had become a game to see who would beg to go back to the room first, and I was certain it wouldn't be me.

There was something about the atmosphere in Las Vegas that allowed me to live in the moment and just be the fun-loving girl I once was. Here, for this night, it was possible to believe that I had no responsibilities and no heartbreaking past. Here, in this godforsaken city, I could live in the moment, be selfish, and do whatever the hell I wanted. And for someone who'd had to do the opposite for years, I was anxious to lap it all up while I could.

"How's your steak?" I asked when our entrée arrived.

"Perfect. It's—" He stopped, his lips falling open when my bare foot landed on the chair between his legs.

I wedged my foot deep between his thighs, only stopping when my toes made contact with something that was starting to twitch into life. "It looks like a choice hunk of meat," I said.

"It is." He stabbed his steak with a fork and cut off a piece, offering it to me across the table. "Try it."

I wrapped my lips around the metal tines and slowly slid away. "Mm-mm," I said with a moan, chewing and wiggling my toes at the same time. "Your meat practically melts on my tongue."

He chuckled, breaking character. "You're really good at this seduction thing," he said, setting his fork down and reaching for the foot between his legs. He pressed a thumb to the arch of my foot and drew heavy circles, causing me to moan in earnest from the pleasure. "I'm afraid I've gotten in way over my head. There's no way I can compete with you in this department," he added, his thumbs pressing a ladder of pleasure up my foot. A hint of a smile played along his lips as he watched me enjoy his ministrations.

"I don't know," I breathed, my entire body on fire. "You seem to be deploying a secret weapon right now."

"I don't know what you're talking about," he said, raising an eyebrow. "Harder or softer?"

"Both." I'd never had a foot rub feel so erotic before and felt the resulting shudder throughout my body. I wanted to throw my head back and lose myself, but remembered in time that we were in a public place. I retrieved my foot and slipped back into my shoes, sitting up in my seat. I took my glass of wine and brought it to my lips, suddenly thirsty.

He stared at me across the table, his gaze so intense I flushed under its glare.

"What do you do for a living?" I asked to relieve the tension.

He took a pull from his beer, then set his hands out on the table. "I'm a freelance software designer. Currently, I'm designing programs for several big companies," he said without pretense. "And you?"

"Dental hygienist." I considered my next question. "Where do you live?"

"Here, there, everywhere," he said with a shrug. "My job doesn't require that I stay fixed in one place, so I put my things in storage and now I just fly around, staying in hotels until I feel ready to move on."

"That's a lonely experience."

"Not really. I get to meet people like you."

"Have you met many people . . . like me?"

"No," he said. "Only you."

Hope bloomed in me. "So where are you going next?"

"I don't know," he said with a smile. "Perhaps a trip to Dallas is in my future."

I smiled into my drink, more pleased than I felt entitled to be. "That would be nice," I said, thinking it would be a good time for Neal to meet Will. Or at least know about him.

I caught myself beginning to paint Neal into my future and quickly banished the thought. We were only at the get-to-know-you stage, nothing more. Sure, he was a nice guy, sexy and smart, but he could turn out to be nothing.

Or everything.

I finally reminded myself to live in the moment, to stop overanalyzing everything and just *be*. "Let's go dancing," I said.

If he was surprised, he didn't show it. "Where to?"

"I don't know. Somewhere loud and crowded." Where one could lose oneself.

"I know just the place."

We went to a club called Cravings, only a few minutes' walk down the Strip from our hotel. The moment we stepped inside the club, I knew we'd chosen the perfect place. It was dark, lit up by only the purple and blue strobe lights mounted at the ceiling. People bounced and writhed on the dance floor, the mass of bodies so thick and so immense I couldn't tell where the room ended. And most interesting of all were the dancers—naked save for tiny black bikinis and Lucite heels—working the poles on top of small platforms around the room.

"We can find another place," Neal called over the music, looking up.

I followed his gaze and gasped when I saw three dancers strung up at the ceiling, wearing little more than a strategically placed harness as they performed aerial acrobatics. Despite their obvious objectification, I found myself admiring their fluid movements, as they spun and twisted in a graceful, gravity-defying dance.

Yes, we were definitely staying.

I grabbed his hand and led him out to the dance floor.

"I haven't had nearly enough alcohol to make me dance," he said, grabbing me around the waist and veering me off course. "You want anything?"

I shook my head and backed away, heading to the edge of the dance floor, starting to move my hips to the hypnotic, thumping beat. He stayed in sight at the bar, and a few minutes later he turned back to me with a beer in his hand, his eyes dark burning embers as I lifted my hands over my head and gave myself over to the music.

A young guy sidled over and started to dance with me, completely oblivious to Neal's glare. I danced with him, flashing a wink at Neal over the guy's shoulder.

Neal chugged his beer, set the empty bottle down on the bar, and stalked toward me. He slid his hand around my waist. "You ready?" he asked, casting a dismissive glance toward the guy before whisking me deeper into the dance floor.

"Trying to make me jealous," he said against my ear. "That's underhanded."

I shrugged, winding my arms around his neck. "That was your own doing."

We danced for a time, only pointed looks passing between us as we moved to the rhythm.

"You're an amazing dancer," he said, grinding behind me. "Better than the dancers onstage."

Drunk on desire and self-confidence, I decided to reveal a little something about myself, something I hadn't told even the Shermans. Here, in this club, it didn't feel like such a dirty skeleton in the closet. "I'm going to let you in on a secret," I whispered against his ear.

"Oh?"

"I used to be an exotic dancer."

2

I sobered immediately when Neal pulled away.

At my confession, his eyebrows drew together and his jaw muscles ticked. "You were a stripper? When?"

"About three years ago, but it was only for several months until I was able to finish school." I held back the fact that I'd desperately needed the money right after divorcing Kyle. Still, after years of self-loathing, I'd finally come to the realization that my past was nothing to be ashamed of. Stripping hadn't been the most respectable way to earn money, but it was the only way I'd been able to make ends meet when Will was barely a year old.

"You couldn't find any other job?"

"Trust me, I tried. Nobody wanted to hire a dancer in Dallas. Except for . . . you know."

He took in a deep breath, his nostrils flaring.

"I have to use the restroom," I said and left, relieved to escape his critical gaze. I found the bathroom at the back of the club, surprised to find the entire place was actually smaller than it appeared. I took my time using the facilities, prolonging the moment when I'd have to see the judgment in Neal's face again. I didn't know what had possessed me to tell him about stripping, but now I wished I hadn't. I'd give anything to have him look at me like an untouched treasure once again.

I hadn't done it for very long. During my short-lived marriage, Will and I had lived in Kyle's house, so it was only natural that I moved out after the divorce. I'd found a tiny one-bedroom apartment in a sketchy part of Flower Mound, but my job creating grocery store ads was just not enough to cover the rent, food, and day care.

"Strippers make a lot of money," a coworker said one day at lunch as I searched through the classifieds for a second job.

She was joking, I knew that, but I couldn't get the idea out of my head. At work that day, I searched online for articles on exotic dancing just out of curiosity. And after work, before I could lose my nerve, I drove to the most respectable club I could find and talked with the owner, meaning to simply ask a few questions—enough, at least, to convince me it was a bad idea—then go on my way.

But sometimes the wind changes direction and we are forced into uncharted territory simply to survive.

I went onstage for the first time a week later, my stomach empty from having thrown up a few minutes earlier. I hated it all, especially the tiny clothing designed specifically for the enjoyment of those leering men sitting at the edge of the stage, holding out their one-dollar bills as if it would somehow make them less loathsome.

After I got home that first night and paid the babysitter, I sneaked into my son's room and watched his peaceful little face with tears running down my cheeks. But despite the urge to sit on the floor and lament the loss of my dignity, I reminded myself of my purpose: I was doing this for Will, the only thing that mattered in my life. So what if lecherous men had to see me degrade myself night after night? As long as my son was happy and healthy, I could endure.

To make the nights bearable, I started to incorporate contemporary dance moves into my performance, eventually earning a name for myself as the "artistic stripper." It wasn't much, but I held on to that moniker with the delusion that it gave me some class. And for a while, at least when the music drowned out all my doubts and the stage lights obscured everyone in the room, I almost enjoyed myself. Dancing was dancing, after all. And the money was good.

I went back to school to become a dental hygienist, and after many months of burning the candle at both ends, I finally graduated and was able to close that filthy black door on my "exotic" life.

I shook my head to clear it of the past, the water streaming into the sink coming back to focus as I finished washing my hands. Leaving the restroom, I noticed a door swing open next to it and was able to get a glimpse of the room beyond, with a leather couch at the back and a stripper pole in the center.

"What's back there?" I asked the person who had just exited, an older Hispanic woman dressed in a black shirt and pants.

"Private room," she said. "Why, you want to rent?"

An idea planted itself in my head and quickly took root. "How much?"

She looked me over. "Are you a celebrity?"

"No, why?"

"Fifty dollars for one hour."

"Okay, can you wait a few minutes?" I asked, already moving away. "I'll be right back."

I snaked through the crowd and found Neal waiting for me by the bar. I grabbed his wrist and shouted excitedly, "Come with me." I pulled him, burning with anxious need to prove myself.

The woman nodded at me when I handed her fifty dollars in cash, then she turned and unlocked the door. "Just sanitized," she said before allowing us inside.

Once Neal and I entered the room, the lock snicked in place, letting us know we wouldn't be disturbed. At least for the next sixty minutes.

I led Neal over to the couch without saying a word.

"Care to tell me what's going on?" he asked, studying the dark velvet-covered walls, the glittery floor.

I put a finger against his chest and pushed, sending him folding to the couch. "I want to show you what I did for a living."

"Julie, you don't have to do this," he said, getting back to his feet. "You don't have to prove anything to me. I'm sorry I acted like a dick. I was just surprised."

"Sit," I said, kicking off my heels and dropping my clutch beside them on the floor. I approached the pole, relieved to see that it had indeed been cleaned. I took note of my clothing, glad that I'd worn a sleeveless dress with a loose skirt that would not impede my dancing. My black lace boy shorts would show him plenty of cheek, but that was a bonus for him.

This dance, this performance, was for me, a way to acknowledge the past and no longer be held back by it.

"Ready?" I asked, grasping the pole with one hand and slinking around it.

Neal sat back and gave a short nod. His face said he was resigned to this, yet the bulge in his pants betrayed his thoughts.

Despite the thumping outside, I focused on a different song in my mind, a slow, melancholy tune that I'd choreographed a dance to. I leaned my back against the pole and gripped it above my head, then slipped down, the movement telling of a girl feeling trapped and demoralized. The choreography came back to me as if only a few days had passed instead of years, my muscles remembering every twist and transition I had to execute.

I kept up eye contact with Neal as I slinked around the stage, using the pole as a means to fly, holding on with two hands as I spun around with my back arched and toes pointed. For the finale, I made my way up to the top of the pole and maneuvered so that I was upside down with my legs outstretched in a split, spinning gracefully down. Halfway down, I twisted so that the bar was clenched between my thighs and I leaned forward, my arms extended as I swirled downward all the way to the floor.

Neal leaned forward, clasping his hands between his knees, and watched me with a dark expression on his face. I knew how my performance was affecting him, how his heart was thumping wildly and sending copious amounts of blood to his dick. But there was something else there, the way his eyes followed my every move, making me feel beautiful in a way I'd never felt before.

I finished with a flourish, a simple spin around the pole with my legs bent that sent my skirt fluttering around, until I came to rest on the ground. Every nerve ending in my body was alive as I sat there, waiting for his response.

Neal rose from the couch with his hand held out and helped me up. "That's how you danced?" he asked.

"Yes," I said, straightening my dress. "The club had a rule that the dancers had to wear pasties and G-strings, so I was never completely naked. And most important, there was a no-touching rule."

"You don't need to explain yourself to me," he said gently. "What you did right there was beautiful. You were grace in motion."

I felt tears stinging my eyes. If only all the men had reacted to my dancing in such a way. "Grace is actually my middle name."

He slid his hands up my shoulders and onto my neck, cradling my cheeks in the palm of his hands and letting out a slow, sighing breath. "Julie Grace," he said, bending down to touch his lips lightly to my cheek. "You are, without a doubt, the most surprising, amazing, confounding woman I've ever met."

"Confounding?"

"Yes," he said with a rueful smile. "I can't figure out how I'm going to keep you when all of this is over."

We left the club not too long after and headed back to the hotel, unable to keep our hands off each other any longer. He touched me, kissed me, from the taxi to the hotel lobby and up the elevator, where he continued eye-fucking me even as we stood with other hotel guests. When the doors finally slid open, he bent down and threw me over his shoulder, taking long, confident strides down the hall.

He set me down inside our room and immediately relieved me of my clothing as easily as if he'd been doing it all his life. When he was done, he stepped back and took me in, devouring me with his eyes as he undressed until we were both completely exposed and unguarded.

"My imagination has been running rampant since you closed that bathroom door on me earlier," he admitted with a dark smile before he swept me up into a kiss that scorched me from the inside out. "But I have to say: the reality far outweighs anything I could have ever dreamed up."

I took hold of his wrists and held his palms against the sides of my neck, sliding them around my shoulders and down my chest. I closed my eyes, overcome with the need to feel his hands all over me. Whether it was my direction or his own, it no longer mattered; his hands traced the undersides of my breasts then slid downward, past my stomach, around my waist, and came to rest at my backside. His fingers bit into the skin of my ass as he jerked me against him.

My skin tingled with the rough handling, but he threw me off guard when he trailed his fingers up the curve of my back, his touch light and teasing. Done waiting, I sat on the edge of the bed and gripped his shaft, bringing him closer toward me. For the first time, I was able to study his cock in all its hard, veiny glory. It was thick and long with a slight curve upward, second only in magnificence to the man who wielded it.

I bent down and wrapped my lips around the large head of his shaft, sliding my tongue through the slit, the drop of precum salty on my tongue.

"Get on the bed," he said with a rough quality to his voice. "On all fours."

I did as he asked, crawling toward him to take him into my mouth again. Gently, he started pumping his hips, fucking my mouth. I took him in deeper and deeper until he was hitting the back of my throat.

"Oh, shit," he groaned, grabbing my hair. He leaned forward, reaching down my back, startling me when his finger slid down the crease of my ass and dipped into my cleft. He fucked me with his finger as I sucked him off, his other digits dragging deliciously along my clit with each pumping motion.

I moaned around the cock in my mouth and squeezed tighter.

"I have to be inside you," he said, and pulled away from my mouth. He grasped my hips and spun me around, pushing my shoulders down into the mattress and leaving my ass up in the air. There was a crinkle of foil, and a few seconds later he was pushing into me, sliding in easily from the moisture that had accumulated all night.

I hissed his name between my teeth, feeling complete. I held my breath when he pulled nearly all the way out then slowly thrust back in, repeating the process in an unbearably slow rhythm, stretching out the thick thread of pleasure.

Then he reached for my hair and twisted it around his hand,

tugging my head back. A whimper was wrenched from my mouth when he pulled out, and I looked back in time to find him getting on his knees. He buried his face in my folds, pulling my ass cheeks apart as he feasted on my sensitive flesh, stabbing me with his tongue and sucking on my clit. To keep me from squirming, he grabbed both my thighs and locked them together, holding me captive against his mouth.

A second later, his cock was back, penetrating me, shoving into me so hard our skin was slapping together. Over and over he thrust into me, letting out deep, rumbling groans that riled me up even more. Still embedded in me, he twisted my hips down to the bed so that I could face him, my legs trapped to one side.

"I want to see you," he rasped, grabbing the side of my head and bringing our faces together. "See your forehead crease in concentration and your mouth turn into a delicious O when I give you the best orgasm of your life."

"That's fairly cocky of you," I breathed, even though I knew there was a definite possibility of it coming true. "What if you can't deliver?"

He grinned and speared into me. "Then I'll just have to try—" He thrust again. "And try—" Another thrust that had me clenching hard. "And try again—" He began pounding in earnest, each stroke long and powerful. "Until I succeed."

My insides quaked and I stared into his eyes, my mouth indeed falling open as the orgasm surged through me. He continued the assault, a confident smile on his lips. He covered my mouth with his own, sealing shut my cries of pleasure.

When I came to my senses, he stilled, waiting for my reaction. "That was damn good," I said. "But not the best."

He grinned, all confidence and sex. "I didn't say I was done."

3

"My turn," I said, getting up and pushing him backward onto the mattress, feeling a rush of feminine power through my veins. "I'm going to take my own *best* orgasm."

He settled farther onto the mattress and folded his arms behind his head. He said nothing, only watched me as I crawled over him, dragging the tips of my breasts along his skin as I made my way up. When I reached my destination, I sat up and turned around, straddling him backward, my wet heat directly on his cock.

"You should see the view from here," he said, massaging my ass.

I looked down between my legs, at his engorged testicles and the thick vein that ran along the length of his penis. "The view from here is not too shabby, either," I said and reached down to take his balls in my hand and give them a firm tug.

He lurched up. "Holy hell!"

"Did that hurt?" I asked, glancing over my shoulder.

"Yes. No," he replied, looking conflicted. "More."

The second time, he let out a hiss, then took hold of my hips and lifted me up. I guided him inside me, taking my time sliding down his shaft, my nerves still raw from my orgasm. I began to rock my hips, taking hold of his sac and allowing my movements to take it with me.

"God, yes," he whispered in a pained voice. His hand reached around and found my clit, stroking me in a circular motion.

"Right there," I said when he found the spot. I bounced on his lap, rising till he was almost out, then slammed straight down, my muscles clutching at him. I leaned back, setting my hands on his chest to support myself. His hands bore my weight when I lifted my hips, and he thrust upward, taking the reins once again.

He hammered into me relentlessly, the friction making my nerves sing until the orgasm started to build once again, taking me by surprise. I'd been able to climax readily and without much help during my sexual prime, but I had never experienced back-to-back orgasms.

I threw my head back, rolling side to side, and noticed the large mirror against the wall. I caught our reflection on the bed—me hovering above him, his ass and thighs flexing with each rapid upward thrust—and suddenly, I was climaxing. My legs quaked as the orgasm tore through me, shooting liquid pleasure through my veins.

Neal paused for a few beats, then thrust into me again, igniting another orgasm that had my entire body shaking, the sensation racing through my limbs down to the tips of my fingers and toes. For a few seconds, I felt removed from my body, as if I were nothing more than just one ball of scorching white fire.

"I'm about to come," he said then let out a loud groan, wrenching me down on top of him as his cock twitched and surged, his body one coiled muscle.

When the aftershocks ebbed away, I lay back on his chest. "Holy shit," I said, my brain completely devoid of rational thought.

He brushed my hair aside and twisted my head around to kiss me, his heart still thudding a heavy staccato beat against my back.

"Okay, you win," I said, biting his bottom lip. "That *was* the best orgasm of my life."

He smiled against my lips. "Now I'll just have to give you an even better one."

"I don't know how that's possible, but I'm game to try."

His chuckle was deep and satisfying, rumbling through his chest. "I knew you would be."

Sleep proved elusive when there was a sexy man in bed with me who couldn't control his thoughts or his hands.

"So tell me about your parents," he said, palming my ass.

I snuggled into the crook of his arm, running my fingernails through the hair on his chest. "They had what you'd call a tumultuous marriage. One minute they couldn't stand each other, the next minute it was like they couldn't breathe without each other. It was a constant 'I hate you, I love you.' It took me a long time to realize that their relationship was abusive in a way, not physically but emotionally, that they did horrible things to each other in the name of love. And I grew up thinking I'd never be like that. Never be so entrenched in someone else that I'd lose all sense of control over my emotions."

"And how's that going for you?"

"So far so good." I cleared my throat. "Anyway, how about you?"

"My dad, Patrick, lives in San Diego. He used to be Navy but got out a while ago and now he's running a small business teaching people how to fly. He lives with my stepmom, Karen."

"And your mom?"

"She died when I was seventeen. Cancer."

"I'm sorry."

"Me, too. Her name was Lori. She was the best person I knew." He stared off into space, lost in his thoughts.

"So tell me more about your dad," I said to steer him away from melancholy thoughts.

He kissed my shoulder. "My parents married young, had me young. Mom was sick for years and my dad took care of her, even quit the Navy to be there for her. He was so wrapped up in my mom and her cancer that he gave up nearly everything else in his life. One night, about two weeks after she was buried, he confessed to me that he was a little relieved that she was gone, and it made me so angry with him. I hated him enough that I left home as soon as I graduated and stopped talking to him. It took me a long time to let go of my anger, to finally think about his words and try to understand where he was coming from.

"On his fortieth birthday, I finally went back home and we talked it all over. He said it was the best birthday gift of his life. And a few months later he met Karen. They fell in love, got married, popped out two more kids."

With his theory about things happening for a reason in mind, I asked, "Do you think your mom died in order for your dad to meet Karen?"

"No. My mom died because it was her time to go. Nothing more, nothing less."

"Something tells me you won't feel that way if it's your life on the line."

"I do. We're all going to die sometime. Why waste energy worrying about it?" He pressed a soft kiss to my forehead. "Anyway . . . so why birds?"

I took to the change in subject happily. "I'm not sure when it began, but for as long as I can remember, I've always wanted to have the ability to fly. To leave everything behind and soar into the clouds, far removed from my life. Once, I climbed a tree to jump onto a trampoline."

"And?"

"I broke my arm."

He lifted my arm straight out above us, skimming along its length with his rough palm. "This one?"

"The other. I was in a cast for eight weeks," I said. "I guess that's why I was drawn to dance. Leaping onstage, defying gravity, it's how I'm able to fly. For those few seconds, time slows and I'm weightless."

"Come with me," he said, getting out of bed. I followed him, enjoying the view of his firm ass as he led me toward the balcony door, noticing for the first time the faded tattoo of wings on his shoulders.

I hesitated by the door, taking note of the glass balcony walls and my distinct lack of clothing.

He sensed my hesitation and held out his hand. "Fly with me."

I walked out onto the balcony, surprised to feel the concrete warm beneath my feet, and came to a stop before the nearly invisible railing. He came up behind me and lifted my hands to the sides, and it was almost as if he were leading me to the edge of the world, two birds ready to soar.

I closed my eyes to the thousands of sparkling lights around us just as the breeze picked up, feeling it sift through my hair and wrap around me like a promise.

"Sometimes I feel like I'm weighed down here on earth," I found myself confessing with my eyes still shut. "But being here with you . . . for the first time in a long time I feel . . . light."

"Why?" he asked so softly I almost didn't hear. "What is it that's dragging you down?"

I took a deep breath and let it out, along with the worries and doubts. Here, thirty-eight floors above the world, it was just Neal and me, without adornments or armor. "Five years ago, I was engaged," I said, rubbing the phantom ring on my left hand. The day Jason had suggested we get married, I'd put on a silver band in anticipation of a real engagement ring and had worn it through the months he was deployed. "We were going to get married after he came home from deployment."

Neal nodded, maybe sensing where this story was headed.

"But he died before he could come home. Killed by a sniper in Kabul." Even after I found out about his death, I'd worn the ring, kept spinning it around and around on my finger while I prayed that the reports were wrong.

Neal's eyebrows drew together, his lips growing tight.

"Life was . . . tough after that. I didn't leave my room, my apartment, for weeks. Eventually my mom came and tried to snap me out of it. It worked for some time. I stayed with her and she tried her best to make me forget. But you can't forget something like that." I swiped at the tear streaking down my cheek.

"But you're here right now, doing well," he said in a pained voice.

I didn't know if he meant it as a statement or a question. It didn't matter either way. "I haven't felt the same since his death. Like he took the best of me with him to the grave. And I'll always resent him a little for that." I opened my eyes and stared down at the streets below. "I probably shouldn't say that about someone who died. It wasn't like it was his choice to go."

"That's bullshit," he said so roughly I whipped my head around in surprise. "Why aren't we supposed to speak ill of the dead? Why should we romanticize their lives, as if they were perfect? If his death took away your chance at happiness then no amount of whitewashing will make that go away."

My chest threatened to cave in on itself, making it difficult to say anything.

He moved away from me and leaned on the railing. He put his head in his hands and was silent for a long time. When at last he looked up, the gloom was gone and in its place was grim determination. Without warning, he lunged forward and took hold of my face, kissing me hard and deep. There was a different texture to this kiss—a new, more desperate kind of need—but for the life of me I couldn't figure out what had changed.

He kissed me on that balcony for a long time, grasping the back of my head to bring me closer, pinning my body against the railing with his own.

His chest was heaving when he pulled away, his gaze almost frightening in its intensity. "I'm sorry," he said before stalking off inside.

4

"Don't go," I said, holding out my hand, hoping this time he'd take it.

But the man before me in camouflage didn't reach out, didn't even acknowledge me. Instead he set the helmet over his blond head and picked up his rifle, holding it protectively over his chest. He turned away from me and faced the flat horizon.

"Come back," I called out, drifting away from him. Tears were streaming down my face, and I sobbed, thinking that if I cried hard enough, he'd turn around and change his mind. I knew if he left now, he would not come back alive. "Please don't go. Please. I don't want you to go."

He looked over his shoulder, flashing me a confident smile. "Don't worry. I'm going to find him," he said with a young boy's voice. "I'll find him for you. I'll come back with Dad."

Then he walked off toward the desert, disappearing into the dusty, tan horizon.

I woke up, my back covered in sweat, my pillow damp from tears. I'd had the dream before and though the location sometimes changed, the outcome was always the same. If I was lucky, like today, I'd wake up before his body was brought back in a coffin.

With trembling fingers, I lifted Neal's heavy arm off my waist and rolled out of bed. I rummaged around in my purse for my cell phone before heading to the bathroom, closing the door behind me. I sat on the toilet lid and took deep breaths, trying to calm my nerves.

I knew it had only been a dream, that Will was not actually going off to war, but my body felt it anyway, as if the absolute horror of watching someone you love die was now part of my muscle memory.

A good five minutes elapsed as I stared at the phone in my hand before finally deciding to hit the call button. I didn't know if seven thirty in the morning was too early, but I needed to hear my son's voice.

John picked up on the third ring. "Good morning," he said. "How are you enjoying your trip?"

"It's been fun," I said, feeling a twinge of embarrassment that John knew where I was, what I was doing here. "I just wanted to check up on Will."

"He's doing well. We stayed up late last night watching *The Lion King*, so he's still asleep." I heard some shuffling in the background, then, "Oh, wait, he's here."

"Hello?" came the sleepy little voice on the line, easing the tightness in my lungs.

"Hi, honey."

"Mom! Where are you?"

"I'm still here," I replied with tears gathering in my eyes.

"When are you coming home?"

"Tomorrow morning. Unless you want me to come home earlier?"

"No, it's okay. Grandma and Grandpa are taking me strawberry picking today at a real farm."

"That's fantastic! What did you do yesterday?" I hugged my knees to my chest and listened as Will gave a blow-by-blow account of his day, sounding so happy it almost hurt to know that it hadn't been with me. It struck me again that he was growing up so fast, and soon he'd be deciding on his future, perhaps even wanting to follow in his father's footsteps. And as much as I appreciate those in the military for their sacrifice, I didn't want my son joining their ranks. The military had already stolen one man from my life; I would fight tooth and nail to make sure it didn't claim another.

"Will, remember to be polite and well mannered, okay? And don't eat too many sugary things. You know how it makes you shaky."

I was sure his eyes were rolling. "Okay, Mom. You know I'm always good."

"Yes, you are." I looked down in time to see a tear drop on my knee. "I love you."

"Love you, too, Mom. 'Bye!"

"'Bye."

I looked around the clean bathroom, a strange feeling of detachment settling over me.

What the hell am I doing here? I should be back in Monterey with my son.

I stood up and started the shower, trying to figure out how to tell Neal that I was ready to end our time together.

When I opened the bathroom door several minutes later, I found Neal lying in bed, his arms folded behind his head as he glared holes at the ceiling. I watched him quietly for a few moments, riveted by the torment in his face, wondering what the hell had put it there.

When he noticed me, his entire demeanor changed: the lines

between his eyebrows eased and his lips curled up into a smile. "Morning," he said in a sleep-roughened voice. "You're up early."

I dropped the towel and slid under the covers beside him. "So are you."

His warm palm found my breast under the sheets. "In more ways than one."

"What were you thinking about just now?" I thought I had finally figured him out, but after the conversation on the balcony the night before, he was once again a mystery to me.

He dipped his head and nipped at the underside of my jaw, tickling my neck with his stubble. "I was thinking about you," he murmured. "Of all the things I still want to do with you."

Even though I remained unconvinced, I laughed and tried to squirm out of his grasp. His hand slid down my stomach and found my heat, his fingers quickly slipping through my folds, further distracting me.

By the time he slid into me, I'd already forgotten about his worries and my determination to leave, my brain emptied of all thoughts save for one: that I wasn't ready to say good-bye.

After eating brunch at the hotel buffet, we went out into the bright Nevada sunshine.

"Where are we going?" I asked, looking down at my gray tank top and white maxi skirt, which billowed in the wind. "Why did you have me dress like this?"

"Secret," he said with a wink as he led me toward a waiting taxi.

I settled into the seat. "You should know that I hate surprises."

He slid in beside me until our shoulders and thighs touched. "It's a good surprise," he said, squeezing my leg.

"Where to?" the taxi driver asked, casting me a long look in the rearview mirror.

"To the Bunny Ranch," Neal said. He burst out laughing at my shocked expression and quickly said, "I'm kidding. To the MGM Grand, please."

"Isn't that right down the road?" I asked.

He grinned. "Yes."

"You baller," I teased.

"What kind of gentleman would I be if I made my lady walk in this heat?" he said. "You're going to need your energy for where we're going."

It didn't take long before we were exiting the taxi and he was leading me through the hotel, past the golden lion, under the golden dome, by the live lion habitat, and finally coming to a stop in front of the Hollywood Theatre sign.

"Are we going to see a show?"

"No, we're not," he said, approaching a lean, good-looking man in a blue button-down shirt, vest, and black slacks. "Hey, man. Good to see you again," Neal said, shaking his hand. "Carlos, this is Julie."

I shook his hand, still bewildered.

"Nice to meet you." He turned to the main theater entrance and unlocked the set of doors on the right. "You have an hour before the crew starts setting up for the show," he said to Neal as he led the way inside.

We walked down the aisle through the overwhelmingly red theater, past the empty seats toward the stage.

"Thank you," Neal said, shaking Carlos's hand again.

"No problem. Happy to return the favor," Carlos replied, heading back toward the entrance. "I'll lock the doors behind me. Just call me on my cell phone if you need out."

When he was gone, Neal turned to me with a pleased smile on his face. "A few years ago he needed to fly to Idaho for a family emergency, so I helped him out," he said.

"Very generous of you."

"He's a friend and I was in town." He shrugged, as if dropping everything and flying someone hundreds of miles was no big thing. "Since I was here, I thought I'd call in a solid."

I looked around. "So . . . what are we doing exactly?"

He motioned to the stage. "This stage—this entire auditorium—is yours for an entire hour."

I stared at the stage, trying to remember the last time I'd danced on one. It was so long ago.

"So what would you like to do?" he asked.

Dance, of course.

I walked up to the raised platform and touched the edge of the polished surface before me, suddenly short of breath at the prospect of performing onstage again.

"What's wrong?" he asked, coming up behind me.

"I don't know," I said, suddenly fighting back tears. "I'm scared, I think."

"It's just you and me here, Julie," he said, his gentle words like a caress on my skin. "You don't even have to dance. You can just stand there and twirl around in your skirt."

I chuckled, blinking away the doubt. "Okay."

Then I felt his hands encircling my waist, lifting me up onto the stage. I chewed on my lip, surveying the land before me. It wasn't a very big area—about three or four leaps across in length—but for someone who hadn't danced in anything bigger than her living room in several years, it appeared to me the size of a football field.

I took my sandals off and set them at the edge of the stage, then performed a quick warm-up before testing the area with a few grand jetés. I came to a dead stop in the center of the stage, finding myself at a loss. I looked down at Neal, who was standing in the same place, and shook my head. "My mind's gone blank."

He smiled and pulled out his phone, playing with it for a few seconds before setting it onto the stage. A few seconds later, piano notes floated through the air as "Gravity" by Sara Bareilles began to play. The song immediately dragged me back to college, to the first time I performed a contemporary dance in front of the class.

I smiled ruefully. "This was the song I used on the first dance I ever choreographed and performed. I was so scared beforehand that I was actually shaking."

"I bet it went well."

"It was a disaster. I kept forgetting moves that I could have done in my sleep, kept falling out of rhythm. Nobody was impressed. I think people only clapped out of pity," I said with a chuckle. "But the next time, the class agreed that I was most improved."

I'd taken an important lesson with me that day that I'd tried to carry with me through life: that each performance was an opportunity to grow. It didn't escape my notice that I hadn't performed in a while.

Neal put his hands in his pockets and smiled up at me, my pensive mood reflected in his face. He reached out and restarted the song. "So dance like you did back then."

I curled into my knees on the ground, a cloud of white gauzy material surrounding me, then slowly rose. I let the melody wind around me like the breeze, guiding me, whirling around me as I spun. My skirt flowed around, billowing gracefully as I moved. My body was nowhere near as limber as it used to be but it felt good to extend my limbs as far as they could reach, to leap across the stage without worry weighing me down.

I was heaving by the time I dropped to my knees, ending the

performance in the same position as before. I got to my feet, exhilarated and anxious, unsure of what I'd see in Neal's face.

He jumped onto the stage and crossed the divide in three long steps, sweeping me up in his arms. He grabbed my face and kissed me like he was drowning and I was a pocket of air and he had no choice but to breathe me in. "I'm sorry," he said after some time. "I couldn't help myself."

"You don't hear me complaining," I said, still fighting to catch my breath.

He kissed the tip of my nose. "Will you teach me a few moves?"

"Sure."

He kicked off his shoes, keeping his socks on, and put his heels together with his toes out to the sides.

"You know first position?" I asked with an eyebrow raised.

"My stepsister used to do ballet," he said with a confident grin. He then brought his hands to the front and lifted them over his head.

"What else do you know?"

He lifted one leg to the knee. "This is called passe?"

I chuckled. "Looks like you're ready for a pirouette," I said, demonstrating the turn.

He spun around but his socks were too slippery and he stumbled out of the spin, regaining his balance before he fell.

"You need to spot," I said. "Give it another try."

He spun again, his head whipping around after the turn, this time executing a fairly decent spin. "How's that?" he asked, raising an eyebrow.

"Let's try a grand pirouette." I held my arms out to the sides and spun around with one leg extended, bobbing up and down on my heel.

Neal laughed then gamely got into position. "Okay, let's give this a shot." He spun around and kicked his leg out, falling immediately off balance and catching himself on one knee. As he stood up, his deep, self-effacing laughter echoed throughout the auditorium, settling over me like a warm blanket. "That's a lot harder than you make it look."

"You are so sexy, you know that?" I asked, wondering how someone could be so goofy and still exude masculinity.

He bit his bottom lip and wagged his eyebrows. "You should see my other moves," he said, stalking toward me.

"Oh, I've seen them," I said, pressing my palm against his hard stomach.

He held me against him, tipping my chin up and touching his lips to mine. "Julie," he whispered, our breaths mingling. "What is it about you that has me dizzy?"

"You mean apart from the spin?" I asked. "Is it my winning smile?"

"That's a big part of it," he said, tracing the outline of my mouth with his finger. "I love the way you light up sometimes when you smile at me, when you look at me like I'm someone amazing."

"You are."

He bowed his forehead to mine. "Hold on to that thought. Don't forget you once felt that way about me."

My throat seized up and it seemed there was not enough oxygen in the room. I pulled away. "Um, what?"

"I just want to make sure you take a snapshot of this moment and file it away in your memory so if something should come between you and me, you'll be able to remember."

"I don't understand," I said, hot prickles bursting on the back of my neck. "What is going to come between you and me?"

He shook his head, his eyes haunted. "I'm the ocean and you're the sky, remember? There's a whole world that comes between us and never will the two converge."

"They meet in the horizon."

"That's just an optical illusion."

"I don't know what the hell is wrong with you," I said, wrenching myself away and stomping toward the edge of the stage. I sat down and grabbed my shoes. "We were having a perfectly pleasant moment before you started talking skies and illusions."

He shoved his feet into his shoes and sighed. "I'm just preparing for the inevitable."

I stalked off up the aisle toward the exit. "Call your friend. We're done here."

5

I had some time to think in the taxi on the way back to the hotel, to chew on his words and figure out why I'd reacted so violently, but by the time we were dropped off, I had already cooled down. After raising a son on my own, I'd become pretty good at reeling in my temper.

Neal didn't say anything when we walked into the hotel. He just grabbed my hand and walked beside me, never letting go, even when we wedged ourselves inside the crowded elevator. As the car ascended, Neal continued to hold my hand and never once took his eyes off me. I kept my eyes trained on the backs of people's heads, wishing it were possible to see through a thick skull to read the person's thoughts.

Once we were back in the privacy of our room, I spun on him. "Something happened last night. When we were talking on the balcony."

He nodded, unbuttoning his shirt.

I reached out and stayed his hands. "Tell me."

He blinked up at me, his eyes a murky brown. "I realized that I'm not good enough for you."

My face twisted in confusion. "What?"

He took hold of my wrists and brought my hands up to his face, holding them against his bristly cheeks. "You are a beautiful, talented, amazing woman who deserves more in life than someone like me," he said. "But you misunderstood me. I wasn't saying good-bye. I'm a selfish bastard and I'll hold on to you until you tell me to go."

It occurred to me then, as I stood on my toes and touched my lips to his, that I didn't want to say good-bye, either. Not yet. Maybe not ever. "I guess that makes us both selfish, then."

"Maybe so." He grabbed me around the waist and walked me backward until the backs of my legs hit the mattress. "Put your arms up," he instructed before pulling my tank top over my head.

"You really enjoy undressing me, don't you?" I allowed him to slip my skirt and panties down.

"Do you blame me?" he asked, his eyes devouring my naked form. "Look at you. You're perfect."

"I don't know about perfect." I no longer had a lean, lithe dancer's body. After giving birth, my breasts became C cups and perhaps weren't as perky as they used to be, my hips were wider, and I no longer had the muscle definition that I'd once been so proud of. But as curvy as I'd become, I was under no illusion that I was out of shape. "But I like my body just fine."

He set his hands on my waist. "Me, too." Then he guided me down onto the bed, positioning my naked form in the middle of the mattress. He bent down over me, his hands burning hot against my skin as he slid them between my thighs then gently pried my legs apart until I lay spread-eagled on the mattress.

I watched and waited, my muscles taut with anticipation. He said nothing, only kept his gaze on me as he straightened up and took off his own clothes without hurry. I felt so vulnerable being laid bare to his scrutiny, but a part of me reveled in it.

When he was completely naked, he stood at the foot of the bed and continued to take me in. His cock twitched but he ignored it and instead set his palms on my shins and skimmed them upward, his touch almost reverent. He crouched over me as his touch continued, his fingers rolling over my hip bones and up over my ribs, flittering over my breasts as they made their way across my chest.

My stomach trembled uncontrollably when his hands cradled my head and he brought his head down to my neck, breathing me in.

"Don't stop, please," I said, feeling short of breath. "I need you to touch me." I gasped when I felt the wet heat of his tongue tracing along my collarbone then sliding down my chest, paying careful attention to the neglected skin under my breasts.

He said nothing as he sat back on his haunches and continued the gentle caress, tracing my every curve with the pads of his fingers, leaving tingling trails all across my body. He wore a brooding look on his face as he raked his nails across my nipples then sat astride me, his balls heavy and ticklish on my mound.

"What are you doing?" I asked, the sight of him over me taking my breath away. My insides throbbed, aching to be filled.

He swallowed, his Adam's apple bobbing up and down. "I'm memorizing you, trying to appreciate you with all my senses," he said in a roughened voice.

"Are you done? Because I'd really like to be fucked now."

A hint of a smile playing along his lips, he rolled off me to get a condom. He settled back between my legs, the unopened package in his hands.

"Wait," I said before he ripped the wrapper. "I want to feel you without it."

His eyes bored into me, and just when I thought he would reject the idea, he said, "I'm clean."

"Good. I can't get pregnant."

He let out a breath and threw aside the foil package. He positioned himself at my entrance, waiting for an answer. "Are you sure?" he asked, his elbows on either side of my head.

I lifted my hips and felt him penetrate my cleft. "Definitely."

He sank down into me with a pained groan, our naked bodies aligning. "Julie," he rasped. "You feel incredible."

I wrapped my legs around his ass, reveling in the pleasure of his bare skin against my channels. I clutched him tighter as he began to rock his hips back and forth, thrusting into me in a steady rhythm. He wrapped his arm around my back and held tight as his thighs nudged my legs farther apart, allowing him to plunge deeper until he found my G-spot. Over and over his thick cock stroked me, ripping ragged moans from my throat.

I gripped his ass, digging my fingers into his flesh, enjoying the sensation of his crotch rubbing against my clit. Then he took hold of my wrists and held them above my head, his gaze holding me in place. It was an incredibly intimate moment, as if our bodies as well as our minds were connected. If it was possible to peer directly into someone's soul, I was sure I could see into his and he into mine.

I had never felt more naked in my entire life.

I felt the climax rip through me the moment I came to the realization that I was starting to fall for this man. A tremor traveled over my entire body but Neal held me down, prolonging the pleasure with his firm thrusts, and I bit into his shoulder to muffle my cries as the orgasm went on and on.

His breathing sped up at the same time as his movements, and his body bowed over me as he pressed into me one last time, his entire body a landscape of taut muscles.

After the end of his climax, he relaxed, supporting his weight on his elbows as his fingers brushed the sides of my face. Tears escaped out the corners of my eyes, and though I tried, I was too weak to rein in my emotions. So I just stared into his eyes, helpless and crying, drawing in ragged breaths.

Neal didn't have to ask what was wrong. I suspected he already knew. "Julie," he whispered, wiping away my tears. "I feel it, too."

After taking a shower together, we ordered room service and ate dinner on the bed, wearing nothing but thick bathrobes.

"Try this," he said, picking up a wedge of pineapple with his fingers and bringing it to my lips.

I opened up and took it in, sucking the juice off his fingers. "This is the sweetest pineapple I've ever tasted." I looked around at the empty plates on the tray, coming to the conclusion that perhaps my enjoyment of this food had something to do with my revelation earlier. Everything, even the pumped-in hotel air, seemed more fresh.

I crawled around behind him and peeled the robe away from his back, exposing the faint lines of his eagle tattoo. I traced a finger along the light brown outline of the stylized bird, its wings spread out over his shoulders.

If I believed in omens, I would think that this tattoo was the universe's way of telling me that this man had been brought to me for a reason.

"You should definitely visit Dallas," I said, pressing my lip to the very heart of the bird.

"Just say the word," he said, twisting around to face me. "But I have to stop in Kansas first. I have to get something from storage."

"What's that?"

He shook his head, tangling our fingers together. "Just some stuff." He studied my hand, playing with my fingers. His gaze caught on my ring finger. "Have you ever been married before?" he suddenly asked.

I let out a long breath. "Yes."

He nodded, urging me to go on.

"I was married once, to a good man. But it didn't last."

"Why not?"

"Because I married him for the wrong reasons. I married him out of loneliness." I could have told Neal about my son in that moment, to explain why I'd felt I needed a husband to begin with, but the words stuck in my throat. The truth was, I was still afraid. "He also grew to resent me for getting my tubes tied. He wanted children, I guess."

"And you don't?"

I pursed my lips and shook my head, searching for the courage to just tell him about Will. But I guess that's the thing when you care about someone, you start to care about what they think of you. "What about you? Have you ever been married?"

"I almost proposed to my girlfriend once after I got back from deployment."

"Oh, that's a pity . . ." His words took a moment to sink in, and then my head was spinning and I felt like I was about to faint.

"But come to find out, she'd cheated on me while I was away and didn't even have the decency to break up with—" He stopped and peered into my face. "Are you okay?"

I scrambled for my champagne flute and took a large gulp, trying to clear the clog in my throat. Suddenly it became clear to me, the eagle tattoo, the reason he knew Henry. I couldn't believe I never saw it before. "You're in the military?"

"I was Air Force but now I'm in the reserves." He spoke slowly as if afraid to spook me.

"Why didn't you tell me before?"

He shrugged as he shook his head. "I thought you knew. I thought maybe Henry or Elsie had told you."

"No, they didn't." I got off the bed and began to gather my clothes from around the room.

"What's wrong?" he asked, getting to his feet. "Why are you packing?"

"I can't . . ." I stopped and took a deep breath, trying to contain the disappointment that was threatening to surge out of my eyes. "I'm sorry. I can't see you anymore."

"Because I'm in the military?"

"Basically." I stuffed my clothes in my bag, not bothering to fold them. I needed out of here before I did something even more stupid, like give him all of me.

He grabbed my hand and wrenched the bag out of my grasp. "Julie, stop," he said in a commanding tone. "Stop and talk to me. What's wrong with being in the military?"

I tried to retrieve my bag, but he held it away from my reach. "I have my reasons," I said between my teeth. "Give it back."

He turned my bag upside down over the bed, its contents tumbling all over the mattress. "You're not leaving until you give me a valid reason." When I lunged for my clothes, he grabbed my wrists and pulled me close. "Talk to me."

I bit my lower lip to keep it from trembling, but there was no hiding the regret in my eyes. "You know why, Neal," I finally said.

His fingers dug into my skin. "Because of your dead fiancé?"

I nodded, averting my eyes. If I looked at him one more second, I might cry. "As much as I like you, I can't get attached if there's even a chance that you'll go out there and die. I can't go through that again."

He took a deep breath, his heart breaking all over his face. “Okay,” he said, that one word soaked with finality. “I’ll fly you home.”

“No,” I said quickly. “I’ll just take a commercial plane.”

I expected him to argue, to insist that he’d take me, but he just nodded and said, “Let me call you a taxi at least.”

6

Neal dressed and waited with me at the front of the hotel for the taxi to arrive. He didn't have to—I practically pushed him back through the sliding doors, I was so aggravated—but he wouldn't budge. He simply stood stoically beside me, his hands folded across his wide chest, casting glances at me as if I were a complex math problem that had him perplexed.

"I'm sorry it has to end like this," I said, seeing the taxi turn off the street and into the hotel driveway. "I appreciate everything you've done for me."

He nodded, though there was pain in his eyes.

I cleared my throat. "You gave me the ability to fly, even for a little while." Hell, I was being sappy, but how was it possible to keep from being sentimental during this gut-wrenching moment? "I'll never forget it."

When the taxi stopped before us, Neal stepped off the curb and opened the door. The move, so chivalrous in nature, just about broke my heart. "Have a safe trip back home."

I set my bag inside and turned to face him one last time. "Be safe," I said, and gave him a brisk hug.

"Julie, before you leave, please tell me your last name."

"Keaton."

He let out a defeated sigh and nodded gravely. "Julie Grace Keaton," he said, my name sounding beautiful in his deep voice.

"Wait, I don't know yours." How was it possible that I'd slept with him, flown to a whole other state with him, and yet we didn't even know each other's names?

"Harding. Neal Harding." He held out his hand and I took it for the last time. His eyes rooted me in place as he shook my hand, then before I could react, he tugged me in and I was engulfed in his strong arms. I buried my face in his chest, breathing in his scent, then he was gripping my hair and kissing me, a desperate man drawing his last breath. "This isn't the end, Julie," he said, bowing his head to mine. "Not by a long shot."

I wanted to believe him, wanted so badly to take back the last hour so I could enjoy our last night together, but knew it wouldn't change a thing. Because come the morning, he would still be the very thing I'd been running away from all these years.

I pulled away, wishing I'd been more careful with my heart. "Sorry, Neal. It has to be."

I arrived in Monterey at midnight, bleary-eyed and numb. Though it had been a direct, three-hour flight, by the time I walked off the plane I felt like I'd been traveling for days.

I took a taxi to the Shermans' house and let myself in quietly, using the key Elodie had lent me. On my way to the guest bedroom, John appeared at the top of the stairs, concern written all over his sleep-rumpled face. "Julie? I thought you weren't due back until tomorrow," he said, padding down the stairs.

"I . . . I missed Will," I said, hoping he didn't notice my puffy, red-ringed eyes in the dim hallway light.

He nodded, looking like a comfortable sage in his blue robe.

I had just turned to go when he spoke, stopping me in my tracks. "You know, sometimes things like these don't work out," he said gently. "But the admirable part is that you gave it a try."

I kept my back turned to him. I didn't want him to see my lips twisted in misery. "Good night, John. Sorry I woke you," I said and walked away.

Instead of going to the guest room, I crept into Will's room and lay beside him, wrapping myself around his little body. He snored softly, unaware that his mother's heart was hurting. I held him to me—my sweet little man—and finally closed my eyes, glad that we only had one more day before returning back to our normal lives.

A while after Jason and I had broken it off, I came to Dallas with the cast and company of *Broadway Across America*, and I invited him to one of our after parties. I didn't think he'd actually come since I hadn't seen or spoken to him in a while, but he made the three-hour drive down from Oklahoma City on his own.

"Well, well, well," he said with a wide smile when he spotted me in the bar. "Look who flew into town."

I gave him a kiss on the cheek, feeling the familiar fluttering in my belly whenever he was around. "I'm glad you came."

He looked good, more muscular and mature than I remembered, and I told him as much while I led him out to the dance floor.

He grabbed my waist, just like he'd done when we first met, and danced from my cue. "If I look good, then you look fantastic."

We slipped into our old ways easily, the dancing leading into touching, the touching making swift way to the kissing. It was easy with Jason because he lacked pretense. He had no secrets and it seemed—at least during that time in my life—that he was the only person I knew without a hidden agenda. He wanted me; that much he'd always made clear.

"I need to sit and I need beer," he said, tugging me away from the dance floor.

"But this is a good song!" I protested.

"I need nourishment!" he growled, bending down to nibble at my neck.

We sat down at a table a few minutes later, laughing and drinking like old times.

"I've missed you," I said, kissing his cheek. "Thank you for driving down here to see me."

"I'd go anywhere for my favorite dancer," he said with a wink. "You know I'm staying the night with you, right?"

"You'd better," I said. "So how's life treating you? Are you seeing anyone?"

"What would you do if I said yes?" he asked, chuckling. "Would you feel bad, considering you've been kissing me all night?"

I smacked his arm. "You'd better not have come down here, kissing and flirting with me, if you have a girlfriend!"

He laughed, giving me a peck on the mouth. "No, I'm not seeing anyone," he said, his blue eyes glittering with meaning. "I had a girlfriend for a little while, but it didn't work out. She didn't like that I was in the Air Force."

I took a sip of my wine, giddy and drunk on his presence. "Why?"

"Because we deploy and we go on unaccompanied tours for a year at a time."

"Why do it, then? Why start a relationship with someone, knowing you'll be leaving for months or years at a time?" I leaned in for the answer, not knowing back then just how it would affect the rest of my life.

"Why wouldn't I?"

"Don't you think it's kind of selfish? You'd be putting her through hell on purpose," I said, feeling so important with my views and opinions.

"Why is it selfish?" he asked, his eyebrows drawing together. "Don't I deserve to be loved, too?"

PART THREE

DIVERT

1

"Will, please eat your cereal faster. We have to get going."

"Okay, Mom."

After preparing his lunch, I zipped up his lunch bag then poured two glasses of orange juice. Before I had a chance to drink it, the dryer beeped and I rushed to the laundry room to get my light blue scrubs. I ran upstairs to finish getting ready, cursing myself for forgetting to put the clothes in the dryer the night before.

It was close to seven by the time I came back downstairs, where Will was putting his cereal bowl in the sink. "Ready?" I asked, wetting a paper towel and wiping the milk off his face.

"Ew, it's all wet," he said, squirming away.

I grabbed him by the collar and inspected his little face. "Do you want to go to your first day of kinderbloom with drool and milk all over your face?"

He shook his head and lifted his face.

"Didn't think so," I said, and continued wiping him down. "Okay, get your backpack. We have to go."

We were already five minutes late by the time we got in the car, and we made it to the elementary school with one minute to spare. I had only a few seconds to take his picture in front of the kinderbloom classroom—a prekindergarten class set up for kids who just missed the age cutoff—before the bell rang.

I bent down, giving him a quick hug. “I love you, Will. Have a great first day.”

“I love you, too, Mom,” he said, pulling away and walking into the classroom. I stood at the doorway, watching as the teacher’s aide showed him his desk and he immediately struck up a conversation with his classmates. Once upon a time, that near-five-year-old was no bigger than a Cabbage Patch doll, and now here he was, learning and making friends and living a life wholly separate from his mother.

I swallowed down the sadness, taking deep breaths to keep from bursting into tears.

“First kid?” someone asked beside me.

I blinked and looked around, not realizing there were other parents around me going through the same array of emotions.

“It’ll get easier,” the woman said with a kind pat on the shoulder.

“I hope so,” I said, though I seriously wondered if that was even possible.

“So this guy offered to buy me a drink, but he was one of those creepy guys at the bar, you know, the kind who looks too old to be there?”

I nodded, listening to my friend Naomi’s story while I ate my salad. I sneaked a glance at my watch and saw that we had only ten minutes left to our lunch hour. “We have to get going soon.”

“Okay,” she said, putting her trash into the paper takeaway sack. “So anyway, I said no but he kept insisting. Then he followed me around the rest of the night.”

"Why didn't you tell a bouncer?"

She shrugged. "I don't know. I just tried to ignore him. I did meet a guy and we made out, but that was it."

I studied my coworker, keenly aware of the five-year gap between us. She was still at that stage in her life when she could get away with partying every night and look no worse for the wear. Me—I fell asleep around ten every night, with the remote control in my hand and a half-drunk glass of cheap wine on my nightstand.

"You should come out with me and my friends sometime," Naomi said as we drove back in my Jetta.

"Yeah, maybe," I said, not giving it another thought as we pulled back into Gentle Dental, the practice where we worked as dental hygienists.

But Naomi would not let it drop. "I'm serious," she said later in the afternoon. "I'm going to take you clubbing this Friday."

"But Will . . ."

"Get a sitter. Done."

At exactly five that afternoon, I rushed out of the office and drove to Will's school, not wanting to go over the five thirty after-school care allowance and have to pay extra.

"What took you so long?" he asked as he climbed into his car seat and buckled his belt.

After I checked that he was properly buckled, I climbed into the driver's seat. "I'm sorry, honey, but this is how it's going to be for a while. I won't be able to get out of work until five."

"But, Mom . . ."

"We don't have any other choice, Will," I said, trying to temper my voice. I took a deep breath. "So how was your first day of school?"

Will talked about his teacher and classmates the rest of the drive home. Once at our house, we only had enough time to eat dinner and do homework before he had to take a bath and get ready for bed.

"Mom," he said as I tucked him in, "can we go back to California?"

It had been nearly a month since we'd come back from Monterey and still he asked the same question night after night. "What did I tell you?"

"No?"

"Why?"

"Because our life is here," he said, reciting my exact words. "But what if we moved our life somewhere else?"

"Don't you like our life here?"

"I do but it's boring here." He chewed on his lower lip. "I want to live near Grandma and Grandpa, or maybe near Aunt Elsie."

I closed my eyes, fighting against the rising frustration. Exhaustion coupled with that emotion that I was desperately trying to put behind me was making me an exposed nerve these days. "I'm sorry, honey. But we're not moving anywhere. Not for a long time," I said, keeping my tone even. "Surely there's something you like about living here."

"I guess," he said with a resigned sigh. "I like my friends and my room. And school's pretty good, too."

I ruffled his hair. "That's the spirit." I kissed his forehead, breathing him in. "I love you, kid."

"Love you, too, Mom."

After closing the door, I went downstairs and stood in front of the open fridge, the fresh bottle of wine in my sight. Then it occurred to me that drinking alone once again—even if I was drinking only a little bit to relax at the end of a long day—was just so . . . pitiful.

We had made a few friends in Dallas, but we had no family, nobody we could really count on through thick and thin. Nobody to sit and relax with at the end of the day. All we'd done for the past month—for the past few years, really—was stick to our routine and maybe, sometimes, stray outside our comfort zone to find adventure. But more often than not, we spent our weekends at home, doing the same old thing.

Will was right. Our life here was boring.

That Friday, I decided that we would try something different. I spoke to Stacy, the mother of Will's best friend from preschool, and she agreed to have him over for a sleepover.

"You sure about this?" I asked her again as I dropped him off that night. "I don't want to impose."

"Please, you're not imposing," she said just as Dennis, her son, came careening around the corner, yelling for Will to follow him. "Dennis has been begging me to allow Will to come for a sleepover."

I crouched down in front of my son, feeling like it was the first day of school all over again. "Have fun on your first sleepover," I said with a reassuring smile that I didn't entirely feel.

He wrapped his little arms around my neck and squeezed. "Thanks, Mom."

"If you need me, just call my cell phone."

"Okay."

"I'll come get you tomorrow morning."

He looked away, preoccupied with his friend's whereabouts. "Okay." He gave me a quick peck on the cheek, bid me good-bye, and took off down the hall.

I went out with Naomi and her former sorority sisters that night, to a dance club by the Stemmons Freeway called Zouk. After a long wait outside, when I seriously began to question my life choices, we finally made it inside and made a beeline for the bar; someone ordered a line of tequila shots.

"I'll just have wine," I told them.

"Come on, Julie, live a little," Naomi said, handing me a full shot glass. "Tonight you are free!"

I took the shot, feeling anything but free, and downed it with the rest of the women. After the second shot I realized, as my eyesight started to blur around the edges, that I hadn't had a chance to eat dinner. In that moment I was faced with a choice: stop there and live my life barely toeing the edge or just say *fuck it* and act like the single woman I was.

So I ordered another round, then led the way to the dance floor and lived it up, whooping when a good dance track started to play. I closed my eyes and lifted my arms above my head, swaying my hips to the thumping beat, dancing with my new best friends.

After some time, a pair of hands landed on my waist. "Hey, beautiful, you wanna dance?" a male voice whispered by my head.

I knew he wasn't the guy I'd been avoiding thinking about for the past several weeks but I leaned into him anyway, pretending for that moment it was Neal who was holding me close, grinding into my backside.

"You are so sexy," he said, his hands roaming over my stomach and down my thighs. I should have protested when his palms strayed upward and cupped my breasts over my tube dress, but I was too deep into my fantasy to care. Neal was here, igniting my body with his touch once again, and any moment now he was going to lead me to a dark corner and bury himself deep inside me.

"J, we need to go to the bathroom," Naomi shouted over the music. I opened my eyes to find her looking slightly horrified at the guy behind me. She grabbed my hand and pulled me away, eliciting a "Hey!" from my Neal proxy.

"What the hell?" I asked once we were in the bathroom.

"Did you see who you were dancing with?" Linda or Larissa or somebody whose name started with an *L* asked.

"Yeah, *dancing*," Naomi said, putting up air quotes. "He was basically trying to hand-fuck you out there."

"I was letting him," I said, leaning against the wall to steady the swaying room.

Naomi gave me this look, a mixture of awed surprise and pity. "If you want to hook up with someone, at least choose a guy who's not so . . ." She looked to her two friends for help.

"Cheeseball," the other girl whose name I never did catch said.

"Greaseball," her *L*-named friend amended. "He's the kind of guy who clubs every night, bobs his head around, thinking he's cool."

"He's Last-Call Guy," Naomi said.

I nodded, pretending to know what she meant. If I thought hard enough about it, I'm sure I would have understood, but in my inebriated state, all I could think of was how much I missed Neal. His laugh, his face, his kiss . . . his everything.

Tears welled up in my eyes. Never more than in that moment did I feel the effects of my decision to walk away from him. And even though I felt deep down I was doing the right thing, beneath that was another layer: a desire to try again, sure that the next time would be different. Maybe if I convinced him to get out of the military . . .

I shook my head to clear it of cobwebs, dabbing at the corners of my eyes. "This is why I don't date!" I cried out. "I should just stick to booty calls and one-night stands."

Naomi raised an eyebrow. "In all the time we've worked together, when was the last time you had either one of those?"

"Since my divorce? Not even once," I said, shaking my head. "And the one time I did, I did it wrong and got too attached."

Naomi took my hand. "Come on, Jules. I'll take you home."

"That sounds like a great idea." I followed her out of the bathroom and waited while Naomi said good-bye to her friends, who were opting to stay.

"It was nice to meet you," I called out to them and turned to make my way through the room to the exit. My eyes sought out every male face I passed in search of something familiar and warm.

I locked gazes with a man who was different from the rest, who wasn't trying to block my way or trying to grope me. He was just talking to his friend when he happened to look over at the exact right time.

I walked up to him and took his face in my hands. "Kiss me," I said and pressed my lips to his.

It took him a second to get over the shock before he opened his mouth and kissed me back, eager and willing.

I closed my eyes and tried to feel something, but even pretending didn't bring back those same feelings. This kiss might have been technically good, but it was definitely lacking.

When I pulled away, the guy wore a bewildered smile on his face. "Damn, girl."

I touched my fingers to my lips, wiping away traces of him. "Nothing. I feel nothing," I said to myself. I moved in for another kiss and, hopefully, for more, when Naomi took hold of my arm and yanked me away again.

"Girl, you are a mess," she said as she dragged me toward the door.

I turned back to the guy longingly, wishing I could finish what I'd started. If I slept with him and still felt nothing, then maybe there was hope for me yet.

But I allowed Naomi to lead me out of the club and back to her car, not because I was too drunk or too meek but because, deep down, I really didn't want anybody else.

2

After a few weeks, Will and I were finally able to figure out a routine so that we weren't always running late. Will seemed happy and thriving at school, even making friends in the after-school program, and all seemed to be going well.

Still, each night after I tucked him into bed, I would sink into the couch with a sigh and wish there were more to life than this.

One Tuesday afternoon, while I was sitting with a patient, flossing her teeth, I felt my phone vibrating in my pocket. While the patient sat up to spit in the sink, I quickly checked the caller ID to make sure it wasn't Will's school. The call was from Veronica Jackson, my best friend and fellow dance major back at New York University.

I hadn't heard from her in years. We'd fallen out of touch a few months after I moved to Dallas, when it became too difficult for either of us to carry on the friendship.

That evening, while Will was in the bath, I finally had a chance to call her back.

"How are you?" she asked as soon as she picked up.

"I'm good. And yourself?" I sat on Will's bed, which was adjacent to the bathroom, feeling a sense of nostalgia upon hearing her voice.

"I'm great. Still dancing my ass off, still lighting up the town."

I smiled, remembering the motto we'd come up with on graduation night, when we'd made a drunken vow to "dance our ass off and light up the town." God, had that really been almost eight years ago?

"So I hear you got knocked up," she said, ever straight to the point. There was no beating around the bush with Veronica, a trait that I'd really admired.

"Over five years ago," I said in amusement.

"And the dad?"

"He died."

"Oh, shit, I'm sorry."

"It was a while ago," I said, an automatic response whenever somebody found out about Jason for the first time, the easiest, most uncomplicated response I could think of.

Veronica was quiet for a moment, probably at a loss for what to say.

"So how are things in New York?"

"Life is good," she said. "That's actually why I called you. I don't know if you've been keeping up with your dancing, but there's an audition in October for a new production. It's a new Broadway musical and they need a lot of background dancers. I really think you should audition for it."

My scalp tingled at her words. "I haven't danced professionally in years. I'm so out of shape."

"You have six weeks to get back in shape. Come on, girl, I know you have a lot of natural talent."

"Why are you pushing for this?" I asked. "We haven't talked in a long time and all of a sudden you want me to audition?"

"I just know you'd be perfect for it. At least say you'll think about it."

"I will, I will."

Later, I mulled over Veronica's words over a glass of wine. It would be a dream come true to start dancing professionally again but even if I did manage to somehow beat out dancers who were younger and more in shape than me, how could I afford to move Will and me to New York City, one of the most expensive cities in the country?

I got to my feet and paced in front of the couch, wondering where I could even practice dancing. The one-car garage was full of stuff, and the living room, of course, had the couch, TV, and coffee table, among other things. I found myself walking through the lower part of the house, mentally eyeing the space. In the formal dining room, my eyes landed on the dining set, which we'd only used maybe twice, as we always ate at the round table in the kitchen.

Struck with an idea, I downed the rest of my wine and fetched my laptop before I could lose my nerve.

The dining set sold the very next day. A newlywed couple from Denton drove down with a trailer that night and bought the entire set, including the buffet. When they were gone, Will walked around the empty dining room, scratching his head. "So what are you going to do in this room?"

"Come with me," I said, picking him up like a football and taking him to the living room. "We're going to move the couch and TV into the dining room."

"And then?"

I spun us around before setting him down. "Then I'm going to use this room as a dance studio."

He gave me a dubious look, then pushed at the edge of the suede couch, managing to move it several inches. "Come on, Mom. What are you waiting for?"

It took nearly forty-five minutes to move everything into the other room. Will was most helpful with the smaller things, carrying the lamps and my bird figurines with care, while I somehow managed to maneuver the large furniture and rug through the narrow doorways.

When we were done, we collapsed on the couch in our new, smaller living room. "What do you think?" I asked, stroking my toes on the rug that covered the tile floor. "It's not too bad, right?"

"I like it," Will said. "It's weird."

"Okay, kid, time for bed."

He groaned. "Oh, man, I wanted to stay up and watch cartoons."

I tickled his side. "Not gonna happen, little man. It's already past your bedtime," I said, pulling his limp body up off the couch. "But thank you for helping me."

That night, I vacuumed the wood floor of the living room and stuck tile mirrors on one wall. It was nearing midnight by the time I was done and I stood in the middle of the room, surveying the space. It wasn't nearly as spacious as a studio, but it was big enough.

I caught my reflection in the mirror, looking weary in my wrinkled and dusty scrubs, and didn't see a dancer; instead I saw a single mom whose face wore lines of exhaustion. How in the world was I going to get back in dancing shape when I was barely getting by? Still, there was something in that woman's eyes, a drive that burned beneath the layers of weariness, a fire that had been rekindled on a stage in Las Vegas.

Making sure the blinds were all drawn, I took off my scrubs and stood in the middle of the living room in my underwear then pulled my hair out of its ponytail. I performed a quick set of stretches then tried a quick choreography to a song, moving my body until I forgot where I was.

When I danced, I lost and found myself over and over.

By the time I gathered my clothes and turned off the lights in the living room, I was filled with a buoyant feeling, something akin to hope.

And even though I had only a few hours' sleep that night, by the time I woke the next day, I was energized, excited for the hours of the day to fly by, for the time when I could dance again.

"Mom, can I dance with you?" Will asked one evening while we waited for the lasagna to heat up.

"Have you finished your homework?" I asked as I sat on the floor, stretching my legs.

"Yep!" He kicked off his shoes and socks then sat on the floor with me, mimicking my moves. "Mommy, I like it when you're happy."

I smiled at him, though his comment took me by surprise. "I'm always happy. Because I have you."

"I know, I know," he said, waving away my comment. "But sometimes you're sad or quiet. But you smile real big when you dance."

I leaned over to plant a kiss on his nose, never realizing just how transparent I'd been with my emotions. "I'm hoping to become a dancer again," I said. "There's an audition in New York in two weeks. Do you think I can make it?"

"Yeah, duh! You're the best dancer I know!"

"I'm the only dancer you know," I said with a chuckle, pulling him to his feet.

"Am I going to New York with you?"

I looked at him sadly, feeling the guilt lodge itself in my chest. It felt like all I'd done lately was leave him. I didn't know if I had the heart to go through with it, even in pursuit of my dream. "I want to take you with me, but nobody can watch you while I dance. So I've talked to Miss Stacy. She'll pick you up from school, then you'll sleep over at Dennis's house. I'll fly right back the next day."

"Yeah! He's got a PlayStation!" he said, pumping a fist in the air.

"But you have an Xbox," I said, his reaction lightening the load.

"But not a PlayStation."

"So I take it you're okay with that plan?"

"Yes."

But later, as we ate dinner, he asked, "Mom, if you become a dancer, you're not going to stay there, are you? You're coming back to get me, right?"

"Of course I am," I said, reaching across the table to squeeze his hand. "If a miracle happens and I somehow land the job, I'm coming back and then you and I are going to talk about moving."

It struck me then what I'd just said. I didn't know when the idea of moving had even taken root in my head, but it had sprouted almost overnight. The idea of moving with Will was no longer an impossibility; now it held some appeal.

I danced extra hard that night, even if my muscles were protesting from the paces I'd put them through the past few weeks. I moved with passion, extending my limbs as though I had something to grab, as though I were reaching for my dreams.

3

The flight to New York was hell.

To be enclosed in such a small space without room to move was pure torture when my body had once again grown accustomed to moving freely. I felt the energy buzzing through my veins, but it had to be tamped down, contained. After the first hour, it finally manifested itself in my restless, fidgety legs, earning me a dirty look from my seat neighbor.

"I'm sorry," I said and turned to the window, taking deep breaths to calm my nerves. Outside, the clouds were thick and fluffy, the sky a light cyan that expanded into oblivion. And even though I could look out the window, I felt claustrophobic, unlike the time I'd flown in Neal's plane.

I sighed, trying not to think of him, but that was a tall order when I had nothing to do for hours. In this enclosed space, feeling caged, it was impossible not to think of the man who had tried his best to set me free.

I pulled out my phone and plugged in my earphones, listening to the song that I'd danced to on that small stage in Las Vegas, when I'd felt uplifted and hopeful. My muscles started to relax as I imagined myself how Neal must have seen me, flying around the stage with my skirt fluttering, and soon I relaxed enough to fall asleep.

I went directly to the audition, my nerves still in disarray. But the moment I stepped into that hallway and joined the other dancers who were waiting to audition, I felt a strange sense of calm wash over me. Being here, with my people—this was my jam.

They called us all into a large studio and taught us the choreography, going over it at a slow pace the first few times. I had always picked up choreography quickly, and this time was no exception as I executed the moves with very few problems. Still, I couldn't help but notice the other dancers in the mirror, couldn't help but compare myself to their lithe bodies and clean technique.

Six weeks was definitely not enough time to get back in top competitive shape, that much was clear. I didn't even know if it was possible to compete—certainly I was no longer one of the young and limber.

After rehearsal we were each given a number to pin to our shirt and, after a ten-minute break, were then asked to come back inside, where three new people sat at a long table, ready to pick the best dancers in the room. I stood near the back of the room and didn't realize until we started to dance that one of the people on the panel was none other than my friend Veronica. She wore her jet-black hair shorter, but everything else about her—her flawless chocolate skin, her wide engaging smile—was still the same.

The sight of her on the panel caused me to miss a step, but I recovered quickly, hoping nobody noticed. Veronica saw and gave an encouraging nod.

We went through the choreography several times, each time moving around the room so that eventually everyone had danced at the front. The people sitting behind the table made notes in their notebooks, eyeing each of us closely but leaving their critiques until the end.

After we were dismissed, I hung around and waited until Veronica was done talking to her peers. Then, with a sheepish smile, she came to me, throwing her arms around my sweaty shoulders as if no time had passed at all.

I hugged her back. "It's so good to see you," I said. "You didn't tell me you were part of the show already. I thought I'd be auditioning *with* you."

"Would you have come if I'd told you?"

I could have lied but she already knew me, knew there was no way I would have come back and auditioned for her. My pride wouldn't have allowed it. "Probably not."

"Didn't think so." She slung an arm over my shoulder and led me out. "Come on, let me take you out for a drink."

After I changed back into jeans and a sweater, Veronica and I went to a bar that we'd frequented back in the day, sitting at "our" table like old times. She filled me in on her life since we'd lost touch, how she had started choreographing and had eventually earned a name for herself around town.

"So how do you think you did?" she asked over a Manhattan.

"I should be asking you that."

She grinned. "You did great."

"Really?" I asked, perking up. "Objectively speaking?"

She rolled her eyes. "Yes. You may be my friend but I'm still a professional. And you, my friend, have still got it."

My face warmed from her words, from the validation of all my hard work recently.

"You'd better stick around for another day or two for callbacks. But you didn't hear that from me," she said, adding a wink.

That familiar jubilation washed over me, the pure exhilaration of knowing you had beat out a large portion of those who'd auditioned. But that feeling was cut short by reality. "I can't," I said almost immediately. "My son."

"Julie!" she admonished. "You of all people know auditions aren't just a one-day thing!"

"I know. I just never thought I'd even survive the day, let alone get a callback."

"Well, fix it," she said as if it were that simple to leave my son for another few days. "You've got a real shot here. You'll regret it if you don't take it."

I stared into my drink, wondering which I would regret more: missing this chance or abandoning my son.

"Julie?"

Veronica and I looked up to find Colin, another dancer friend, approaching us. "It's you!" He clapped his hands together then threw his arms around me, talking animatedly the entire time. "You dropped off the face of the earth! I heard you were living in some bumfuck town in Alabama."

"Bumfuck, Texas, actually," I said, swept away by his enthusiasm.

He put his fingers to his lips and let out a sharp whistle, gaining the attention of the entire bar. "Hey, Shawna, Carolyn! Look who I found!"

Several other people joined us at our table, friends and acquaintances from my life a million years past. It was good to see them but I couldn't help but feel like time stood still here, that I'd aged while I was gone but my friends had not.

I wondered, for the millionth time, what would have become of me had I not stayed in Dallas. No doubt I would still be dancing, still hanging out at the same places with the same people. I might have become like Veronica, moving up in my career, or perhaps I'd still be doing the same thing, jumping from job to job, without any real security, destined to be put out to pasture before I was even past my thirties.

I knew then what my answer had to be.

I'd just opened my mouth to tell Veronica I wouldn't be coming back, when my cell phone began to ring. I excused myself from the revelry at the table and went outside to take the call, hugging my arms around myself in the chilly autumn night.

"Hello?"

"Julie!" Stacy said in a tone that immediately dropped my stomach to my feet.

"What happened? Is Will okay?"

"We're at the hospital—"

"What happened?" I practically shrieked. "Tell me he's okay!"

"The boys were just watching a movie when Will said his stomach was hurting. I thought it might have just been an upset stomach, but then he started running a high fever. We took him to the ER—"

"And?" My hands were trembling, my fingers struggling to hold the phone up to my ear. Every atom in my body wanted to start running, and to keep running until I was in Texas with my son.

"His appendix ruptured," Stacy said. "He's in the operating room right now."

I covered my mouth with my hand, unable to utter a word.

"I'm sorry, Julie. It happened so fast," she said, her voice full of worry.

"Thank you, Stacy," was all I could manage to say.

"I'll be right here, I promise," she said. "So he'll have a familiar face to see when he comes out from under anesthesia."

Bile rose up in my throat at the sudden thought that something might go wrong during the surgery. "I'm headed to the airport right now," I said. "I'll let you know the details in a few minutes."

I put away my phone and ran back inside the bar to grab my things.

"Where are you going?" Veronica asked, rising from her seat, no doubt alarmed by my panicked appearance.

"Family emergency back home."

A look of concern rumpled her features. "But what about—"

I stopped her with a look. "I can't stay, V. I have to go."

I barely managed to utter an explanation to the others before I was rushing out the door and hailing a taxi.

"What do you mean?" I practically shouted at the ticket agent. "Are you seriously telling me that none of the airlines here in this airport have any flights going to DFW right now?"

"Ma'am, I can't speak for the other airlines, but the next United plane leaving for DFW won't be for another four hours."

I leaned my head down on the desk, no longer able to hold it up, and fought the urge to sob into my arms. "It's an emergency."

The agent shook her head at me, genuine regret in her eyes. "I'm sorry. I can find a different route for you, but honestly, it would get you there the same time or later than the next DFW flight."

I shook my head and walked wearily back to the American Airlines counter, resignedly purchasing a seat on the flight leaving in three hours. I honestly couldn't remember the next hour; I was on autopilot from the moment I walked away with my ticket.

I arrived at the deserted gate and took a seat, sinking down into it, covering my face with my hands. I refused to think about Will, sure that if I even entertained the idea of his death, fate would somehow find a way to make it come true. Hell, it had happened before—when I'd scoured the news outlets for news on Jason—it could happen again.

I remembered it vividly, the moment I'd found the clip on CNN .com mentioning that an Air Force officer had been killed by a sniper attack in Kabul. Even later, when his name was printed in black and white in the newspaper underneath his picture, I'd refused to believe it. Instead I'd crawled under the covers and lived in my fantasy world where the father of my child was still alive.

I was saved from the sorrow spiral by the ringing of my phone. I pulled it out of my pocket, surprised to find Neal's name appear. "Hello?"

"Julie. Hi."

To hear his voice after all this time, admittedly, had a soothing effect on my chaotic mind. "Neal."

"Are you home? I'd like to come over and talk."

"No, I'm stuck in New York," I said. "I'm trying to get home because of an emergency but the flight doesn't leave for another million fucking hours."

"What's going on? Are you okay?"

I blinked the tears away. "It's my son. He's at the hospital and I can't get to him."

"You have a son?"

I took a deep breath, not having the energy or heart to lie about Will, especially not when he was on the operating table. "Yes," I said, sure that, any moment now, Neal would hang up.

He was quiet for a few beats then finally said, "What can I do? I'm in Dallas, so just tell me what I can do to help."

"You're in Dallas?"

"Yes," he said. "Do you want me to come and get you?"

"By the time you get here, the plane will already be boarding."

"Okay, so, what?" he asked, his voice all concern. "Where is your son?"

"He's at Medical City Children's Hospital."

"Okay, I'll head on over there right now."

"Will," I said before he could hang up.

"Will?"

"My son's name is Will."

He let out a breath. "Okay. I'll call you when I get there."

"Thanks, Neal," I said softly then hung up and dialed Stacy, letting her know that a friend of mine might show up.

When all was said and done, I put the phone away and leaned back in my seat, still rattled but able to breathe a little easier.

4

The moment I stepped inside the hospital, I started running. My bag was bouncing everywhere and I looked like a raggedy mess, but I didn't care. I ran past the information desk and up the stairwell, no longer patient enough to wait for the elevator.

At the children's ward, I stopped at the front desk to tell them my name and then headed to Will's room. I opened the door as quietly as I could manage, my eyes immediately finding the little body tucked under the sheets on the bed.

I fought to contain my breathing as I entered the room, setting my bag down on the floor, and approached the bedside. With teary eyes, I bent down to kiss his forehead, fighting down the sobs that were threatening to erupt. He looked so tiny in the bed, so helpless.

"Mom?" Will cracked open his eyes, blinking up at me. "You're back?"

"Yes, I'm back," I said, sitting on the bed and giving him a careful hug. "I got back as soon as I could."

"It really hurt, Mom," he said, his chin quivering. "I tried to be tough but it really hurt."

I bent my head down and cried silently into his hair, the guilt finally proving too much. "I'm sorry, sweetheart. I should have been with you."

"Neal was here. He stayed with me even after Miss Stacy had to leave."

I looked up and was surprised to find Neal asleep in the chair in the corner, his tall frame slumped over uncomfortably.

"It's okay, Mom. Neal said you tried your best to come back." He patted my shoulder. "I know you got stuck at the airport."

I glanced over at Neal again. "I couldn't get a flight back sooner."

"Mom," Will said, tugging on my sleeve until I bent down. He brought his lips to my ear. "Is he your boyfriend?" he whispered.

"No," I said, hoping Neal wasn't listening. "He's just a really good friend."

"You could marry him," Will said sotto voce.

I shook my head. "I don't think so, honey. He's not that kind of friend."

Our conversation was cut short when Neal began to stir. "Hey," he said with a tired smile as he stretched his neck side to side. He rose to his feet, unfolding to his full height, and walked to the bed. "I thought we agreed you'd wake me up when she got here," he said to Will with a smile, squeezing one little foot under the sheet.

"Sorry. I forgot."

Neal's gaze found mine and we stared at each other across the bed for a long, charged moment. My eyes ate him up; I'd almost forgotten just how attractive he was. His wavy hair was a little shorter, the sun-bleached tips shorn off. It was a relief to see that I hadn't just imagined his masculine beauty.

"Thank you," I mouthed.

He smiled at me, but his eyes were intent, letting me know that we had plenty to discuss. "You're welcome." He cleared his throat and looked at Will. "You good?"

"Yeah." Will's face lit up. "Hey, Mom, did you know Neal has no appendix, too? He has a scar on his stomach and everything."

I faked a smile as Neal lifted his shirt to show me the scar that I'd already seen.

"Cool, huh?" Will asked. "I'll have a scar just like that."

Neal grinned at my son, a genuinely warm smile that caught me unaware. "We'll be scar buddies," he said and ruffled his hair. "Hey, I'd better leave you and your mom alone."

"No, she doesn't mind—right, Mom?"

"Neal probably needs to get some sleep," I said. "Where are you staying?"

"At the Hilton downtown," he said. "And yeah, I need a shower and a shave," he added, rubbing a palm along his scruffy jaw.

"I'll call you later?" I asked as he stepped away from the bed.

"Sure," he said, picking up his jacket from the back of the seat. "No rush."

"You *are* staying in town, right?"

He stopped at the door and gave me a meaningful look. "I'll be here, Julie. When you're ready to talk, just come find me."

I slept in the room with Will. When the nurses saw that I wasn't about to leave his side, they brought in some sheets and a pillow, showing me how to turn the bench seat into a bed. I lay in that uncomfortable makeshift bed that night and tried to sleep, but my eyes kept popping open to watch my son sleeping; I found myself staring at his chest to make sure he was still breathing.

We'd stayed the night in a hospital only once before, back when Will was only a year old. We'd just moved into our own apartment and he was crawling on the floor while I was unpacking the kitchen. Apparently he'd found a paper clip on the floor and he swallowed it.

I would never forget the instant panic when I heard him start choking, and the short-lived relief when he swallowed the paper clip then smiled.

I rushed him to the hospital that afternoon and there we stayed overnight to prepare for the procedure in the morning. I held him in my arms, so small and afraid, as we slept in the armchair.

The next day I called Kyle during the procedure, out of sheer loneliness. I just needed someone—anyone—to talk to, else I would have gone crazy from the wait. It was the first time it occurred to me that I was well and truly a single parent.

Kyle rushed over, like he always did, riding in on his white steed, trying to save the damsel in distress. "I haven't taken you off the insurance yet," he said the moment he entered the waiting room. "I can go to the front desk and fix it."

I shook my head because I knew what Kyle wanted. "I'll find another way to pay for it."

"Julie, this will set you back tens of thousands."

"I know."

"Just let me help, okay?"

"I know you mean well, but Will is my responsibility."

He shook his head, his eyes never leaving my face. "That was always part of the problem. You never really let me in, never really allowed me to become a real father to Will."

"Kyle, I didn't call you because I wanted your help." I was tired and didn't want to rehash the reasons why I'd wanted a divorce after only a year together. "Let's not do this today, okay?"

I told Kyle to go home, and when Will came out of the OR, I was the only one there to greet him. I took him home on my own with some difficulty, accepting that I would have to do everything on my own from then on. I didn't yet have a plan on how I would pay the bills, but I was determined to make it through somehow.

I couldn't sleep. My mind raced with memories and thoughts, with wants and regrets. Finally, at around four in the morning, I got up and took a shower in the room's private bath, glad that I had toiletries and a change of clothes with me. When I came out of the bathroom, a nurse was standing at Will's bedside, looking at his charts.

"We caught it early," she said as she checked the IV fluids. "It hadn't spread too much. And the surgery went smoothly and without problems."

"That's good to hear."

"He'll recover in no time," the nurse said. "You're welcome to go get some coffee or breakfast. I'll be here for another twenty minutes or so."

"Thank you," I said, realizing I hadn't had anything to eat for twenty-four hours, since before the audition. I bent down and pressed a kiss to Will's head. "If he wakes up, could you please let him know I'll be right back?"

"Sure thing."

I stepped out of the room, closing the door soundly behind me, and walked to the elevator. When the metal doors slid open, I was surprised to find Neal standing there with his hands in his pockets, a backpack slung over his shoulder.

"Um, hi," I said, running a finger through my damp hair.

He put his hand against the door to keep it open. "I couldn't sleep," he said. He hadn't shaved and he wore his exhaustion like a mask, hiding his feelings.

"Me, either."

He pursed his lips and gave a nod. I stepped inside the elevator, both of us knowing that it was time to start talking.

But neither of us said a word the entire way down to the cafeteria. I was keenly aware of his solid presence, felt both energized and apprehensive just walking beside him. A few times our hands brushed, and it took everything in me to keep from reaching out and grabbing him like I really wanted to. I'd made my decision about Neal three months before, and I needed to stick to it, no matter how much I missed him.

We bought some coffee and took it to a table in the far corner of the cafeteria, away from the rest of the world. There was a moment, before we sat down, when we said nothing but felt everything passing between us.

"Come here," he finally said, grabbing a handful of my sweater and pulling me into him. My arms went around his waist of their own accord; I closed my eyes and pressed my cheek to his chest. I felt him take in a deep breath then let it out, the sound as calming as rolling waves. I could have stayed there longer, enfolded in his arms, but he kissed my head then let me go.

"So . . ." he said, holding out a chair for me.

"So . . ."

We sat down and sipped our coffees, watching each other over the steam.

"So you have a son," he said softly.

"I do." I set my cup down, keeping my eyes fixed on its inane coffee bean design.

"Why didn't you tell me?"

"For many reasons. But mostly because you and I were supposed to be a simple fling."

He blinked a few times. "He's a great kid."

"I know. I raised him."

"How old is he?"

"He'll be five in December."

Neal looked away, his nostrils flaring. "He told me his dad died in Afghanistan."

"Yes. I was pregnant with Will when his dad was killed."

He was quiet for a long time, a tormented look on his face as he sipped his coffee. I could sense the turmoil in him as he struggled to make sense of the situation.

"So you said you came here to talk."

He blinked a few times. "I did. I came here to give you something."

"What is it?"

He stared at me for a few beats, then, without warning, he leaned forward, taking my face in his hands and kissing me. He tilted my head and deepened the connection, and I responded, a moan rising up from my throat. He tasted like coffee and mint, his tongue reaching deep as if he couldn't get enough.

Then I came to myself and pulled away, gasping for air. "Neal, this can't happen," I said, keeping him at bay with a hand to his chest. I could feel his rapid heartbeat under the palm of my hand as he leaned into me, could feel his muscles straining to keep control.

The skin between his eyebrows furrowed and he said nothing, only allowed me to keep him an arm's length away.

"Julie!"

Neal and I turned to find the owner of the voice stomping across the cafeteria floor, his dark hair mussed, lines bracketing his mouth.

"Kyle," I muttered.

"Why didn't you call me?" he asked, walking toward us at a fast clip.

I stood up. "What are you doing here?"

"You didn't think I deserved to know about Will having an operation?"

I closed my eyes and took a deep breath, fighting to control my emotions. "We're not married anymore, Kyle. I know you mean well, but Will is not your son. You don't have to feel responsible for him anymore."

"Is that what you think this is?" he asked in a hurt voice.

Neal stood up then and pressed his hand into the small of my back. "Hey, man, I'm Neal," he said, holding out his other hand to Kyle.

Kyle was frowning but he shook the outstretched hand anyway. "Kyle."

"My ex-husband," I said, in case Kyle was planning on saying otherwise.

"I want to see him," Kyle said, turning back to me. "Please."

I turned to Neal, giving him an apologetic look. "We'll continue this later, okay?"

He nodded, his fingers squeezing at my back gently. "I can wait." He bent down and whispered, "Just call me if you need me. I'll be right here."

I nodded, though I knew it wouldn't be needed. Kyle Manning was the most even-keeled person I knew, so patient and eager to please.

Kyle and I were quiet on the way back up but the moment we stepped inside the hospital room, his face broke out into a wide smile. Will seemed apprehensive at first, knowing Kyle really only from photographs and stories I'd tell, but he quickly warmed up when Kyle started telling funny stories of when we were all together. I stood back and watched them interact, seeing the genuine affection in Kyle's eyes as he talked to my son. In that moment it was plain to see that he really cared for Will, that he'd come because he genuinely cared.

"Thank you for coming to see him," I said to Kyle out in the hallway some time later.

"Of course. Believe it or not, I love that kid." He looked at me, his brown eyes drooping down at the ends, giving him a sad puppy-dog look. "I loved our family."

I took a deep breath to quell the burn of guilt in my chest. "I'm sorry things didn't work out between us."

"Me, too."

"It wasn't your fault."

"It was. I should have been a better husband, a better everything."

"Kyle," I said, touching his arm, "it wasn't your fault. Really."

He nodded as he looked down at my hand, and again I was struck with regret that this gentle, wonderful man couldn't have been a bigger part of our lives. He was handsome and loving, without baggage or damage, and he had a big heart. Any woman would be lucky to have him. "Kyle, you're welcome to come and visit Will sometimes."

"You mean that?"

"Yes. Just, you know, don't overdo it."

"You sure Neal won't mind?" he asked as we walked toward the elevator.

"He and I aren't together."

"Huh."

"What you saw in the cafeteria . . . that was a good-bye kiss."

"You giving him the heave-ho, too?"

"Kyle . . ."

"Okay, okay," he said, holding his palms out. "It's none of my business."

"Thank you."

He stepped into the elevator. "I'd like to visit Will when he comes home from the hospital."

"Sure," I said. "I'll let you know."

5

After lunch, Neal came back up to the room holding a book in his hands. "Hey, bud," he said to Will as he approached the bed.

"What book is that?" Will asked, his face lighting up.

"This was the book my mom read to me when I had my appendix out," he said. "It's about a kid who had to stay in the hospital for a long time because he was sick, but then all sorts of strange people came to visit him. Your mom told me you were an advanced reader, so I thought you might want to read this."

"I am a good reader," Will said without pretense. "But I want you to read it to me."

Neal looked up at me, apparently unprepared for that request. "Um, sure," he said, dragging a chair closer to the bed.

I shrugged, trying to ignore the warning bells in my head. Neal shouldn't have been there, shouldn't have been sitting with my son, reading him a book. But at that moment I was too exhausted to care. So I sat on the bench and leaned back, listening to Neal read the book to my son like a seasoned pro. I closed my eyes and allowed his deep, soothing voice to wash over me, ironing out the wrinkles on my forehead and in my heart.

"He didn't like it in that room where he was all alone," Neal read. "He didn't like the needles in his arms and the machines beeping all around." He turned the page. "But then one day, there came a knock on the door and that was the beginning of a strange and wonderful day . . ."

"Julie?"

I opened my eyes, surfacing from the depths of a dreamless sleep, and saw Neal looming over me. For a moment, I couldn't figure out where we were, why it was that I felt completely secure in his presence. I wanted to close my eyes and go back to sleep, but Neal squeezed my shoulder.

"Julie, I'm going to head back to the hotel," he said in a whisper. "I have some work to do."

I sat up, our faces inches apart. "Okay." I reached for a water bottle on the side table and took a long pull, feeling like it had been years since I'd drunk anything. "I'll walk you out."

I glanced at Will, who was asleep once again, as I stood up and straightened my clothes, sure that I looked rumpled regardless. "Thank you for reading to him," I said once we were out in the hallway. "He's been reading since three, but he loves it when people read to him."

Neal smiled tightly. "No problem. I told him he could keep the book."

"Wait, that was your book?"

He smiled sheepishly. "Yeah. I had it with me, so I figured he'd like to read it."

"You travel around the country with a picture book from your childhood?" I asked, feeling the warmth spreading across my chest.

He shrugged, but though the gesture was nonchalant, his voice was anything but when he said, "It was the last book my mom and I read together."

I don't know why, but I followed him into that elevator. "Neal," I said as the doors swished shut, "I don't think you should come back."

He didn't say anything for a few seconds. Then his hand shot out and he punched the emergency button, halting the elevator. "Explain," he said, setting his backpack on the floor.

"It's for the best," I began, trying to unjumble the words in my head. "I don't want Will getting more attached to you. It's not in his best interests."

"Why is getting to know me such a bad thing?"

"Because I don't want him looking up to a military guy, thinking fighting and blowing things up is so cool."

"I don't fight or blow up things but I can assure you that my job *is* cool," he said, folding his arms over his chest. "But this isn't about Will, is it?"

"Actually, it is," I said. "He can't get attached to you."

"Are you pushing me away to protect your son or yourself?"

"Both," I said, lifting my chin. "I can't have you wedging yourself into our lives only to have you deploy and die on us."

"Pushing me away isn't going to keep me from dying, you know," he said, his jaw muscles flexing. He sighed and took a step closer until we were almost touching, lifting his hand to my cheek. "Julie, you need to stop fighting this. Because there's something here between us, and it'll still be here whether I'm with you or not."

I shook my head, tears blurring my vision.

"You take that leap of faith and I promise I'll be there to catch you." He ducked down and pressed his lips to the corner of my mouth. With my face cradled in his hands, he tilted my head back and pressed soft kisses along my cheeks, my nose, and finally to the wrinkled skin between my eyebrows. "I want to be in your life. Yours and Will's."

"Why?" I whispered, barely able to breathe. God, he was everywhere, overwhelming me with his scent and his touch and his sweet words.

"Because I've been flying all over the country for years and only when I met you did I feel the need to stop and stay." He brushed his lips against mine, a tender touch full of promise. "Because you're the most amazing woman I've ever met and I haven't been able to stop thinking about you since that morning on the beach. Because your son is a cool kid who told me yesterday that I should just be brave and tell you why I'm here."

I lifted my hands and covered his. "And why are you here?" I asked, my gaze steady and true.

"To tell you that I think I'm falling in love with you."

The breath caught in my throat, but something niggled at me. "What, you're not sure?"

He let out a chuckle. "Oh, I'm sure." He dipped his head and took my mouth captive once again. The kiss went on for a long time, both tender and urgent. I closed my eyes and let his words soak in, allowing myself to believe that his love was enough to overcome everything else, even his dangerous line of work.

"Maybe you should come by later," I said, deciding to take that leap of faith.

He smiled, the skin around his eyes wrinkling. "I definitely will."

6

The hospital released Will after lunch the following day. It was a Monday but, thankfully, my boss gave me the day off to bring my son home and take care of his needs. Neal arrived just as they were taking the stint out of Will's arm and was helpful in lifting Will out of the wheelchair and into my car.

Back at home, we settled Will onto the couch in the new living room, doing our best to make him comfortable.

"Do you need your blanket?" Neal asked him.

"And my Buzz Lightyear toy, please."

Neal turned to me but, before he could ask, I said, "No, it's okay. I'll get it."

"What else do you need, bud?" Neal asked, sitting on the arm of the couch while I tucked Will in.

"Some milk," Will said with his eyebrows up. He then glanced at me. "And chocolate chip cookies?"

"We're all out of cookies. I haven't had a chance to go to the store."

"I can go," Neal said, already reaching in his pocket for the keys to his rental car. "What else do you need?"

"I think I have the fixings to make fresh cookies."

Will's face lit up. "Oh, yeah!"

"Okay, well, it will take a few minutes." I handed the TV remotes over as well as the Xbox controllers.

"You need help?" Neal asked, getting up.

"I'm good," I said automatically. "You can play Xbox with Will."

"Do you know how to play Mario Brothers?" Will asked as Neal settled on the couch beside him.

"Mario Brothers? Now we're talking."

I went to the kitchen, casting long looks at the two heads visible over the back of the couch, feeling a strange sensation wash over me.

"Mom, Neal knows how to play it!" Will cried out in excitement.

Neal turned his head and cast me a quick wink. "I used to play this nonstop when I was a kid," he said. "See, I'll show you a little secret over here . . ."

The two played for several minutes, Will occasionally squealing with delight or gasping when he learned a new secret. While it was Will's turn, Neal got up from the couch and said, "Let me just see if your mom needs help with the cookies." He came over to where I was balling up the dough. "Hi," he said, his face all lit up.

"Hi."

He bent down and kissed me, nibbling on my lower lip before pulling away. "Do you need a hand with your cookies?" he asked with a flirtatious wag of an eyebrow.

I stifled a laugh. "Sure. Just dive in. Don't be afraid to get your hands dirty."

He dipped a finger in the batter and lifted it up to my mouth. I wrapped my lips around his finger, running my tongue along his skin as I sucked off the batter. His face was impassive but I could see the desire simmering just below the surface of his light brown eyes. He dipped his finger in again and brought it up to his mouth. "So sweet."

"My cookies always are."

He stared at me, running his tongue along his lower lip.

"Hey, Neal!" Will called, rousing us from the moment. "Your turn!"

"I'll be right there," Neal said, never taking his eyes off me. He set his hands on the edge of the counter and leaned closer until our faces were a mere hairsbreadth apart. He touched his finger to my chin and, just when I thought he'd kiss me, he leaned his forehead onto mine. "I know you're used to doing everything yourself," he murmured. "But I'm here. Let me help."

I nodded, still unsure, still waiting for that moment when everything felt right.

Neal spent the rest of the day with us, watching old *Tom and Jerry* cartoons while we ate the cookies with glasses of cold milk. He and Will shared an easy rapport, as if they'd known each other for years instead of days. Every now and then, Will looked at me with a wide smile, wrenching my heart tight with his joy.

After we ate Chinese takeout in the living room, I gathered up the plates and was about to stand up when Neal grabbed them from me. "You stay right there. I've got this," he said, squeezing my shoulder.

I sat on the couch with my head slightly turned, watching Neal from the corner of my eye as he rinsed the dishes and put them in the dishwasher. He must have sensed me watching him because he turned around and flashed me a toothy smile.

I don't know what it is about a man cleaning, but to see him standing in front of my sink was sexy as hell. All he needed was to take off his shirt and flex as he ran the dishes under the water and it might as well have been porn.

"I could really get used to this," I told him when he returned to the living room.

He raised an eyebrow. "Yeah?"

"Are you also available to vacuum?"

"Any time."

At around seven thirty, we brought Will upstairs to get him ready for bed.

"I'll go downstairs and do some work," Neal said in the doorway to Will's room. "Good night."

"'Night!" Will said, easing off his T-shirt. I helped him into the tub and gave him a quick wash, using the detachable showerhead to keep water away from his stitches. After he was in his pajamas and tucked into bed, he asked for the book that Neal had given him.

"Hold on. I think it's in my purse," I said, heading out the door and down the stairs.

"How's it going?" I asked Neal as I walked past the kitchen.

He looked up from his laptop. "Can't complain."

I came back with the book in my hand and trailed a finger on his shoulder as I walked by. "I'll be back in about five minutes."

"Take your time."

I headed upstairs and stopped outside Will's room when I heard him talking to someone. With a pounding heart, I went inside and found he was alone.

"Who were you talking to?" I asked, sitting on the bed.

"Dad," he said matter-of-factly.

"Like, for pretend?"

"No, for real."

"When did you start doing that?"

"At the hospital. After the operation," he said. "A nurse told me that if I was scared or lonely, I could ask my guardian angel to watch over me."

"You think your dad is your guardian angel?" I asked, having a hard time speaking past the tightness in my throat.

"Yeah," he said, nodding. "He's definitely my guardian angel."

I bent down and kissed him on the forehead. "So what were you telling your dad just now?"

"About all the things Neal did while you were gone."

"Oh? What did he do?"

"He sat by me and helped me eat when I couldn't sit up. When I was crying because my stitches hurt, he held my hand and asked the nurse for a Popsicle to see if that would help."

"And did it?"

"Yeah," he said. "We're gonna have to get some of those fudge Popsicles, Mom, in case anyone else gets hurt. They're like magic."

I chuckled softly. "Okay."

"He also told me stories about where he flies. Did you know he has an airplane? Like, by himself?"

"I did know that," I said.

"He told me that if I wanted to, he could fly us to the beach so he can teach me to surf." He looked up at me with those blue eyes. "Can we do that, Mom? When I'm all better?"

I started to say that surfing was dangerous, that all it took was one wipeout and a strong undertow to snuff a life away, but bit my tongue. Neal would be there and he'd never let anything happen to my son, I was sure of it. "When the weather is warmer, okay?"

"Okay." He snuggled deeper under the covers. "Mom, you like Neal, don't you?"

"Yes. Why do you ask?"

"Because I want him to stay."

I hugged him to my side, kissing the top of his head. If I had any reservations about welcoming Neal into our lives, they all but dissolved right then. "Yeah, me, too, sweetheart."

"So what are you going to do after I go to sleep?" he asked, all wide-eyed innocence. "Are you going to kiiiiiss?"

I pinched his nose and laughed it off. "Never you mind."

At the bottom of the stairs, I stopped and took a deep breath before going to the living room. But Neal wasn't in there. "Hello?"

"In here."

I found him standing in the middle of the dance room, barefoot, with the lights turned down low. Soft, slow music was playing from the small CD player on the mantel. He held out his hand. "May I have this dance?"

I kicked off my shoes and walked over, taking hold of his hand.

He pulled me in and held me against his body, his hands splayed on the curve of my back. I wound my arms around his neck, rubbing my fingers along the short hair on the back of his head. We looked at each other for long moments as we began to sway, the air charged around us.

"Julie," he said, his fingers clutching at the fabric of my shirt. His brows were drawn together, his face dark with worry.

"What is it?"

He contemplated me for a few more seconds before blinking it all away, bringing forth the affable guy once more. "It's nothing," he said. "Nothing that can't wait, anyway."

"Why are you being so ominous?" I asked, pulling away. "Why don't you just tell me what you're hiding?"

He jerked me back against his body and, instead of an explanation, he simply molded his mouth to mine and tried to erase my doubts with a searing kiss. And though I didn't want to be distracted, a part of me gave in anyway because deep down, I sensed that what he was hiding was something that could ruin what we had right now. So I tilted my head back and kissed him, content in the knowledge that, at least for now, all was good.

"Do you want to stay the night?" I asked after we pulled away.

"But Will . . . what will you tell him?"

"I'm not sure," I said, swallowing hard. "But I don't want to think about it right now. Right now, I just want to dance."

"Then let's dance," he said and swung me around. His hands roamed up my back and all around, caressing me, wandering over my curves and edges. In his arms, I felt supple, as if he could mold me with his touch.

"God, you're so beautiful," he breathed.

"I think you were right."

"About what?"

"About the universe putting us in the right spot at the right time."

He smiled, but there was a sad undertow in his eyes that I tried to ignore. "There is no doubt in my mind that we were definitely meant to meet."

I took his hand and led him upstairs, turning off all the lights, never more glad than in that moment that Will's room was at the other end of the hall from mine. I led Neal into my bedroom and closed the door quietly behind me, hearing the satisfying click of the lock.

Neal surveyed the room, wordlessly taking in my off-white bed and my cream-hued curtains and furnishings.

"I know it's a girly room," I said, surreptitiously sliding some clothes off the dresser and stuffing them into a drawer below.

"Not at all," he said, turning to face me. "I feel like I just walked into a cloud."

His words stretched my mouth until the smile took up half of my face. How was it possible that this man—whom I'd only known for a short time—somehow understood me?

Neal closed the distance between us and took my hand, pressing my palm against his chest, and suddenly it was as if my every sense was heightened—the feel of his heartbeat under my hand, the scent of him that reminded me of the ocean after a thunderstorm, the sight of his handsome face made even more attractive by the scruff on his cheeks.

I lifted to my toes and touched my lips to his mouth, eager to taste him, needing to hear him make that sexy noise from low in his throat. The moment I parted my lips to his, a moment of piercing clarity washed over me: Neal was unlike any man I'd ever met. Nobody, not even Jason, had ever made me feel this alive, this free. That fact alone drew me to him, but there was something more, something inscrutable and indefinable about him that meant only one thing.

"I hope you're ready to catch me," I said against his lips.

His arms went around my waist right before understanding lit up his eyes. "I'm here. I've got you." Without warning, he swooped down and lifted me off my feet, carrying me across the room and lowering me to the middle of the bed. He lay down on his side and ran the pad of his thumb along my lower lip. "You have no idea how badly I want to have you naked underneath me right now."

I ran my nails along his crotch. "Then what's the holdup?"

He let out a soft chuckle. "I want to make sure Will is asleep so we don't get interrupted."

"You can kiss me until then."

"Yes, ma'am." He rolled until he was partly on top of me, slinging one leg over mine. He kissed me, feather-soft touches that spoke of his capacity for tenderness. I grasped the back of his head and deepened the kiss, greedy for more.

"I think he's asleep enough," I said and rolled over onto him.

"Yes. Definitely."

Taking my time, I pulled my sweater up over my head, swiveling my hips in the process. His hands sneaked around to my back and unclasped my bra, pulling the cotton fabric away from my chest.

"You're unusually good at that," I said, biting back a smile. "Must have had plenty of practice."

"No, I just have nimble fingers."

I followed his gaze down to find that he'd already undone my button and zipper without my knowledge. He raised an eyebrow smugly.

I got up off the bed and took my pants off then took the opportunity to do the same to him. He sat up to lose his shirt then lay back down, beckoning me over. When I crawled over and resumed my seat on his lap, he hooked his hands on the back of my shoulders and urged me down for a kiss. One of his hands snaked between our naked bodies and moved to my mound, his fingers sliding easily through my folds.

I gasped when two digits pushed at my entrance then thrust inside. "You weren't lying about your fingers," I said, sitting up. I set my hands on his chest and began to rock to and fro, fucking his fingers.

"That's so hot," he hissed between his teeth. He moved his thumb to the front so that each time I swayed, it rubbed against my clit. I closed my eyes and continued to ride his hand while his cock lay throbbing beneath me, begging for attention. I reached up and played with my breasts, tweaking my nipples, enjoying the way it made Neal's jaw flex.

Then his fingers were gone and he was lifting my hips and lowering me onto his shaft. I let out a slow breath as I sank onto him, feeling so full and complete. I had missed this. No matter how much I'd tried to ignore my feelings, my body still craved the feel of Neal inside and around me.

I sat still and squeezed at him with my inner walls until his forehead broke out into a sheen. "I want it hard and fast," I said, running my nails down his chest.

He let out a low growl before grabbing me and flipping me over until I found myself staring up at him. He stared down at me with a heated look in his eyes and his nostrils flared as he found my entrance and speared me with no amount of gentleness. Gone was the tender guy of before; this man above me was once again an aggressive sexual creature who demanded as good as he gave.

Then he pulled out but refused to push back in, the head of his cock resting at my entrance. I pulled at him but he refused to sink down. He shook his head, teasing me until I was a whimpering mess.

"I want to hear what you want," he said in a low, husky voice.

"I want you back inside me," I said. "I want to be fucked hard."

He leaned down, shaking his head. "I didn't hear you ask me nicely."

"You want me to beg?"

He raised an eyebrow and nudged me with the tip of his cock. "Yes."

I gripped his ass and pulled him hard, gasping as he slipped back inside me. He tried to back off but I wrapped my legs around him and locked my ankles together, effectively trapping him in place. "Now you'll have to beg *me*."

One side of his mouth curled up. "I'm not going anywhere," he said and nudged into me.

"Oh, fuck."

"I love your dirty mouth," he said, kissing me hard, retreating slightly then slamming back into me. He kissed my jaw, my neck, my collarbone. "And pretty much everything about you."

I relaxed my legs and allowed him room to maneuver; he started pounding into me, deep, savage thrusts that pierced to the heart of me. He was everywhere, kissing me, touching me, possessing me.

He hooked his arms under my knees and lifted my legs, rocking his hips faster even as he went deeper. The entire time he never once took his eyes off me. He kept me captive with the intensity of his gaze, the raw passion that sparked in his eyes.

The orgasm tore through my body faster than I'd ever experienced before, stealing the breath from my lungs. My muscles seized up for a few seconds and then I was flying into a shower of sparks.

Neal grunted as he came to the crest, thrusting faster and harder until he, too, was coming, his back bowing as he emptied himself into me. He twitched from the aftereffects, and then he lowered my legs to the bed and kissed me long and hard.

Neal was insatiable that night, making love to me twice more before we finally fell into an exhausted sleep, my back to his front as he wrapped himself around me.

Sometime before six, I felt him lifting my leg and nudging at my cleft. "I'll never have enough of you," he murmured against my ear.

I reached back and gripped his ass, welcoming him into me once again. With his arms gripping me to his chest, he made slow, deliberate love to me, his breathing ragged against my ear. And when his nimble fingers drew lazy lines up and down my folds, I came completely apart, trembling with the knowledge that the all-consuming love I'd feared my whole life had finally, and completely, found me.

PART FOUR

CONTACT

1

Neal didn't move in. He switched to an extended-stay hotel and only came over early evenings after Will and I came home.

Sometimes Neal stayed the night but that didn't happen as often as I'd have liked. Will still had no clue, or if he did, he didn't say anything about it.

"Could you grab the napkins, bud?" Neal asked as he reached in the top cabinet for three plates.

"Getting plates was my job, too," Will said, watching Neal with awe. "I always have to get a chair, though."

"Here, why don't you put these on the table," Neal said, handing him the stack. "And I'll get the silverware."

"The silver what?" Will asked, carefully carrying the plates to the table.

"Silverware. Forks, knives, spoons."

"We just call it forks, knives, spoons. That's just easier," Will said.

I watched the exchange from the stove, grinning to myself. It had been a week since Will had come home from the hospital and I'd allowed Neal into our lives. A week of growing and stretching beyond our comfort zone, of Will and I welcoming another person into our lives. And so far, apart from having to cook twice as much food, the changes had been barely noticeable.

"Mmm, my favorite!" Will cried as I spooned mac and cheese onto his plate.

"We also have vegetables and chicken, so you'd better eat some of that," I said.

"Yes, sir," Will said, performing a small salute.

I tried to ignore the pang of unease and went back to the stove, aware of Neal's eyes following me.

He came up behind me and pressed a gentle kiss to the back of my neck. "Here, I got it," he said, taking the strainer full of vegetables from my hands. "Go sit down and let me take care of the rest."

Neal served the rest of dinner and we ate in comfortable silence. Will kept glancing over at Neal, trying to mimic his movements, eating heartily, no doubt trying to impress his new idol.

"Good job eating, man," Neal said after Will had taken his last bite. "If your mom says it's all right, I have a treat for you."

"What? What is it?"

Neal leaned close and whispered, "I got him some ice cream."

"When did you get that?"

"I snuck it in earlier when nobody was looking," he said with a grin.

I turned to my son, who wore a yellow-cheese smile. "Okay, but just this once."

Neal left the next Friday and headed to Homestead Air Reserve Base in Florida for training, promising to be back on Sunday night.

"Why did he go there?" Will asked on Saturday morning while he stood on the stool, whisking eggs in a glass bowl. "Does he have to go all the time?"

"He's training," I said, flipping the pancakes. "From what I understand, it's only one weekend a month and two weeks a year. At least, that's what the commercials say."

"But what does he do there?"

"I'm not sure," I said, glad that I truly didn't know any details so that I wouldn't have to tell my son. I could only imagine what he'd think if I told him Neal was shooting sniper rifles or learning how to drive a tank.

"Why does he live in a hotel?" Will asked, pouring the bowl's contents into the pan. "Why doesn't he just come live with us?"

"Because I want to take it slow. I don't want to rush anything."

"He's your boyfriend, right? I heard Miss Stacy tell the nurses at the hospital that he was your boyfriend," he said, taking over the skillet and putting the cooked pancakes onto our plates, ever the eager helper.

"Yes, Neal is my boyfriend."

"Do you love him?"

I took a deep breath. "I do."

"Do you still love my dad?"

"That's different. I love your dad, but not the same way I love Neal."

His little eyebrows drew together, making him look surprisingly mad. "You can't love Neal more than my dad!"

"That's not what I said."

"My dad was the best guy. Better than Neal!"

"Hey," I said, turning to face him on his perch. "Why are you getting so worked up?"

He swiped at his eyes with the back of his hand. "Because."

"Will, there are many different kinds of love. We'll never love one person the way we love someone else."

"Do you love Neal more than me?"

"Of course not, silly!" I said, hugging him to my chest. "Out of everyone in the whole world, I love you the most. That will never, ever change."

He sniffed. "Okay."

"Where's this coming from? I thought you liked Neal," I asked, stirring the eggs.

"He's okay," Will said. "I just don't want you to forget Dad."

I set the spatula down and took hold of his hands. "Honey, I can never forget your dad. No matter what happens, no matter how old I get, I will always love your dad. You know why?"

"Why?"

I kissed his forehead. "Because he gave me you."

Friday night a week later, Neal and I took Will and Dennis to Chuck E. Cheese's.

"This place is . . ." Neal began, looking around the crowded, loud place full of hyped-up kids.

"Horrible?" I finished helpfully.

He grinned. "That. But I was going to say interesting."

"You've never been to one before?"

"Can't say I have."

We set our things down at a plastic booth and let the boys loose with cups of coins. Neal squeezed into the booth beside me, laying an arm across the backrest, his fingers resting on my shoulder.

"This is an unconventional date location," he said.

"You don't have to stay," I said, feeling guilty that I'd dragged this single guy into the seventh circle of parental hell. "If you'd rather go somewhere else."

He leaned down and kissed my cheek. "I'm good right here."

While we were eating pizza, Stacy called to check up on her son.

"Neal, come play with us," Dennis said, tugging on his hand.

Neal gave my leg a squeeze under the table before sliding out of the booth and following the boys into the maze of machines and lights and the din of falling coins.

"Dennis is not being too crazy, is he?" she asked. "He tends to get hyper at that place."

"No, he's doing fine," I said. "We'll drop him off tomorrow morning around eight if that's not too early."

"That's perfect," she said. "Shane and I are enjoying the silence. We're about to put in a DVD and drink some wine."

"Sounds wonderful." I scanned the room until my eyes landed on the boys standing over at the basketball games. Neal was demonstrating how to hold the ball, correcting Will's form before throwing it into the hoop. "I know it's only been a short time, but I think Neal really, genuinely cares about Will," I thought out loud.

"Of course he does. Will is a lovable kid. I think it'd be a warning sign if he *didn't*."

I grinned to myself as Will jumped up, giving Neal an elated high five. "But most guys don't want to date women with children, in case it means they'll end up at Chuck E. Cheese's on a Friday night. So what's wrong with Neal? What the hell is he still doing here?"

Stacy laughed. "He does seem a little too perfect. But, girl, with the life you've had, you deserve some perfect."

"And when I discover his deep, dark secret?"

Stacy was quiet for a while. "I don't know. Just keep crossing your fingers and hope he doesn't have one."

"We all have one."

She gave a short chuckle. "You're overthinking this. Just relax, okay? Enjoy your time."

After we hung up, I went in search of my boys, finding them at a game that involved shooting large insects onscreen. "How's it going?" I asked Neal, who was watching from outside the game enclosure.

"Excellent. I got them some more coins but it looks like they'll be using all of it on this one game," Neal said, his eyes fixed on the screen. "Okay, Dennis, shoot the legs. See the target on his leg? Yeah, shoot that."

I tugged him aside and gave him a hug. "Thank you. You've been so patient."

He kissed the tip of my nose. "It's no big deal. I'm having a good time."

"It's really okay if you're not. I know this isn't every guy's ideal Friday night."

"Are you kidding? I get to spend the night eating pizza, playing video games with my buddies, and then, later, hopefully spend time with my girl. Sounds perfect to me." He leaned close and whispered, "If I'm lucky, I might even get to put a coin in the slot."

"I heard the ride can get pretty bumpy. I hope you can handle it."

"Oh, I'll handle it all right."

Later, after the kids had changed into their pajamas and were set up in Will's room, Neal said, "I meant to ask earlier: is Will in any type of after-school sports?"

"No. Why?" I asked, settling down on the couch with my glass of wine.

Neal sat down beside me with his beer. "I was just wondering. He seemed unsure of himself when we were playing the basketball game."

"I've never had the chance to take him to any after-school activities."

"Has he shown any interest in it?"

"No, but earlier this year he was asking me if he could play soccer," I said. "But practice is right after school and there's no way we can make it work."

"I can take him."

My head snapped around to him. "You will?"

He took a swig of beer. "Yeah. I can pick him up after school and take him to practice."

"Why would you do that?"

"Because I want Will to experience sports."

I stood up just as my eyes began to burn. "I'm going to get more wine," I said quickly and left the room. His suggestion had filled me with so much guilt and so many conflicting emotions. I knew going in that being a single parent meant Will would have to miss out on some things, but I was trying my best. To hear someone confirm what I'd always secretly feared—that I was somehow depriving my son of a normal childhood—made my heart hurt.

Still, a part of me knew that Neal meant well. I should be happy that he wanted good things for my son, right?

After gathering myself, I rejoined Neal on the couch. "Yes. I'd love it if you could take him to an after-school sports program."

"Sure?" he asked. "It was just an idea."

"It's about time Will experienced other things. I've sheltered him long enough."

He sat up and took my glass, setting our drinks down on the coffee table. "Julie, you've done a phenomenal job with your son. It's time you give yourself some much-deserved credit."

I shrugged, not sure how to answer. So I just kissed him instead, pouring into it all my gratitude. He leaned forward and deepened the kiss, tangling his fingers through my hair.

I pulled away. "Does this mean you're sticking around for a little while? An entire soccer season lasts three to four months," I said. "Are you sure you want to make that kind of commitment?"

He gave me a soft kiss, lingering to nibble on my bottom lip. "Yes. I'll stay as long as you need me." He pressed light kisses along my jaw and up to my earlobe. "As long as you want me."

In that moment, I couldn't imagine a time when I would never *not* want him. "Then you're probably sticking around forever."

He ran his tongue along the shell of my ear, making my entire body tingle. "Forever it is," he rasped.

Our heads snapped around when we heard giggling coming from the stairs. We pulled apart and turned to find Will and Dennis crouched at the landing.

"Told you they'd be making out," Dennis said, nudging Will.

Will stifled his laugh behind a hand.

"You guys are so busted," Neal said, getting up, causing both boys to jump up and run upstairs. He chuckled and turned back to me. "I guess I'd better go."

"You don't have to. We can just watch a movie and be chaste," I said, patting the space beside me.

He raised an eyebrow. "I can't sit beside you and be chaste, Julie. That's not possible."

I walked him out the front door. As soon as the door closed behind us, Neal had me up against it, his hands on either side of my face as he kissed me. My hands went around his back, pulling on his butt while our tongues tangled.

"I'd better go," he said even as he ground his hips into my crotch, the hard length in his pants divulging just how unchaste he wanted to be.

"You don't have to. You can just stay here, at my front door, forever."

He let out a pained chuckle and pushed away from the door. "I'm just going to go take a cold shower," he said, dropping one last kiss on my nose. "I'll see you tomorrow."

"Okay," I said, straightening my shirt and trying to recover my senses.

"I hope he likes the surprise."

"The kid thinks you're so cool. You could give him a piece of gum and he'd think it was the best thing ever."

He leaned down until our faces were a hairsbreadth apart. "And what about his mom? What does she think of me?"

I slid my fingers into his jean pockets and tugged, planting one last kiss on his lips. "She thinks you'd better get going before she mounts you right here in front of the neighborhood."

"Kinky. I like it." And with one wink, he went on his way, leaving my body prickling from his absence.

2

The next morning, after we dropped Dennis off at his house, Will and I drove to Neal's hotel. We rode the elevator up to the fifth floor and knocked at his door; he greeted us with his bag in hand, closing the door behind him.

"Can I use the bathroom?" Will asked, starting to do the potty dance.

Neal hesitated, glancing at the door behind him. Finally he said, "Okay," and, with some reluctance, let us inside.

"Just hurry up, okay? We have to get going," Neal said then turned to me, looping a finger into the waistband of my skirt and pulling me close. "Hi."

"Hi," I said, nuzzling into the soft skin of his neck, inhaling his fresh soap scent. I gave him a quick kiss then pulled away, looking around the room that he'd been staying in for the better part of a month. I took in the rumpled covers on the bed and the desk in the corner with his laptop, programming books, and papers all crowded on it. "So this is where you live."

"I just sleep here," he said, wrapping me in his arms again. "I do my real living with a beautiful woman and her son."

"So where are we going?" Will asked when he emerged from the bathroom, wiping his hands on his pants.

"Secret," Neal said, heading toward the door once again.

"Are we going in your plane?" Will asked, all wide-eyed wonder.

"Yes."

"Cool! I call shotgun!" Will skipped the entire way to the elevator, with Neal laughing alongside him, and I followed behind, nagged by a vague notion that there was something in that hotel room Neal hadn't wanted us to see.

At the Denton airport, Neal conducted a thorough preflight check, explaining the purpose of each step, while Will followed him around with wide eyes. When the check was nearly complete, we climbed into the plane, Will taking the front seat. He was very nearly bouncing with excitement when Neal set the headset on him, but he listened closely while Neal gave him safety instructions. As we started off for the runway, I relaxed in the backseat and watched in contentment as Neal taught my son about the instruments and their various purposes.

I fell asleep about an hour and a half into the flight and jerked awake some time later with a thundering heart, thinking for a moment that we were crashing.

"We're here, Mom," Will said, looking over the seat at me. "We're in Florida!"

We called a taxi and headed toward the water, Will bouncing excitedly when we turned a corner and saw the wide ocean spread out before us. "It's the beach!"

Neal and I exchanged an amused glance over his head.

"Are you teaching me how to surf?" he cried.

Neal laughed. "You guessed it!"

The taxi dropped us off at a rental store, and a few minutes later we three were trekking toward the sand with surfboards tucked under our arms, already starting to sweat in our jeans and T-shirts.

After we stripped down to our swimsuits, Neal began the lessons on the sand, showing us how to paddle and how to go from a prone position to jumping up on the board. While Will and I practiced, Neal talked about safety and what to do when you fall in the water.

"Enough talking," Neal finally said, dusting off his hands. "The only way we'll learn how to surf is to get in there and do it."

Will grabbed his board and ran to the water with a whoop, with Neal and me close behind.

"And now for the true test," Neal whispered to me, watching as Will hesitated in shin-deep water, still clutching his little surfboard under his arm. I knew what was going through his little mind because, without meaning to, I'd instilled in him the fear that danger and death were always lurking, waiting to claim him.

But then a wonderful and scary thing happened: Will took one step deeper in the water and then another; then he positioned himself on the board and began to paddle against the waves.

"Not too far," I said purely by instinct, trying hard to ignore my rising panic.

Neal squeezed my shoulders and followed Will into the water. "I chose this beach specifically for its gentle waves, and there's virtually no undertow today. And I'll be close by. I won't let anything happen to him," he said.

"How did you know? Is it showing on my face?"

"I can tell you're trying hard not to freak out," he said with a grin. "Your 'mom face' is on."

I laughed as I followed him in, splashing him when he was nearby.

The water was warm when we entered, only knee-deep for a long way. Neal was right; the waves were gentle enough that I didn't worry myself to death when Will would try to get on the surfboard and fall into the water. The first time he succeeded in getting on the board, we all whooped then he immediately fell off. Neal was always nearby when that happened, helping Will up before retrieving his board. The next few times, Will was able to stay on until he reached the shore, then he jumped off and punched the air in jubilation.

"Mom, did you see that?" he asked, running up to me.

"I'm so proud of you!" I said, giving him a huge hug, the smile breaking my face apart.

"You going to dive in?" Neal asked with a boyish smile. "Or do you need some persuading?"

"Give me a minute," I said, contemplating wading deeper.

The last time I'd swum in the ocean was with Jason, during spring break many years back. The day after we'd slept together, we ran into each other at a beach party. My friends and I were lying on our towels, content to just bake in the hot Florida sun while everyone around us danced and drank, when Jason sat down beside me.

"You want to swim with me?" he asked.

"No, thanks. I'm good."

"Come on. Are you scared to get your hair wet? Your makeup ruined?"

I put my sunglasses on. "Basically."

He tugged on my big toe. "Come on. Let's cool off in the water."

I sat up with an exaggerated sigh. "Fine."

When I held out my hand to his, he grabbed it, and before I knew what was happening, he had me up and over his shoulder. He ran to the water's edge, laughing as I tried to catch my breath. The next thing I knew, I was in the warm water, scrambling to get back to my feet.

Jason was laughing when I found my balance, but he froze when he saw me stand up and quickly pulled me against him. "Your bikini top is floating away," he whispered.

I pressed my breasts into his bare chest. "You'd better get it, then."

He looked around at all the spring breakers. "But you'll be exposed."

"People have seen breasts before. They're not exactly in short supply around here."

With a huff, Jason spun me away from the beach and its many pairs of eyes then leapt into the waves to catch my errant top. He came splashing back a few moments later and handed it to me.

"Can you put it back on me?" I asked with a flirtatious smile. I pulled my hands away from my chest and he fumbled with the strings behind my neck then very gently laid the triangular pieces of fabric over my nipples, the backs of his fingers brushing along my skin.

"There. Done." He smiled down at me, and in that moment it became abundantly clear to me that Jason Sherman was someone I definitely wanted to see again.

"Do you have a fear of deep water?" Neal asked, wrenching me away from the past.

"In a manner of speaking," I said, contemplating the nearly endless depths of the ocean. Love had managed to pull me under once and I had barely broken the surface in time; I didn't know if I could survive sinking again.

Neal took hold of my hand. "Come on, I'll go in with you." And he led me out deeper and deeper until we were up to our necks in salt water. "Not so bad, right?"

I held on to him and smiled. "Yeah. I don't know what I was so afraid of."

When Will took a break from surfing to build a sand castle, Neal excused himself and took his own board out. He paddled out farther than Will and I had dared, chasing waves that were obviously too tame for his level of expertise. Still, he tried to make do, doing the same tricks I'd seen him perform once before.

I sat on the wet sand and watched his masterful display, reminded of that first morning we met in Monterey, when the sky and the sea conspired to bring us together. It didn't seem all that long ago. He was beautiful out there in his board shorts, his muscles stretching and contracting with each swing of the board, his skin golden brown and his hair tinged gold from the sun. He looked in his element, carving into waves as easily as walking, looking like some sort of water god with his easy command of the water.

After Neal came in, he helped Will dig a trench from his castle to the water's edge. Will squealed when the waves came in and filled the lopsided moat, and the two marched around the perimeter of the moat, pretending to be knights.

"This was the best day," Will said later as we took a taxi to a hotel that I had booked ahead of time.

"I'm glad you had fun, bud," Neal said, ruffling his hair then looking over to me with an infectious smile.

At the hotel, we went into our room and appraised the two queen beds.

"Which bed are you taking?" Will asked Neal. I half expected Neal to say he'd share a bed with me, but he said, "You and your mom can take the right and I'll take the left."

"You'll sleep in that big bed all by yourself?"

He grinned. "What can I say? I'm a big guy."

I found it hard to sleep that night, partly because I kept getting kicked by little gangly legs, and partly because I could see Neal sitting at the desk, rubbing his chin as he worked on his laptop on code that made absolutely no sense to me.

At around eleven fifteen, I finally crept out of bed and walked over to Neal, bending over the chair and dropping a kiss on his bare shoulder. "Why aren't you asleep yet?"

He reached back and grasped the back of my head, twisting his head around to kiss me. I melted into him, dropping down onto his lap. "I've been staring at the same code for hours," he said, sliding his palms up and down my thighs. He leaned over and took my earlobe between his teeth and whispered, "But I can't concentrate with you lying there, sexy and untouchable."

I wiggled around in his lap, riding higher up until my hip was rubbing against his erection. "I'm sorry to be such a distraction."

He tilted my head back, kissing along the column of my neck. "Oh, you are the sweetest kind of distraction." His hand was starting to slide up my leg when the bed across the room rustled.

"Meet me in the bathroom," I whispered and stood up.

He was behind me in two point five seconds, flipping the lock behind him and pressing me against the door. "All fucking night, Julie," he rasped, grasping my hands and holding them above my head. "I've been craving you the entire night."

I straddled his thigh and ground into it, trying in vain to scratch an itch. I tried to pull my hands down to touch him, but he refused to give, his fingers tightening around my own above my head. He chuckled when I made a whining noise low in my throat.

"In due time," he said, nipping at my lips.

"Get in me. Now," I growled, wrapping one leg around his back.

He gripped me by the ass cheeks and lifted me up, grinding me into the door. "Too . . . many . . . clothes," he gasped, burying his face in my neck. He carried me away from the door and set me on the marble counter, letting me go long enough to pull down his shorts and underwear.

I lifted my nightgown and drew aside my panties, welcoming him inside me with a hiss. He yanked me closer to the edge of the counter and held my legs up over his arms, opening me up further. "You're so deep," I whispered as he drew away then slammed back in.

He increased the pace, gasping and groaning by my ear. I started moaning, unable to keep from making noise, not when my entire body was electrified with pleasure. He put one hand over my mouth. "Shhh, he'll hear," he said, making me giggle.

I bit down on his hand and squeezed at his cock harder, vindicated when he gasped a little louder. "Oh, shit." He stopped, his jaw muscles tightening. "That's going to make me come too fast." Without warning, he pulled out and was on his knees in a flash, his face between my legs as he lapped at me.

He placed his hands on either side of his head and spread me bare on that countertop, my legs trembling as he worked me over with his tongue and lips. I leaned back, the back of my head hitting the mirror, tipping over the tiny toiletries as my body coiled tighter and tighter. I bit my lip when he thrust two fingers inside my cleft and flicked them upward to a steady rhythm, intensifying the pleasure.

When I was close, he stood up and thrust back inside with a loud groan, sending me over the edge. My climax traveled through me like a tidal wave, roaring through my body and cresting at the point where Neal and I connected.

He continued the assault, his breathing growing more ragged. Then his entire body tightened as he thrust hard one last time; his back bowed and his face pressed into the hollow of my neck, muffling his groan. He came hard, hips bucking, cock pulsing inside me.

He held me tight while our throbbing slowed and eventually stopped.

"I hope you'll be able to concentrate now that you've been sated," I said when he eventually helped me down off the counter.

"Not even close," he murmured, taking hold of my jaw and kissing me. "I don't think I can ever get enough of you."

3

When I opened my eyes the following morning, I found Neal standing by the bathroom door in his pajama pants, watching Will and me sleep.

"Morning," he said with a smile.

I sat up and ran a hand through my tangled hair. "What time is it?"

"Nearly ten."

I wiped a palm down my face, feeling like I could sleep another ten hours. "Were you just watching us sleep?"

He grinned. "You two looked so sweet. It was hard not to," he said and went back inside the bathroom. "Let's go have brunch before we head back. They stop serving breakfast at eleven," he called through the open door.

Will stirred beside me and a second later, he was jumping out of bed and racing across the room. "I gotta pee," he said and ran into the bathroom before I could stop him. I heard him talking to Neal as he peed, then a flush.

"What are you doing?" I heard him ask Neal.

"I'm shaving."

"Why?"

"To get rid of the hair on my face."

"Does everybody have to shave their face?"

"No. Just men."

"Am I a man yet?"

"Not yet. You have a few more years."

"Can you teach me how to shave when I'm a man?"

"I can teach you now if you'd like."

I sneaked closer, listening as Neal told Will about the shaver, the shaving cream, and all the intricacies of being a hairy man. Finally, unable to keep my curiosity at bay, I crept to the door and watched, unnoticed for a time, as my son finally experienced a rite of passage. He stood beside Neal at the sink, smiling up at him as if he were the most fascinating person in the world.

I stood there, leaning against the jamb, seeing before me the life I could have had.

"Hey, Mom." Will turned to me with shaving cream smeared all over his face. "Are you going to shave, too?"

I laughed as Neal grabbed me around the waist and pulled me inside, to where my son stood. He squirted some shaving cream onto his fingers then slowly dabbed it onto my nose, grinning at me through the mirror.

Will squealed with delight and gave me a foamy kiss, adding to my white mask.

"This means war," I said before grabbing the can and starting a full-fledged shaving cream fight that I was sure housekeeping would be cursing us for later.

As the days moved into the holiday season, Neal became more and more a part of our lives. He started taking Will to soccer practice every Tuesday and Thursday afternoon and then we all went to the games on Saturday mornings.

Neal, however, never pushed to move in, never even suggested it. Each night he said good night and went back to his hotel, and each night I stood at the front door, wondering why I was letting him go.

"Hey, Neal," I said to him one sunny Saturday as we stood off in the sidelines and watched Will's team getting annihilated on the field.

"Great hustle, Will!" Neal shouted then turned to me. "Sorry, what were you saying?"

"I just wanted your opinion on something."

"What is it?" he asked, still distracted by the game. He put his hands on his head when our team took a shot at the goal and was blocked. "Oh, man, that other team is really good."

I shielded my eyes from the sun and followed his gaze, to the girl expertly dribbling the ball down the field. My eyes flew to the other end of the grass, where my son was standing with his hands on his waist. He caught my gaze and gave me a crooked grin.

"He's really enjoying it, isn't he?" I asked.

"He loves it," Neal said. "And with a little more practice, I think he can really be good."

"You think so?"

"Definitely," he said with a resolute nod. "I've researched some drills that he and I can work on in the afternoons. He sounds very eager to start."

I looked at up him, dazzled, the sun framing his face so that his hair looked like a bit of a halo. "You're coming over after the game, right?"

"I have some work to finish today. But I'll be over tomorrow."

"Okay," I said, wrapping one arm around his waist. "I have something I'd like to talk about."

He raised an eyebrow. "That sounds ominous."

"Believe me, it's terrifying."

I didn't get a chance to ask him my question until much later the next day, after Will went to bed. Then finally, at the foot of the stairs, he turned to me and said, "Okay, now, what did you want to talk about?"

I stepped up on the bottom step until we were almost at eye level and took his face in my hands. "Come upstairs. I have something I want to show you."

He broke out into an intrigued smile. "I like where this is going."

I tugged him upstairs, not that Neal needed much persuading, and led him into my bedroom, where a brand-new pillow sat on the bed. I chucked it at him, the plastic packaging crinkling when it hit his chest.

"You got me a pillow?" he asked.

"A firm one," I pointed out. "You won't have to use two pillows anymore." I ripped it open and started to put a pillowcase on it, one that matched the light blue sheets already on the bed. I pulled the quilt aside and set his pillow beside mine then walked over to the dresser and opened the drawer that I had prepared the previous night.

"Hmm," he said, walking over to inspect the drawer where I had put the few pieces of clothing—a T-shirt, a pair of socks—that he'd left behind. He set his hands on my shoulders and leaned his chin on the back of my head. "Julie . . ." he said on a sigh.

"I can also give you a quarter of the closet, but not much more," I said with a teasing tone.

He let out a long breath; not exactly the excited reaction I'd been hoping for. At the very least, I was offering him a reprieve from mundane hotel life. At the most, I was inviting him into my family. Shouldn't he be more excited?

"Are you asking me to move in?" he asked.

I reached into my pocket and handed him the new set of keys I'd had made earlier that morning.

He looked down, the metal jingling as he turned it over in his hands. "Julie," he said, placing the keys back in my palm and folding my fingers over them one by one. "I can't take this."

I stiffened, not at all prepared for this outcome. "I just thought you might want to stay sometimes."

"I would love nothing more than to move in," he said, kissing my forehead. "But . . ."

I needed air, to take a step back and get a clear view of the situation, but was trapped in place by the dresser. "But what?" I asked, lifting my chin despite my trembling lips.

He grasped the sides of my face. "But before anything can progress between us, there's something I need to give you first."

My eyebrows drew together. "What is it?" I asked, deathly afraid of the answer. If he was planning to give me a ring—well, I didn't know what I'd say. I'd vowed after my failed first marriage that I would never marry again, but, then, I'd also vowed that I would never get involved with a man again, and look what had happened.

Neal ducked down and kissed me, tenderly at first then deepening into something more needy. The kiss went on for a long while, and if he was trying to distract me with desire, then I decided I would let him, because honestly, I didn't want to have to face that possibility just yet. Moving in together was hard enough; getting married presented a whole other set of issues.

After long moments, he finally pulled away, wiping at the moisture on my lips with his thumbs. "Tomorrow. I promise," he said before kissing me again.

He swung me around and set me on the bed, undressing and entering me with equal parts tenderness and need. He kept me glued to his gaze, the intensity of which rendered me helpless to look away. And when the orgasm rolled through my body, he ground his hips into mine and groaned through his climax, his arms steel bands holding me captive. Even before we had both recovered, he leaned up on his elbows and kissed me over and over, burning kisses onto my skin, my nose, my eyelids until I was drowning in him, inside and out and all over.

And before he tiptoed out at thirty minutes past midnight, he kissed me one last time and whispered against my forehead, "Tomorrow."

I had never been good with surprises or anticipation. I hated waiting, hated the way my brain thought up a million different scenarios and made the wait that much more unbearable.

The hours dragged at work the next morning, exacerbated by lulls between patients so that I was struggling to find office work to keep my mind off what was to come.

Every time the bell over the door chimed, I looked up, half expecting Neal to come in with a bouquet of flowers and get down on his knee in front of the entire clinic.

"What is it with you?" Naomi asked over lunch. "You're acting all squirrelly today."

"I'm not."

"Yeah, yeah, you are. You look like a fugitive on the run." She gasped. "You're not in the witness protection program or something, are you?"

"No," I said, chuckling. "I'm just expecting a surprise from Neal."

Her eyes went wide. "Oh, my God, is he proposing?" she asked, grasping my hands. "He's proposing, isn't he?"

"I hope not."

She threw my hands down in disgust. "What? You are a single parent who's found a fantastic guy. And you're telling me you don't want him to give you the big fat ring?"

"That's what I'm saying," I said. "I'm just not marriage material. I've tried it before and I'm pretty sure it's not for me."

"Please. Just because you married the wrong guy the first time doesn't mean this guy is wrong, too. They can't all be wrong."

"And I can't marry them all until the right one comes along."

She shot me an incredulous look. "So you're just going to say no even if there is a high probability that this guy is the One?"

I stuffed the rest of my burrito in my mouth, chewing quietly. What if she was right? What was I so afraid of? This was Neal, after all, a man who had managed to pierce my armor and get to the heart of me. If he wasn't Mr. Right, then who was?

"I don't need a Mr. Right," I finally said as we drove back to the clinic. "I'm happy with the way things are right now."

"Bullshit. Hey, I'm down with the feminism mantra of not needing a man. I mean, you fucking did it on your own for all these years," Naomi said. "But just because you don't *need* a man doesn't mean you can't want one."

4

I was a complete mess that afternoon as I headed home from work. When I drove up and saw Neal's car in the driveway, my heart started to pound a million miles a minute because, like it or not, it had become a part of the landscape here. I had even taken to calling it his spot, careful to park on the right side of the driveway so that he had his space.

And there I sat in my car, staring at the rental car beside mine, my fingers clutched around the steering wheel as I thought about my future and that of my son's. I was paralyzed with fear, unable to bring myself to go inside the house and face the future that Neal was about to offer.

I jumped in my seat when the front door opened and Will came rushing out. He knocked on the car window and shouted, "Are you coming in or what?"

To see that little face pressing against the glass, making squashed faces at me, made all my doubts melt away. I had my answer. "I'll be right there," I said, knocking on the glass against his piglike nose.

When I finally found the courage to go inside, I found Neal pacing in the dance room, rubbing his head with one hand and the other stuck firmly in his pocket. He looked so worried, I was compelled to stand off to the side of the doorway and watch him, wondering what was going through his mind.

"Hey," I said finally, setting my purse down and walking over. "Thanks for picking up Will."

He gave a small smile. "You thank me every day."

"Because I'm grateful every day." I wrapped my arms around his waist and stood on my toes to kiss his nose. The doorbell rang just then and I pulled away to answer the door.

"Hey," Stacy said when I opened it. "Is Will ready to go?"

"Where is Will going?" I asked, glancing back at Neal.

Stacy looked confused. "I thought we were taking Will out to dinner." She looked over my shoulder to watch Neal approaching. "Neal set it up this afternoon."

"Oh, that's right," I said, playing along. I called up the stairs for Will to get his things.

"Here, I'll get him," Neal said, going up the stairs two steps at a time.

I turned to Stacy the moment Neal was out of earshot. "What is going on?"

She shrugged, but the smile on her face said otherwise.

"You know something."

"No, I really don't," she said with a chuckle. "All I know is that he asked me to take Neal for a few hours because he had something important to discuss with you." She nodded, her eyes bright with excitement. "Is he doing what I think he's doing?"

I glanced back up at the stairs, my stomach trembling. "I don't know. I think so."

A few minutes later, after I'd closed the front door, Neal and I stood in the foyer and stared at each other.

"Um, I'm going to go change out of these," I said to break the silence and headed upstairs. "I'll be right back."

I didn't hear him follow me. I only felt him touch me after I'd taken off my scrubs, felt the wide expanse of his palms on my shoulders as he bent down and kissed the base of my neck, felt his warm breath as he let out a ragged breath. "I love you so much, Julie Grace Keaton," he murmured.

Tears sprang to my eyes at the raw emotion in his voice. "I love you, too, Neal," I said, taking his hand and holding it over my thundering heart.

I felt him turn to stone behind me. "You've never said that before."

I turned in his arms. "Well, I've felt it. For a long time now."

He blinked several times and then he was kissing me, pushing me back onto the bed. He took off my bra and panties and proceeded to kiss and touch every inch of my body, his movements desperate and frantic.

I pushed against his chest. "Slow down. We have time."

He stared down at me, breathing hard. "We're out of time, Julie," he rasped, dipping his head to take my breast in his mouth. "And tomorrow I'll feel bad about this, but right now, I just want you. I want to take you and possess you and imprint my memory into your brain."

He crawled backward, dropping kisses down the valley of my breasts and onto my stomach, his destination clear. Then he stopped and stared at me, his handsome face creased by anguish. "I can't do this."

"What? What can't you do?"

He slid his hands under my waist and bowed his head to my stomach, clutching at me. "I'm sorry, Julie," he whispered before he straightened and reached into the back pocket of his jeans, producing an envelope folded in half. "I shouldn't have kept this. It doesn't belong to me."

I leaned up on my elbows. “What is it?”

He swallowed hard then unfolded the envelope so that the name on the front was visible, written in messy, scrawling cursive.

Julie Grace Keaton

“Who is that from?” I asked, my breath stuck in my throat. I’d lost all feeling in my toes and I was pretty sure a headache was on the way. “Tell me who the hell that letter is from.”

Neal’s face was full of apology, but he didn’t offer me the envelope. He continued holding it between his fingers as if he never intended to let it go. Finally, he said it, the name I’d somehow known all along:

“It’s from Captain Jason Sherman.”

5

My body didn't know how to react to the appearance of that letter. My skin broke out in a cold sweat even as my insides overheated, so that I was a shivering, sweaty mess.

"What did you say?" I asked, even though I knew I hadn't misheard him. I'd recognized Jason's messy handwriting the moment before my brain put a name to it.

"Please tell me you don't know who that is," he said, lines bracketing his mouth.

"Jason Sherman is the name of my dead fiancé."

Neal let out a defeated breath and, with head hung, held out the envelope to me.

I looked down at it, not knowing how to proceed, simultaneously dying to open it and yet afraid of what I'd find inside. I turned it over and saw that the envelope flap had not been sealed. "Did you read it?" I asked.

He didn't meet my eyes when he said, "I did. I'm sorry."

"What is it?" My hands were shaking and my vision was blurry from unshed tears, and for some reason I couldn't bring myself to open that envelope and look inside.

"It's Jason's good-bye letter to you."

My body, my entire being, turned to stone at the revelation.

"I found it in the room I moved into when I deployed to Bagram. It was at the bottom of his closet, hidden under his clothes."

I was light-headed and having trouble pulling air into my lungs. Neal's words were not making sense. "Jason died over five years ago. You've had this for five fucking years?"

"Yes."

"And you're just giving this to me now? Right when everything had gone back to good and I was finally feeling like my old self again?"

"I've wanted to give it to you for a long time," he said.

I stared at the wrinkled envelope in my hand then up at the man who had delivered it too many years too late. "You need to go, Neal."

He gave a small, resigned nod. "I'm sorry, Julie. I kept hoping that there was some other Julie Keaton out there somewhere," he said, getting to his feet. "I guess I'm still hoping that."

"Get out," I whispered, trying to hold on to the last vestiges of my temper.

He said nothing as he slipped back into his shoes. I couldn't look at him, couldn't bear to see the look on his face. I'd trusted him, had opened up to him, and all this time he'd been keeping this secret from me.

When he was fully dressed, he bent down to give me a kiss but I turned away. "'Bye, Neal," I said with more sadness in my voice than I wanted to reveal.

When the front door clicked shut, I got out of bed and put the envelope on the dresser then got dressed. I sat on the bed, staring at that envelope, until I heard Stacy's car pull up outside.

I took a deep breath, gathering myself before going downstairs and greeting my son as if nothing had happened.

"Where's Neal? I drew something for him," he said as soon as he came inside. He held up a kid's restaurant menu, on the back of which he'd drawn three stick figures—of a kid holding the hands of the two adults beside him.

I dropped to my knees and tried to control the expression on my face. "Oh, honey, I don't know if he's coming back."

"What? Where did he go?"

"Um . . ." I looked at that drawing he'd so earnestly done and found I couldn't do it. I couldn't break his heart. Not like this. "He had to go."

"That's okay. I'll give it to him tomorrow after soccer."

Oh, hell. "Okay. Give it to him next time you see him."

"Hey, Mom," he said that night as he pulled the shower curtain aside. "Check out my scar! It looks just like Neal's! Cool, huh?"

I gave his scar the scrutiny he expected, talking about how scar tissue forms, how much stronger it is than normal skin, anything to steer his thoughts away from the man who refused to leave mine. "Lots of other people have the same kind of scar, too, you know. Not just Neal."

"Yeah, but Neal and I are twins. He called them our battle scars."

I leaned against the wall, thinking about my own wounds and whether, if ever, they would heal and scar over.

After Will had gone to bed, I called the one person who might understand what I was feeling.

"Elsie," I said as soon as she picked up. "Did I wake you?"

"No, not at all. I'm still working. What's up?"

"I just wanted your opinion on something." I paused. "Something happened."

"Hey," she said, taking note of the tone of my voice. "What's going on?"

"Remember that guy I told you about?"

"Neal?"

"Neal."

"What about him? What happened?"

"Turns out he was hiding something," I said. "Jason's good-bye letter."

"Jason's what?"

"You know the letter military members write in case they're killed in action?"

Elsie gasped on the other end. "He had it all this time?"

"Yes." My eyes flew across the room to the letter still lying on the dresser.

"How? Did he even know Jason?"

"I don't know. He said he found it in Jason's room in Bagram."

"What does it say?"

"I don't know. I haven't read it."

"Then why are you talking to me? Read it."

"I'm scared," I said softly.

She sighed. "Why? It's just a letter."

"I was happy, Els. I'd moved on with my life."

"A letter won't change that."

"It already has." I thought I'd moved on from Jason's death, but my reaction to the existence of that letter proved that I hadn't. I couldn't even imagine what its contents would do to me. "I wish this letter was for you instead."

"You're lucky, Julie. I would give anything to have a piece of my brother back," she said. "So please, just read it."

"Okay . . ."

"Go. Then call me tomorrow when you've processed it."

I hung up and made my way across the room, feeling as if every step took hours to complete. When I stood over the letter, I reached for it and took it out of the envelope before I could lose my nerve.

I sat on the edge of the bed and unfolded two wrinkled pages.

Dear Julie,

I don't like letters like these. Hell, guys like me don't need letters like these because our jobs are considered relatively safe. But after you told me about being pregnant, I'm feeling sentimental enough to want to write one. Not because I think I'll die here—I'm sure I'll live to be ninety like Grams—but because I hate the thought of leaving you with nothing if I do. I'm not worth anything and I only have about five thousand in savings, so maybe I could leave you and our baby my words and hope that's enough.

I had a dream about you last night. You were in this big room, surrounded by mirrors, with a lot of kids around you. You were teaching them a move, that one where you jump and do a split in the air, and the kids were copying you. It was nice to see you surrounded by dancing children. You looked so happy. I guess now I know what that dream meant.

Did you know that I started falling for you that first night in Panama City, when I asked you how many people you'd slept with and you said, all beautiful sass, "Does it matter?" Yes, it did matter, but somehow you made me believe that I was the only one who did. I'd never met anyone like you, so full of life and light, so confident and adventurous.

I shouldn't have wasted so much time over the years pretending I wasn't in love with you, allowing you to push me away whenever you got scared. Oh, yeah, I knew what was up. You were afraid of getting too close to someone, but I was determined to make you let go and let me in so that I could show you there's more to life than casual sex and shallow relationships. I wanted to show you there's a deeper love out there and that we could have it if only you'd let your guard down and let it in.

And I think we're almost there. I think I've gotten under your skin and it's only a matter of time until you accept that I'm the one for you.

You asked me once why I haven't told my family about you. You think it's because I'm not sure about our relationship, but it's the opposite: it's you who's not ready. I don't want you to freak out and run again. So I'm waiting until you let me know, until I'm absolutely sure without a doubt that you want everyone to know about us.

I'm hoping it's only a matter of time. Hopefully when I get back from this deployment, I can make my way to you during homecoming, drop to one knee, and give you a ring worthy of you. Because you deserve more than a quick question over the phone.

Ah, shit, I'm supposed to be dead when you receive this letter, but that's the last thing on my mind. Only this morning you told me that you're pregnant, that I'm going to be a dad. How can I possibly think of death when all I can think of is that amazing thing growing inside you? I know nothing about that peanut, if it's a girl or a boy, but I love it already.

I can't even imagine not being there the first time he or she cries, or not being there to compare what features the baby inherited from you and me. Or not being present for the first step or the first word, or any of the firsts. I refuse to entertain the possibility of my missing all of that.

I am not worth more than my fellow airmen—we all have our reasons for living—but knowing that you are carrying my child gives me more drive to succeed. I'll make you this promise, Julie: I won't go down easily. I am going to fight tooth and nail to survive, to be the last man standing. And if by some slim chance I do get killed, then know that I died loving you with everything I had.

Life is full of pain and heartbreak, but it's also filled with surprises and love. I've been lucky enough to love and be loved by you for a time, and for that I'm the most fortunate guy in the world. Despite your fears, I know you'll be a terrific mother. And I know there's more out there for you, more love and dance and laughter. If it's not with me, then I hope you find it with someone else, because you deserve to be happy.

All the same, I hope you never have to read this letter.

I love you, Julie Grace Keaton. With everything I have.

Jason Sherman

6

I needed to pee, but it was safe and dark under the blanket, serene even, and God knew I needed some peace. My eyes were puffy and stinging, and my throat was dry. I peeked out from under the blanket at the clock: 5:23 A.M.

Shit.

I held my fists up to my eyes, the silver ring back on my left hand, trying to force myself to sleep the last hour before I had to get up. But try as I might, my brain wouldn't stop whirring with Jason's last words. I'd heard his voice as I was reading the letter, had heard the hopeful tone coming through his writing. If I closed my eyes, I could almost imagine him alive in Afghanistan, sitting in his plywood room, writing me that letter.

Five years had gone by since he died. Five years of thinking that he had left me without anything. And only now was I finding out that he had left me his love, his thoughts, his words.

Neal had robbed me of that closure for over five damn years.

With adrenaline surging through my veins, I threw aside the blanket and reached for the phone.

"Hello?" he said after the first ring. "Julie?"

"When did you know?" I asked. "When did you know I was the Julie in this letter? Did you know from day one, on that beach?"

He cleared his throat. "No. Not that day. I didn't even have a clue until we were talking on the beach after the wedding reception, when you told me that your fiancé had died."

"Why didn't you give it to me then?"

"I don't know. I guess I was hoping you weren't *that* Julie," he said. "I didn't know for sure until you told me your name in Vegas. By then I didn't want to give the letter to you anymore. You'd been through so much, I didn't want to put you through another emotional upheaval."

"What the hell were you thinking?" I cried, starting to feel my sanity slip. "What, you thought you could just insert yourself into our lives? Try to be Jason's replacement?"

"No," he said without any fight in his voice. He sighed. "It wasn't like that at all."

I took in a shaky breath, tears filling my eyes once again.

I looked around the room, at the darkened walls boxing me in. "When I first read Jason's name on that news article, I just got in bed and crawled under the covers. I didn't want to move. I thought that if I stayed there long enough, it wouldn't be true. Then if I stayed there long enough, I wouldn't be pregnant. I wanted to sleep it off. Everything."

"Julie . . ."

"You know what was the last thing Jason said to me?"

"What?" he whispered.

"He said, 'I'll see you soon. I can't wait to go to that first ultrasound with you.' " I covered my mouth to hold back the sob that erupted from my throat. "I haven't slept. All I keep hearing is his voice, how shocked he was when I told him that I was pregnant, then his ridiculous laugh. He sounded so happy."

When Neal said nothing, I kept going. "He wrote that letter the same day he was killed. He didn't want to die. He had so much to come home to. And then there's you, the guy who proudly courts death," I said. "How is it Jason died while you lived?"

He didn't argue, didn't tell me I was being unfair. In many ways his silence made it worse.

There was a rustling on his end. Then Neal said, "I'm coming over."

"No. Don't," I said, sitting up and glancing at the clock. "I have to take Will to school and I have work . . ."

"I don't care. I need to be with you."

"Neal, we're not . . ." I sighed. "I shouldn't have called you."

He let out a frustrated breath. "Julie—"

"We're over, Neal. Once and for all."

"I don't think so. Not by a long shot," he said with some grit in his voice.

"Well, fortunately, that's not up to you."

After dropping Will off at school, I called off from work and just started to drive around. Pretty soon I was driving north on I-35, toward Oklahoma. I'd never once taken this drive to see Jason, was never even asked.

The entire time we were dating, I thought he hadn't introduced me to his family because he was ashamed of me. Turned out he had just been waiting for me to make the first move.

So I finally made the drive up that long stretch of asphalt that tied Dallas to Oklahoma City as I should have done a long time ago. I tried to recall each and every time we were together but five years had burnished some of the memory's edges, made it hard to remember every detail until only faces and words and feelings were left.

With help from the GPS in my phone, I found the park that

Jason had often told me about. I parked the car and got out, finding the running path that bordered the grassy area. Even though it was only a few degrees above freezing, I walked along that path, staring down at my feet, imagining I was retracing Jason's very same steps.

"He was here," I murmured, fingering my ring. "He was real."

I must have looked strange—this woman huddled in her coat, staring at the frosty ground as she talked to herself—but I didn't care.

"You'll love this park by my apartment," Jason had told me once. "Earlywine. It's always full of activity, people running and walking, kids practicing soccer, families enjoying the playgrounds. It's always so alive."

"I'll stick to my treadmill in the gym, thanks," I'd said just to be ornery and he'd tickled me until I'd thrown my hands up in surrender. "So when are you planning on taking me to this park of yours?"

He'd studied me for a moment before saying, "Whenever you like."

I'd misunderstood him back then, had allowed fear and insecurity to keep me from hearing the truth: that Jason was ready to give me everything. I'd just needed to say the word.

As I walked back to my car, I passed by a mother pushing her child on the swing. I wondered about her little family, about the father of her child. Was he in the armed forces or did he work a civilian job? Most important, was he alive, and if so, did she know just how lucky she was?

PART FIVE

STRIKE

1

NEAL

Thirteen Years Ago

The day my mom came home from the hospital I was convinced she was getting better. But I was only seventeen and didn't know squat.

Dad carried her in from the car, settling her into his favorite recliner. He was still really strong then but it wouldn't have taken much strength to carry my mother anyway. The never-ending chemo and radiation had done a number on her; she was stick thin, her skin pale and paperlike, and she looked about twenty years older.

But still, I thought for sure she was kicking cancer's ass. She was Lori Harding, former firefighter for the Navy and all-around badass. For the longest time, I was convinced that she was some sort of superhero, that there was nothing she couldn't overcome. Turned out I was wrong.

I brought in Mom's bags from the car then helped Dad make her comfortable, tucking her in with her favorite fleece blanket, setting drinks and magazines by the side table within easy reach. We even gave her free rein of the TV, which, for two men who had lived on their own for a long time, was something like giving up an important organ.

"Are you quite done?" she asked, swatting us away with remote controls.

Dad's lips twitched under his overgrown beard. He hadn't shaved in so long, I'd almost forgotten what he looked like under that brown bush. "I'm sending Neal to the grocery store. Do you need anything?"

"Why don't you go instead?" she asked. "I'd like to spend some time with Neal."

Dad shrugged and took the keys from me. "So what do you need?"

"I'd like a big bottle of Yoo-hoo," Mom said with a smile. "I suddenly have a hankering for an oversugared chocolate drink."

Dad smiled. "Anything else? Twizzlers to go with that?"

"Twizzlers will gunk up my system. Better make it Red Vines," Mom said, and suddenly it was like we were back in the old days, back when Mom hadn't yet been diagnosed with cancer and our lives were still fun and easy. For the first time in years, I felt the weight lift off my chest. Maybe it was really going to be okay.

After Dad left, a quiet contentment settled over the room. I sat on the end of the couch closest to Mom and we watched some lame soap opera where the guy got this woman pregnant but she turned out to be his sister or something.

"See, Maurice fell in love with Paulette," Mom explained with a knowing smile. "Then he learned she was really his sister but the kid she was pregnant with really wasn't his. It was really his best friend's baby, who is currently lost in the Sahara Desert."

I gave her a look that conveyed just how ridiculous I thought it was.

"I know," she said with a laugh. "But it's good to escape once in a while."

I rolled my eyes approximately fifty times during the next two minutes. When I couldn't take the show's absurdity anymore, I turned to Mom. "So are you ready to see your only child graduate?" I asked. "For a while there, I thought you might not be able to make it."

Mom turned off the TV. "When is it again?"

"In May. Three months till I'm free."

"Until you go to college," she said in a happy tone that seemed forced. "Will Gia go with you?"

"We're staying here, going to San Diego State. You know that." I'd come to the hospital almost every day, telling Mom everything about my life so she wouldn't feel left out. One of our most frequent subjects was my girlfriend since junior year, Gia Hedlund, and our plans for the future.

"You're still young, Neal," Mom said. "You have many more years of living ahead of you."

I scrunched my eyebrows together, not sure what she meant.

"You don't have to pin yourself down in one place so soon." Her gaze wandered to the window, a faraway look on her face. "Travel around, see the world. Go kiss the Blarney Stone, walk the Great Wall of China, surf the waves of Hawaii." She blinked a few times and turned back to me. "Your dad always told me I had a gypsy soul. I think you do, too."

I jumped up and ran to my room, grabbing the oversized world map that I'd glued onto a foam-core board. "Look," I said, holding it up before her. "These are all the places I want to go once Dad and I are done building the plane. I've got a notebook with information on each country, the best time to visit, the best sights to see."

She reached out and touched every single red pin, reciting each location under her breath. When she was done, she looked up, tears shining in her eyes. "Yes. This."

We looked at each other for a long time, understanding passing between us.

Finally I set the board down at my feet. "You're not going to make it to my graduation, are you?" I asked, my voice cracking at the end.

She shook her head. "I think it's nearly time to start saying good-bye."

My chest hurt. I knew her death had been coming, but knowing hadn't made it easier to deal with the reality.

"Neal," she said, reaching out to take my hand. She pulled me closer. "I know it hasn't been easy for you and Dad. And it might get a little harder after I die. But I promise you that it will get better as time goes by. You'll see."

How could that be? It didn't seem possible. "Who's going to listen to me ramble on and on now?" I asked. "You're like a diary except you talk back and lecture me."

She gave me a sad smile. "You know you can talk to your dad, too."

"Not like I talk to you." I crouched down in front of her, trying to keep it together. "He's not very good at talking back."

"But he's very good at listening." She took my face in her bony hands, her skin scratchy and thin. Still, I nuzzled my face into it, trying to memorize everything about her from here on out. "Everything happens for a reason, Neal."

"Aren't you scared?"

"No. Not anymore," she said. "It's inevitable. We're all going to die, just some sooner than others."

I bent my head at her lap, my tears darkening the blanket that covered her. I felt her fingers through my hair, stroking it like she used to do when I was little and she'd sing me to sleep. It felt like a million years ago.

"My only regret is that I couldn't be a better mother to you," she said, her voice unsteady. "But I know you and your dad are going to be okay. You guys need to take care of each other, okay? He won't ask for help, but try to give him a hand anyway."

I nodded, the vision of my mother hazy through my tears. I wiped at my face with the back of my hand to see her more clearly.

"Don't be so sad," she said, bending forward to kiss my forehead. "This isn't a permanent good-bye, Neal. We'll see each other again."

Five Years Ago

I shielded my eyes from the intense sun and looked up at the small wooden structure—the B-hut, as they're called on Bagram Airfield—wondering what the hell I was in for. I was not prepared for the windowless darkness that welcomed me when I opened the door, with nothing but raw plywood walls greeting me on both sides, the tops of which didn't even reach the ceiling. There were six doors in all in this narrow hallway, three on each side, with a dirty rectangular rug lying skewed on the cement floor to tie the shitty décor together.

I walked in and found my assigned room at the end of the hall. With a small push, the door flew open and slammed against the wall. Hell, I could have breathed on it and it would have blown open, it was so flimsy.

The room itself was roughly seven feet by seven feet, with a rumpled bed that looked as if its previous occupant had just gotten up to go take a leak, a wooden bookshelf above overflowing with books and various other things, and a horrendous maroon rug covering most of the cement floor. The closet, if you could even call it that, was nothing but a rectangular niche in the wall covered by a piece of plywood on hinges.

"Homey." I set my boxes down on the middle of the rug, suspecting it hadn't been vacuumed in several deployment cycles, if ever. The wall that the bed butted against also didn't reach the ceiling, but the occupant next door had stapled a piece of black fabric up there for some semblance of privacy. All in all, this was typical Bagram accommodations. Hell, at least it beat the tents. At least I no longer had to jack off in the latrines.

I walked over to the narrow shelf, looking over the books the previous tenant had left behind. *Faith of My Fathers* by John McCain, *The Art of War* by Sun Tzu, *A Game of Thrones*, a few James Patterson novels, and a book on poker. I held an empty box at the end of the bookshelf and slid everything over into it, then changed my mind and took out the largest book. I'd read the entire Song of Ice and Fire series before but this deployment was going to be long and I'd need something to fill the hours.

I made my way to the closet, finding it completely full of clothing, most of them folded, some not so much. But as long as a scorpion—or worse, a big-ass camel spider—didn't jump out at me, I considered it a good day.

It felt strange to be going through this guy's stuff; I'd never even met this Captain Sherman. I'd only heard stories about him, about what a great guy he was, smart and a good leader. People were saying if his unit had only gone a different route that day, if they hadn't stayed to talk to the locals, Sherman would still be alive, as if they could have saved the poor guy from his fate.

Death wasn't something we could avoid when there were people out there plotting against us daily, whose main concern in life was to kill as many of us as possible. All you could really do out here was hope to prolong the inevitable.

It took a while to empty the closet as I folded everything neatly before setting everything in the box, knowing nobody else would repack it before it was shipped back to his parents or wife. When I was almost done, I spotted a plain white envelope at the very back of the tiny closet.

Julie Grace Keaton, it said on the outside.

I flipped it over and found the flap unsealed. I looked at the name again and wondered why Sherman hadn't sent the letter. Perhaps she was an old flame, someone who'd decided to leave her man during the deployment, or maybe she was "the other woman."

Whoever this Julie was, she obviously wasn't important enough to get this forgotten letter.

I didn't know what possessed me to do it—why I thought it was okay to read this dead man's words—but I sat on the bed and opened the envelope, unfolding the lined notebook paper without too much hesitation.

It became clear, after the first line, that this was no ordinary letter. This was a freaking death missive, a man's last words before he went out to die in battle. Except, in this day and age, save for a few sentimental guys out in the front lines, nobody writes these anymore.

Still, that didn't stop me; in fact, it made me all the more fascinated. I'd never read one, never even thought about writing one of my own. What would I even say to my girlfriend, Shari? Would I tell her to move on with her life, even though I was still alive? Why would I even need to write one when my job entailed never having to leave the base?

Here at Bagram we'd get mortar attacks about twice a week, and though a lot of the times they were duds, a few still managed to cause trouble. A rocket lit up a truck recently and did some damage to a nearby building. We were lucky there were no casualties, but it could have just as easily killed someone, a service member or contractor who thought we were safe within the walled confines of this base. In that sense, writing a death letter wasn't so far-fetched.

Still, the man in that letter wasn't ready to go. Hell, he didn't want to go. His desire to live and get back to his girl was as clear as day.

I put the letter back in the envelope but something kept me from dropping it in the box along with the rest of his stuff—an image of a woman reading this letter, and the tears that would surely follow when she realized he could never make good on his promises.

Before I could change my mind, I folded it in half and stuffed it into my camo pants pocket, ignoring the fact that I was stealing from the dead, preferring instead to think that I was doing them both a favor. I was saving her from even more heartache and he from becoming a man who didn't keep his word.

For years I held on to that letter, trying to understand why this Jason Sherman was so opposed to the idea of dying. It wasn't until much later, when I finally met Julie Grace Keaton, that I finally understood his reason for living.

2

Now . . .

I fucked up. Big-time.

I spent all this time procrastinating, hoping that somehow there was another Julie Keaton out there, when I should have just done the right thing and given her the letter the moment I was sure. And hell, I'd been sure for a long damn time now. I'd tried to deny it, even tried to avoid asking her full name, but the truth was that I'd had a hunch since I spotted her marching down that aisle on the beach, preceding Jason's sister.

I sank down into the hotel's armchair, a near-empty glass cradled in my hand, and continued staring at the computer screen. I scratched at my chest, then my head, trying to force my brain into focusing, but I couldn't think past Julie and that damn letter and her accusation that I'd wanted to replace Jason.

It wasn't true. At least, it didn't start out that way. And if being with them, enjoying being a part of their little family unit, was considered wrong, then I was prepared to be wrong for the rest of my life. Julie deserved to have someone take care of her for once, to love her like she should have been loved all these years. And Will . . . that kid deserved to have a real father figure in his life.

I jumped, nearly spilling my drink, when a sharp rap came at the door. I stumbled out of the chair and somehow made my way across the room.

"Julie," I said as I opened the door, before I made out the woman standing there.

"No," said the hotel clerk. She held out an envelope. "Here's your receipt. If you need anything, please don't hesitate to let us know."

I stuck my head out the door and looked up and down the hall, expecting Julie to emerge from somewhere, but of course she wasn't there.

The next morning, I woke up with the sun too bright, the birds outside too loud. I folded an arm over my eyes and tried to go back to sleep, but the ringing in my head kept going, so loud it was filling the room.

It stopped suddenly and then a minute later started again, until it finally dawned on me that it was the phone making all that racket. I reached over and grabbed the receiver. "Hello?" I barely croaked out.

"Come over," said the soft voice over the line.

I sat up, wincing as my head tried to split right down the middle. I wasn't even sure if I was just hallucinating Julie's voice.

"You okay?" she asked.

"Yeah, just hung over."

"Well, this can wait. Just go back to sleep."

Like hell it could. "I can be there in about thirty-five minutes," I said and tried to move as fast as my protesting body would allow.

"Hi," Julie said when she let me in. "Will's coming home soon, so this needs to be fast."

I took hold of her shoulders and soaked her in, feeling like it had been years since I'd seen her light blue eyes, her lovely face. "I'm sorry, Julie. I wish I could convey just how sorry I am," I said, squeezing her to my chest.

"I understand," she said, twisting out of my arms. "I just wanted to give you this." She picked up a box by the stairs and held it out.

Inside were my things, those little articles that I'd accidentally left behind. Or perhaps I'd consciously left them so that I would be remembered, even after I was no longer welcome in her home.

It took a few moments but it finally pierced through my sludgy brain that this was no reunion. "So we're not even going to talk about this? You're just going to end it like this?" I asked, staring down into that box.

"How should I end it, then, Neal?" she asked, folding her arms across her chest. "Should I have just dropped your stuff off at the front desk of your hotel? Maybe just thrown it away?"

"Come on, let's not do this," I said.

When she looked up, there were tears in her eyes, making me feel like even more of an asshole, if that was possible.

"No, Julie," I said, touching her cheek with the pad of my thumb.

"I wish I'd had that letter a long time ago," she said, all the sarcasm and anger gone from her voice until all that was left was anguish. "It would have made a world of difference."

"Really? It would have made a difference knowing he never kept his promise?"

"I would have had some closure," she said. "My life would have been different."

"But then we might never have met on that beach."

"We would have met when you handed me the letter."

"And you would have said thank you and gone on your way, and I would have never seen you again."

"Wow," she said with a humorless laugh. "You weren't lying when you said you're a selfish bastard."

"Only when it comes to you."

"I knew it was too good to be true. It was all too good to last," she said with a sad shake of her head. "I should have known better. But we had fun at least."

"We had more than fun between us," I said, taking a step forward, needing to be as close as possible. Maybe then I could convince her to give me another chance. "Much more."

"I thought so, too. But I was wrong," she said, taking a big step back.

This was excruciating, this back-and-forth. I'd much rather do SERE training again than endure this torture. "Look, Julie," I said, "I know that withholding that letter was wrong, but one fact remains: I began to fall in love with you before I knew your real identity."

"But if you had really loved me, you would have told me. You would have given me the letter the moment you figured it out. Instead you chose your own self—your own needs—over mine."

I bit back a groan of frustration then lunged forward, kissing her in greed. If she wanted selfish, then she would get selfish. But no matter how hard I mashed my lips against hers, she held firm, refusing to open up to me. I gave up, leaning my forehead against hers. "I haven't ever felt this way about anyone, Julie. But even if this is all new territory to me, I am sure of one thing—that I love you. And there's not a doubt in my mind that you love me, too."

"I love you. But I no longer trust you."

I should have been prepared—I mean, what else did I expect?—but to hear it coming from those lips felt like I'd just been punched in the gut.

She walked to the door, her hand on the doorknob. "You'd better go. Will's coming home soon and I don't want him to see you."

"You haven't told him?"

"What, that the man he idolizes has been keeping a huge secret from us all this time? No, I haven't told him."

I nodded, a tiny bit relieved. "Thank you."

"I didn't do it for you."

"I know, but thanks all the same." I stared at her, trying to figure out how to fix the situation. I could create the most complex codes, set up phone and Internet access in the most remote places of the world, but Lord help me, I couldn't figure out how to appease this woman. But, as with all things in life, I'd learned that in order to figure out a problem, I first needed to step away and get a different perspective. "Okay. I'll go."

"That's a good idea."

I turned toward the door then stopped before I crossed the threshold. "If you or Will ever need anything, just ask. I'll be around."

"Are you staying in town?"

"I don't know." I searched her face for any clues that she wanted me to, but the mask was back on. "I think I'll dust off the plane and just . . . go," I said, though now that I'd known her, I had nowhere else to go.

The front door closed behind me soundly, Julie not even bothering to watch me drive away like she used to do. I went to the car and put the box in the passenger seat, unsure of where to go next.

I could just get on the plane and fly until I needed gas—it wouldn't be the first time I'd done that. I'd lived a nomadic life not too far back, but somehow the idea of flying around the country no longer held appeal.

I was still standing in the driveway, trying to figure out my next move, when Stacy's minivan drove up to the curb. The van door slid open and Will came bounding out of the vehicle, waving good-bye to his friend before running to me. "Neal!" he cried, throwing his arms around my waist. "Where have you been?"

"I've been working, bud," I said, which was technically not a lie.

"I have something for you," he said, and before I could tell him I had to leave, he threw his backpack onto the grass and ran into the house.

I looked around and found Stacy still at the curb, watching me. When she got caught watching, she turned her head and quickly drove off.

Will came back waving a piece of paper in the air. "I drew this for you."

That picture, so roughly and lovingly drawn, made my heart clench. I crouched down and smiled. "Thank you. This is a really good drawing."

"See, it's you and me and Mom."

"It's really great."

"So come on, let's go practice soccer."

"We can't do that anymore, Will," I said, watching his little face go from happy to confused in one point zero second. "I won't be back for a while. I'm sorry."

"Where are you going? Did you and Mom have a fight?"

"I'll let your mom answer all those questions, okay?" I said, squeezing his little shoulder.

"When will you come back?"

"I'm not sure."

"But . . . can you come back to teach me the soccer drills? And teach me to shave for real?" Will asked, slightly panicked.

"I think your mom will be able to handle all that stuff."

"But she'll teach me to shave my legs," he said, throwing his hands up in frustration.

I fought back a smile. God, I was going to miss this kid. "I know, I'm sorry. Things just didn't work out."

His chin started to quiver. "You said I was your buddy."

I held him by the shoulders, willing him to look at me. "You are."

"But soldiers don't leave their buddies behind."

I bowed my head, the realization that Julie was not the only person I was letting down weighing heavy on my conscience.

"Do you want to come back for my birthday party?" he asked with a little hopeful lilt to his voice.

"I can't," I said then remembered the gift I'd bought him. "Hold on a second. I have something for you," I said, and I got the box from the backseat of the car.

Will didn't waste time. He ripped open the wrapping and didn't even bother looking at the box before ripping into that, too. I helped him take the pen out of the plastic packaging and put in the battery for him. "Wow. Is it like yours?" he asked.

I nodded, crouching down. Will had always been curious about my smartpen, oftentimes taking it when I wasn't looking and recording funny little voice messages for me. "You can do voice recordings here and if you write in the special notepad, it will also turn your drawings into computer art." I took the pen and pressed record. "Will Keaton, this is Neal Harding. I want you to know that I've had the best time with you. I think you are a really cool kid, and I'll miss you. I hope you won't forget me."

Will listened to my recorded message. "Thanks, Neal," he said, wrapping his arms around my neck. "You're really cool, too."

My chest constricted at the finality of the hug. "'Bye, buddy."

Will hung on, sniffing by my ear. It was almost too much to take. Then Julie saved me from completely losing it. "Will, time to come in."

I stood up and turned around. "'Bye," I said, leaving so much more unsaid, and with one last sad wave, I got in my rented car and drove away.

3

I flew out of Dallas that afternoon and headed to the shores of San Diego. I hadn't been back home in a while, but I really needed to be by the water and clear my head.

It was dark by the time I exited the hangar at Montgomery Field and caught a taxi to my buddy's pub ten minutes away.

"Hey, long time no see," Lonnie, the owner and my friend, said as soon as I entered the establishment. He reached across the bar to clasp my hand and give my shoulder a pat. "Where the hell have you been, man?"

"Oh, you know, here and there."

"And back again," Lonnie said as he handed me a bottle of beer, reminding me of the geeky kid I'd known back in high school. It was the reason we'd been friends. Geeks of a feather and all that.

"How's Bill Gates?" he asked, leaning on the bar. "You taking over his empire yet?"

"Not anytime soon," I said, taking a big gulp of the beer. It tasted extra good considering the day I'd had.

Another guy walked in and Lonnie greeted him with a jerk of

the head. "'S up." He turned to me. "Mark here will take care of you," he said to me.

"You're not staying?"

"No, it's my wedding anniversary. The wife and I are doing the whole thing—got a babysitter, booked a fancy dinner, the works."

"How long have you been together? Five, six years?"

"Six," Lonnie said. "I still don't know how she fell in love with my nerdy black ass, but I'm not going to question it. I'm just going to make her very happy tonight. *Very* happy."

I raised the mug. "Hey, congrats, man."

"What about you? Still single?"

I worked on peeling the label off the bottle, shaking my head. "It's complicated."

He pushed away from the bar. "Duly noted." He uncapped another ice-cold beer and slid the bottle over. "Hey, man, take care of this guy, okay? Anything he wants. Within reason," he said to Mark.

After Lonnie left, Mark took up his spot. I drank my beer and avoided his prying gaze. He was watching me, waiting for me to say something. When I didn't speak, he finally said, "So what's your sob story?"

I raised an eyebrow.

"You know, your tale of woe, your reason for being drunk at a bar at seven on a Monday night."

"It's Monday. Isn't that enough?"

"There's always a reason why people hate Mondays. For most people, it's because they hate their jobs." He folded his elbows on the bar, leaning too close for my liking.

"I hate Mondays because I do."

"Hmm." He studied me for a long moment, his head cocked to the side. "So what's your damage?" When I gave him a confused look, he waved a hand. "You know, everyone's got something. An abused childhood; they accidentally killed someone; some deep, dark secret that causes them to shy away from the world. What's yours?"

"I have nothing. I'm just a regular guy, completely boring and unexceptional."

"That's it," Mark said, slapping the bar and pointing a finger at me.

I sighed, beginning to wish I hadn't come here at all.

"You don't think you're worth loving."

I got to my feet, the stool screeching beside me. "You know, if I wanted to be analyzed, I would go to a real shrink."

"I am a real shrink," he said with a shit-eating grin. "I like to practice in my off-hours on unsuspecting handsome strangers."

I tried to hide my surprise but didn't know if I was successful. "Well, I'm flattered but I don't need therapy. I just came here for beer."

"Well, you're in luck, therapy is free." When I didn't return his smile, he finally backed off. "All right, I'll leave you alone."

I fixed my attention on the television up in the corner of the ceiling; it was playing the eighties movie *An Officer and a Gentleman*. It was at the iconic point of the movie where Richard Gere was stalking through the factory in his whites, intent on literally sweeping Debra Winger off her feet.

I snorted. "It'll never work," I said to nobody in particular. "She'll always be paranoid that he'll leave her, because if he did it once, he'll do it again."

"You know," Mark said, coming back over, "even trust issues can be overcome, provided both parties are willing to work on it."

I stared down at my empty bottle. "Yeah, therein lies the rub." I looked up. "Give me another one. Keep them coming."

A cab dropped me off at my father's house a few hours and several beers later. I took my bags and knocked on the door, regretting that I'd called ahead, wishing I could just sneak in and hide in the guest bedroom unnoticed instead. I looked up at the second-story window, remembering how easy it used to be to climb up there from the balcony railing, but in my inebriated state, I'd probably fall flat on my ass and land myself in the hospital.

"Neal," my stepmother, Karen, said, ushering me inside. "We thought you were coming earlier."

I bent down to give her a hug, hoping she didn't smell the alcohol on my breath and the lingering cigarette smoke on my clothes. But that was just a drunk man's wishful thinking, because the sober notice everything.

"Have you started smoking again?" she asked, looking stern.

"No," I said, taking my smelly jacket off and balling it up. "I went by Lonnie's bar first, and his bartender is a smoker."

"Well, that doesn't seem right," she said, leading the way to the living room. "Isn't smoking banned in all public places?"

"Yes."

"Well, that's not legal."

"You know what should be illegal? Hitting on and psychoanalyzing the only patron in your bar while you smoke," I said, collapsing onto the suede love seat.

My dad, who was sitting in the same recliner my mother had spent her last days in, looked at me over his glasses. "You look like hell, son."

"I feel it," I said.

"Things didn't go well with Julie?" Karen asked, all motherly concern. "Oh, did you eat already? Do you want a sandwich?"

"Things are over with Julie." I blew out a breath and turned to Karen. "I'd love a sandwich, Karen."

"Be right back," she said and disappeared off into the kitchen.

Dad raised a bushy eyebrow. "What happened?"

"It doesn't matter."

"It does. That's why I'm asking."

I leaned my head on the back of the couch. "I withheld something from her, something that I should have handed over the moment I knew it belonged to her."

"Son," he said with a sigh. "Let me guess, you thought you were keeping it from her for her own good?"

I gave a miserable nod.

"So if everything was going fine, why give it to her? Why ruin a good thing?"

"I couldn't have it hanging over our heads anymore. She wanted to build a life with me, and I didn't want any secrets between us."

Dad gave me a narrowed, suspicious look.

"No, I wasn't self-sabotaging," I said. "I really love her. I want to be with her."

"Isn't that what you did with that Shari girl?"

"Hell no. Shari cheated on me while I was deployed. There's nothing similar between the two situations at all." I sighed, wishing there *were* a correlation between my past relationships and what had happened with Julie. Maybe then I could collect the data and track the trends to see where I had gone wrong.

But as it was, the only recurring fact was that all my relationships had ended. If I was a more insecure man, I'd probably deduce that the problem was me.

I pushed up off the couch. "Do you still have my surfboard?"

He jabbed a thumb toward the side of the house. "All your stuff's in the garage. In the back by the fridge."

"Thanks for letting me crash for a few days, Dad," I said and headed to the kitchen to eat my sandwich and try to soak up the alcohol in my belly.

The next day, I woke up before sunrise, surprisingly free of a headache and that groggy feeling that usually came after a night of heavy drinking.

I took my surfboard from the garage and gave it a coat of wax, finding the constant circular stroke calming. After, I borrowed my dad's truck and drove the short distance to the Torrey Pines State Reserve and walked the two-mile-long path to my favorite surfing spot, Black's Beach.

The sun had risen by the time I made it down to the beach but it was still cold as balls. I stuck my longboard into the sand and took a moment to soak in the view of the massive swells rolling in, smiling as a dozen surfers tackled another fifteen-foot wave. It had been a while since I'd taken on anything that big, but my body was already raring to go, already anticipating the rush of dropping in on a wave.

I took in deep breaths, feeling revitalized as I drew into my lungs the fresh salty scent of the ocean. This was sanctuary. This was home.

A seagull flew by and pulled my thoughts back toward the sky, toward the woman who wanted nothing more than to fly.

"Get it together, Harding," I said, slipping my arms into the sleeves of my full-body wetsuit and zipping up the back. Willfully clearing my head, I took hold of my board and ran toward the water, meeting the freezing waves with an exhilarated shout. My arms sliced through the water as I paddled out to sea, and when I dropped in on that first wave, I felt that familiar rush of joy that comes when I'm communing with the ocean.

As I caught wave after wave, the voices of doubt were silenced by the roar of the ocean, and it was there inside an immense barrel of falling water that I was finally able to make sense of my problems.

I came up with a plan just as my board hit a gurgle in the water and I went flying off my board, landing on my back at the base of this enormous wave, staring up at death.

Come and get me, I thought right before hundreds of pounds of salt water pounded me into darkness.

4

When I came to, I was twisting around underwater as if I were a rag doll, my bearings screwed up as I tried to make sense of up and down. I tried to remain calm, even as my lungs began to burn, biding my time until the water calmed.

It would be easy enough to close my eyes and just let go. I could think of worse ways to die than drowning inside the biggest wave I'd ever surfed. For nearly my entire life I'd been ready to square with death, but I would not die today. This much I knew with all certainty.

Finally, when the wave had passed, I kicked up toward the light and broke the surface, sucking in air to fill my lungs.

"Good morning," Karen said when I came into the kitchen after a hot shower. She looked up from the newspaper, studying me over her glasses. "Did you go surfing?"

"Yes. I went to Black's Beach." I gave her shoulder a squeeze as I walked by to get to the coffeemaker. While I poured myself a cup of coffee, I told her the story of how I'd bit it, and lifted my shirt to show the resulting bruise on my back.

"Saw your board out back. Both pieces of it," Dad said from across the table. "That must have been some wipeout."

I sat down at the table, shaking my head. "I guess it was time to get a new one," I said. "I've had that one since high school."

"I remember. You saved up for it for a long time."

"Actually, Mom paid for half." I took a big sip of coffee, trying to swallow down the lump in my throat. "But it died a valiant death, helping me figure out how to proceed with my life."

"And?" Karen prompted.

"I'm not giving in so easily."

Dad gave a short nod. "Good."

After a long pause, Karen said, "So, are you staying till Thanksgiving?"

"If you'll let me."

"You kidding?" Karen asked. "We haven't seen you in forever. Randy and Catherine will be thrilled."

"Okay. I'll stay."

Thanksgiving was a rowdy affair. Dad and I tried to watch the game but my half siblings, Randy and Catherine—ten and nine respectively—had other ideas for the wide-screen TV, begging to play their newest Xbox game.

Eventually, Dad relinquished the remote control and sat back, shaking his head. "These kids today, they're so technology savvy," he grumbled. "Must take after you."

They put on a dancing game and it wasn't long before Catherine was tugging on my hand, begging me to play.

"He won't," Randy told her, glancing at me. "He's too chicken."

"I'm not Marty McFly—I won't rise to that taunt," I said with a laugh.

"Who's Marty McFly?"

I caught my dad's eye across the way and we both let out exaggerated sighs. "From *Back to the Future*?" I prompted. "Never mind." Still, maybe I was a little bit of a McFly because I ended up getting to my feet anyway.

"Neal, it's okay if you don't know how to dance," Randy said right before the game began.

"Not likely," I said, and I began to make a fool of myself in front of my family. It took only one round before I got the hang of the game and flinging my limbs around actually started to make sense.

"Ha!" I cried out when I finally won a game. I bent down and picked Randy up by the waist, twirling him in a circle while he laughed. "Who can't dance now, sucker?"

Catherine got on the couch and joined in, jumping on my back and clasping her hands around my neck. Despite the weight, I twirled them around until we fell in a dizzy heap on the carpet.

I rolled away and got to my feet. "Hey, let's see if Karen needs some help with the food," I said. "Who wants a piggyback ride to the kitchen?"

The next day, I said my good-byes to Karen and the kids, then Dad took me to the airport.

At Montgomery Field, Dad followed me inside the hangar to take a look at the plane we'd built. "Looks like you're taking good care of her," he said as he slid a hand along the plane's smooth side, not so much a gesture of tenderness as a way to detect any damage on the aircraft's skin.

"Yeah." I removed the tail chock and inspected the elevator and rudder, checking their range of motion.

Dad helped me complete the preflight safety check, going so far as to sit in the cockpit. He put the headphones on and listened while I communicated with the radio tower.

"When do you think you'll get tired of this life and settle down?" Dad asked after preflight had been completed. "I mean, it's gotta get lonely, right?"

"It wasn't." I leaned back in the seat and looked out the windshield, considering my future. "Until Julie."

"So where exactly is it that you're going?" he asked with a lift to his eyebrow.

I turned my head and grinned.

"Well, good luck winning her back, son. You know we Harding men are not the best at grand gestures. Remember that time I tried to ask Karen out?" He chuckled. "Whatever you do, a salsa band is never a good idea. For anything."

"I'm taking notes," I said, deadpan. "No salsa band. Check."

"I'm serious. If I've learned anything, it's that you just need to speak plain and from the heart."

"That's the only way I know how to speak." I gave him a pat on the chest. "Learned from the best."

He looked around one last time, gazing fondly at the various instruments before us. "When you get your affairs in order, let's have a cross-country trip, just you and me."

"Sure thing, Dad," I said. "I say we go to Alaska. Go salmon fishing."

"Okay. I'll start mapping it and you tell me when you're available."

I smiled at my dad, suddenly struck with the realization that somewhere along the way, he'd grown old. His hair was thinner now and more gray than brown, the lines around his eyes and mouth more pronounced, his skin seemingly pulled down by gravity. But despite the physical changes, he was still that same man who'd taken care of my mother during her last years, who'd kept her company at the hospital and read her favorite books aloud when she was too tired to lift her head. Then he'd turned around and come back home to take care of me, being both mother and father to a kid who was still trying to make sense of life.

"It'll be okay, Neal," Dad had said one night as we drove home from the hospital.

"I don't know why you'd think that," I said, folding my arms across my chest. "Mom's not doing so well."

He patted my leg. "I meant, you and me, we can make this work."

"How?"

"Neal, there's life after Mom."

I turned away, furious with the world, especially with the man who was telling me he would be okay without my mom. How could he possibly be okay when the love of his life was about to die? If it were my wife, I'd be beside myself. I might even consider dying with her.

"You know how we're always talking about building a plane?" Dad asked a few miles down the highway.

I slouched down farther into the seat, not saying anything.

Dad glanced over. "Let's do it. Let's buy a plane kit and build one already."

I hadn't believed him at the time, but sure enough, he had come home with a magazine full of propjet planes the next day and we had perused the entire catalog of kits, making a spreadsheet comparing all the planes before finally making our choice.

We'd started building the plane before Mom died, but we didn't finish it until years after her death, when I finally understood what he'd been saying about death and life and love.

"Thank you, Dad," I said, speaking as plainly as possible. "For being a great father. For your sacrifices in order to take care of me and Mom. I know it couldn't have been easy to separate from the Navy at the height of your career."

Dad focused on the windshield through narrowed eyes, blinking fast. "It wasn't much of a choice between my career and my family. What was I gonna do, just leave you on your own to become a hoodlum?"

"I know. But some kids aren't lucky enough to have a dad at all," I said, thinking of Will and the woman who was trying her best to make sure he didn't feel the loss. "And here I am, with an embarrassment of riches."

"Save those pretty words for your woman," Dad said, rubbing his nose. "You'd better get going if you want to get there before dinner."

I gave him a quick hug before he climbed out of the plane. He waved as I taxied out of the hangar, his figure getting smaller and smaller as I headed off onto the runway.

5

I landed in Dallas at around five thirty in the afternoon, and by six thirty I was getting out of the cab in front of Julie's house. I hesitated at the front door, going over the plan in my head.

Step one: Fly back to Dallas.

Step two: Make big huge declaration of love.

Step three: Sweep her off her feet.

Step four: Live happily ever after.

The plan would require some improvisation, but I was sure it would work. It had to.

I had just lifted my fist to rap on the door when it suddenly swung inward, with Julie looking back in the house, saying, "Hurry, Will. He's about to arrive." She squeaked when she turned and ran smack-dab into my chest; I took hold of her shoulders and steadied her, fighting the urge to hold her against me.

"Neal," she cried out, jumping back. "What are you doing here?"

"You weren't expecting me?" I asked before hearing the car door slam behind me. I turned to see Kyle—the ex-husband—coming toward us with a bouquet of red roses in his hand. I spun around to Julie. "What's he doing here?"

She looked abashed for a moment then squared her shoulders, letting me know it was none of my business. "He's visiting," she said and walked around me to greet Kyle with a kiss on the cheek.

My face flamed as I turned on a heel. I was about to leave when I heard a little voice call out my name. I spun around in time to watch Will as he launched himself at me. "Where have you been?" he cried, pressing his face into my stomach.

I wrapped my arms around him, painfully aware of the two pairs of adult eyes trained on us. "It's good to see you, bud," I said, patting his back.

"I've been using that smartpen you gave me."

"Oh, yeah? What are you using it on?"

"Practicing writing and doing drawings. But Mommy has to help me upload them to the computer."

"That's awesome."

"Hi, Will," Kyle said, reaching around me to rub Will's head. "Good to see you, little man."

Kyle crouched down with arms held out; Will looked at his mom before giving in to the awkward hug. "Hi, Kyle," he said, not bothering to hide his lack of enthusiasm.

"Come in, Kyle," Julie said, ushering Will and Kyle inside. When it was just the two of us out there, she closed the front door and faced me. "What are you doing here, Neal?" she asked, looking so put together in her skinny jeans and soft sweater that matched the blue of her eyes, her hair twisted in a pretty knot behind one ear.

"What am I doing here?" I asked, folding my arms across my chest. "What is *he* doing here?"

"He's coming for a visit."

"With roses? Already?"

She sighed, her eyes filled with sadness as she gazed at me. "I'm sorry you had to see this."

"Was I that forgettable that you've moved on already?"

She frowned. "You know you're not."

"Then why . . ." I motioned to the door, letting the sentence hang incomplete in the air between us.

"He's just visiting."

"That man is still in love with you, Julie. Surely you see that." And she knew full well that he wasn't the only one. I took hold of her left hand, staring hard at the silver band on her ring finger.

"That's not what you think it is," she said, gently prying her hand loose. "I'm not getting back together with Kyle, if that's what you're thinking."

"Then why are you wearing a wedding band, Julie?" I asked through clenched teeth.

"To remind me of the past," she said softly, twisting the ring around her finger. "And to remind me to be strong in the future."

I felt suddenly short of breath. "Do you still love me?"

She hesitated, clearly trying to decide how much to confess. Finally she let out a soft breath. "I've only loved—I mean, really loved—two men in my life," she said. "And you are one of them."

I felt buoyed by her confession, until it dawned on me who the other man was. I took a step toward her and again took careful hold of her hand. "I know I destroyed your trust in me. But if you give me another chance, I know I can earn it back."

She glanced at the door, then at me, conflicted. "I want to talk, but not right now." She squeezed my fingers. "Dinner tomorrow night?"

A smile spread across my face and Julie's features finally eased up.

"I'll call you later," she said and put her hand on the doorknob.

Before she could disappear inside, I wrapped my arms around her and brought her back against my chest, burying my face in the back of her neck. I closed my eyes and whispered, "I miss you."

She held still, her heart thumping wildly under my hands. "Me, too," she said before she stepped out of my hold and went inside.

At seven o'clock the next night, I found myself in the exact same spot, but this time I knew I'd be invited inside. At least, I hoped I would be.

"Come in," Julie said when she answered the door, still wearing that damned ring on her finger. She'd said it was a reminder, but from where I stood, it looked like she was using that ring to keep her feelings for me reined in.

I entered and gave her a kiss on the cheek, lingering when I caught a whiff of her scent: vanilla and fresh breeze. I straightened and put my hand in my pocket. "I brought you something from San Diego."

"What is it?"

I held out my hand, offering a small white box. "It's just a necklace," I said quickly, trying to avoid an awkward guessing game about the contents.

She took off the lid and lifted the silver necklace out. I set the box aside and said, "Can I put it on you?"

"Sure." She lifted her hair and turned around as I clasped it shut at the back of her neck. When I was done, she turned to the entryway mirror, running the pads of her fingers over the tiny silver bird flying across her collarbone.

I ran a hand through my short hair. "I saw it at a market in San Diego and thought of you."

She touched it again, giving me a warm look. "It's perfect. Thank you." Our moment was interrupted when something beeped around the corner. "Dinner's ready."

"Is Will around?" I asked as I followed her into the kitchen. Seeing that the table was only half set, I went to the cabinet over the microwave and took out three plates.

"No. He's having a sleepover." She took a casserole dish out of the oven and set it on the stove.

A sleepover—now, *that* was a hopeful little development. I put one plate back and handed Julie the rest.

"I figured we needed some privacy to talk."

I leaned against the counter, watching her. "So let's talk." I looked pointedly down at the steaming food on our plates. "We have time until the food is cool enough to eat."

She took a deep breath, nodding. "You were right about Kyle," she said, diving right in. "I invited him over just to visit, but he thought it meant something more."

I got a sick feeling in the pit of my stomach. "I knew it."

"He wanted to get back together. He said he missed us, that he wanted us back." Julie leaned on the counter beside me, refusing to meet my eyes.

"What did you tell him?"

"Kyle's a good man. He's honest and hardworking and would do anything for us."

"All great qualities," I said.

She looked up at me, amusement playing along her lips. "Yeah, I bet you really think so."

"So what did you tell him, Julie?" I asked, starting to lose patience. I'd hate to think she had invited me over just to tell me that she was getting back with Kyle, but hell, it could happen.

"Our food's ready," she said, evading the subject and taking our plates to the table.

We ate in silence, glancing at each other over our meals. I knew she was trying to torture me—and I probably deserved it—but I was nothing if not patient. I could wait.

"You have room for dessert?" she asked after we were done with the casserole.

"I have room for more talking," I said with a raised eyebrow.

She chuckled softly before gathering the dishes and taking them to the sink.

I followed her, coming up from behind and setting my hands on her hips. "You're playing with me," I said, squeezing her sides until she laughed. I set my chin on top of her head and breathed her in, taking pleasure in holding her again.

"Neal," she said, twisting out of my arms. "I told Kyle the same thing I'm going to say to you."

I froze. "That you'll see us both?" I asked, hoping a joke would change her mind. Or at the very least, ease the pain in my chest.

She shook her head. "I'm sorry. I think Will and I are better off alone. We need to uncomplicate our lives."

I reached out and touched the bird at her neck, thinking it such an appropriate symbol for that moment. "Is this what you really want?" I asked, sliding my hand down so that my palm lay above her heart.

She swallowed hard as her heart rate sped up. "No, it's not what I really want. But it's what my son and I need."

"I thought we had something good going."

"We did." She met my gaze squarely, almost accusatory in nature. "But that was my fault. I shouldn't have let it go that far."

"Let it go that far?" I echoed incredulously. "You asked me to move in with you."

"Look, Neal," she said, taking my hand and leading me to the couch. She sat down, but I remained standing, getting ready to fight for her. Or maybe getting ready to leave. "I think that what happened was probably for the best," she said.

"Oh, how do you figure?"

"I've been thinking about it. It's all I've thought about lately," she said, her eyes fixed on her lap. She picked at an invisible spot on the dark denim. "It wouldn't have worked in the long run between us. You're still in the reserves—that never changed."

"I thought you'd gotten over it."

"I just ignored it, hoping the issue would never rear its head. There's a difference," she said. "It's probably good that we break up now, before we get in too deep."

I crouched in front of her, setting my hands on her knees. "I'm in love with you. I don't know how much deeper I can go."

She covered my hands with her own, meeting my gaze. God, she was so beautiful, with her eyes the color of the midafternoon sky. "That's why this needs to end. Before either one of us drowns."

I stood up and paced in front of her, rubbing my forehead while I tried to figure out what to do next. A good-bye wasn't in the plan. We were supposed to be at step four already.

I could feel her eyes on me, following me while I paced the space between the couch and the TV.

"Sit down, please," Julie finally said. "You're going to wear a hole in the rug."

I turned to her, completely at a loss. What could I say or do that would convince this amazing woman to let me stick around?

"Neal, what if . . ." She bit her lower lip, hesitating. "I mean, would you ever consider getting out of . . ." She looked away, letting the sentence float away.

I twisted around to face her, my brain filling in the rest. The solution was so simple and yet so complicated. A part of me wanted to be with Julie and Will, but I wasn't sure if I was willing to give up that part of my life to do it. "You're saying that if I separate from the military, you'd forgive me and take me back?"

She blinked a few times then began to nod. "When you love someone, you have to make some sacrifices," she said. "Like how I gave up dance to be with Jason."

I ran a palm down my face, not sure how to articulate my connection with the military. It's hard to put into words the need to serve your country, to be more than one person and become part of a greater whole. "Julie, that's . . ."

"I know it's a big thing to ask. I'm being selfish."

I let out a humorless laugh. "I guess that makes two of us."

"This is not an ultimatum. It's just a suggestion," she said quickly, getting to her feet. "Jason's letter was hard to read, but it was good in a way. Cathartic. It gave me the peace of mind that I'd been searching for."

I reached out to touch her cheek but let my hand slide down her arm instead. "I'm sorry I didn't give you that peace sooner."

"But it also solidified my opinion on never dating another man in the military," she said. "I can't go through that again, Neal. I won't."

"The chances of that happening to me are very low."

"You never think you're going to die," she said, a sob escaping from her lips. "Until you do."

"And so you're going to live your life in this little bubble? Death-proofing your life won't work. You'll only end up missing out on all the good that comes before death."

"I'm just being careful." She lifted her eyes to mine. "I want everyone I love to be safe. So if asking you to get out of the military makes me a selfish bitch, so be it. I'll do anything, be anything, to make sure you don't die like Jason."

I took a step toward her and took her face in my hands, touching my lips to hers gently. The kiss was tender, a show of appreciation for the courageous woman who wanted to save everyone. I tilted my head and deepened the kiss, my anguish tainting my every gesture with desperation. We were gasping for air when I pulled away, but I couldn't let her go, knowing that I was on the verge of losing her.

"You can't always protect me," I said, holding the back of her head and pressing our heads together.

"I can't help it. I'm a mom," she said with a tiny smile.

I swallowed hard, preparing to pull the pin from the grenade. "Julie," I said, taking a deep breath. "I love you—so much—but I can't separate from the military."

"Why not?" she whispered.

"Because I *want* to serve my country."

She closed her eyes, lines forming between her eyebrows. With pain etching her lovely features, she began to nod in acceptance. God, this wasn't how I wanted this to go.

My phone rang right then, sending goose bumps crawling up my spine. I wouldn't have checked were it not for the strange feeling that suddenly had come over me. One glance at the caller ID confirmed everything I feared. "Hang on, I have to take this call," I told her and went outside the front door.

Julie met me at the door the moment I stepped back inside. "What is it? What happened?"

I stared at her, unable to form words.

Her face crumpled with worry. "What is it, Neal?" she asked, grabbing a handful of my shirt. "You're scaring me."

I looked down at the phone in my hand, still willing that phone call to be a mistake. But it was no mistake. A recall roster was an organized system that had been in place for decades, with one person calling the next one on the list, and that person calling the next, until everyone had been notified.

"That was my buddy Kevin Staley," I said, grasping her wrist to keep her from running. "They're deploying our unit."

6

Of course I was getting deployed. And of course I received the news the same moment I was trying to convince Julie that being in the military wouldn't affect our relationship. Fate is a fucking asshole that way.

Even though she didn't move, I felt Julie pulling away the moment I delivered the news. She kept her eyes trained on my chest, her fingers still clutching at the cotton fabric of my shirt.

"My unit wasn't in the bucket to deploy, but I guess . . ." I stopped, deciding on how much to reveal. How could I even begin to tell her that we were deploying to replace a unit that had had major life loss from a successful mortar attack? Right on base, no less? "They need us to replace another unit at Bagram ASAP."

She finally found her voice. "Why? Why so soon?"

"There was—" I cleared my throat. "There was a mortar attack that caught a row of B-huts on fire."

"People died?"

I took a deep breath and nodded.

"So these people died while in the safety of the base?"

This was so painful, I could actually feel it making my stomach turn. "Yes."

She watched me quietly. “But . . . ?”

“There is no but. There are mortar attacks on base almost on a weekly basis. Sometimes they hit something, but most of the time they’re duds. B-huts are flimsy and dry and catch fire easily. The attack happened in the middle of the night. You can be in a nuclear bunker but if it’s your time to die, then there’s nothing you can do to stop it.”

“And what if it’s your time to die this time?”

I wrapped my arms around her and gathered her close even as she resisted me. “Then I will die with regret, knowing that I couldn’t give you and Will the life you deserve.”

She pressed her forehead into my chest and took in deep breaths. A moment later, I felt her tears dampen my shirt. Eventually she pressed her cheek against my chest and began to sob. “How long?”

“A year.”

I held her to me, my fingers tangled in her hair, my chest aching. “I’m sorry, I’m sorry,” I said, wishing I never had to hurt her, wishing I were bulletproof, wishing that love alone could fix everything.

“This can’t be happening again,” she said softly. “It’s not fucking fair.”

“Not, it’s not. That’s why I can’t ask you to wait for me.”

She looked up then, her cheeks damp with tears. She opened her mouth to say something but thought better of it and nodded instead.

I bent down and crushed my lips against hers, kissing her like it was the last time. She eased out of the kiss and swiped a finger at the corners of her eyes.

Needing to be closer, I grabbed her and grasped her against my chest.

“Neal,” she whispered.

“Mmm?” I sifted my fingers through her hair, trying to savor every last second we had left together.

"Please don't send me letters or e-mails," she said. "It's not that I don't care or don't want to hear from you. It's just . . . I can't . . ."

"I understand," I said, rubbing her back. "But promise me something."

"What?" she asked, looking up.

"Don't torture yourself looking for news about me."

I left a few days later to do a week of combat skills course to prepare me for combat communications. When that was over, our unit went through two weeks of training and deployment preparation, and then we were ready to go.

On Christmas Day, I flew back to Dallas to make my final good-bye. Julie hadn't told me to stay away, and there was no way I was going to go twelve months without seeing her face again. Besides that, I couldn't leave the country without first saying good-bye to Will.

"Neal!" he cried as soon as I stepped in the door. "Merry Christmas!"

I gave him a big hug and handed over the gift-wrapped box I'd brought with me. "I'm surprised you guys didn't go to Monterey for the holidays," I said to Julie.

"We figured you might come by," she said with a sad smile.

"I would have flown there for you," I said. "Or anywhere, really."

"When do you leave?"

"I have to go back to Homestead tomorrow," I said. "Then we fly out on the twenty-seventh."

"Where are you going?" Will asked.

Julie looked at him. "He's deploying, remember?"

My eyes flew to her. "I didn't know you'd told him," I said to her a few minutes later when Will ran upstairs to get something.

She gave me a meaningful look. "I didn't want to lie to him. He asked me why you'd just disappeared again."

"How did he take it?" I asked. "Does he know it's the same place as . . ."

She nodded. "I don't think he's worried about it. He said you were going to shoot the bad guys." She frowned.

"Julie," I said, taking her hand, "you can't shield him from everything."

"He's not my worry right now," she said, looking at me pointedly.

Will came back wearing a white soccer uniform and bright new cleats, holding a new soccer ball in his hands. "Look what Mom got me for Christmas!" He turned around and showed me the KEATON emblazoned across his back. "Sweet, huh?"

"That is very sweet," I said with a smile, reaching for the ball and spinning it on my hands. "Have you been practicing the drills we talked about?"

"Yeah. Mom's been helping me."

I turned to Julie, who just shrugged. "We practice a few minutes before getting ready for bed. Mostly we do it on the weekends," she said. "He has really improved."

"Will you show me?" I asked Will. "I'd love to see it."

We put on hats and jackets and went out to the backyard to play soccer on the winter-dried grass. Julie stood off to the side at first while Will and I went through the drills, wearing a pleased smile on her face when I suggested a few tiny changes and Will completed them without problem.

"Look what I've been working on," he said and bounced the ball on his foot once, twice. He grinned up at me. "Piece of cake."

I tucked him under my arm and spun him around. "Fantastic job!"

"Come on, Mom, let's play soccer!" Will cried once I set him down, running to Julie and tugging on her hand. With a laugh, she joined us, moving light on her toes as she passed the ball with her feet. I purposefully lost track of time as we played, laughing and playing with this little family I'd come to wish was my own, pretending that time stood still out here.

When our cheeks were red and Will began to sniffle, we went back inside and made hot cocoa. With our mugs, we all sat together on the couch, Will wedged between Julie and me, and watched *A Christmas Story*.

At about the time Ralphie was getting kicked down the slide by Santa Claus, Will yawned and laid his head on my lap. I rubbed his head as he drifted off and when I looked over, I saw that Julie was watching me with an unreadable expression. I flashed her a hopeful smile that she didn't return.

"You all right?" I whispered.

When she pursed her lips and shook her head, I reached across the back of the couch and kneaded the side of her neck. She kept her eyes on me the entire time, the muscles on her face immobile save for a slight tremble on her lower lip. Then a tear slid down her cheek and it was all I could do not to climb over her son and take her in my arms. Instead I wiped the tear with my thumb. She turned her face into my hand and kissed my skin, closing her eyes as she nuzzled into my palm.

I couldn't take it anymore, the space between us was far too much. I pulled her toward me and kissed her, taking no heed of the sleeping child between us, only showing this amazing woman that she was loved.

We didn't say much more the rest of the evening, and when I stood up to make my way back to my hotel room after that perfect Christmas Day, she rose with me and walked me to the door.

"I guess this is good-bye," she said with some finality. The day together had been our last hurrah; there would be nothing else for us after this.

"I wish things could be different," she said, pulling away.

"Me, too." I kissed her forehead one last time. "'Bye, Julie. I wish you the best in life."

I gave one last nod before turning away, noticing the bright constellation of stars in the sky. I'd unlocked the car and had my hand on the door when Julie suddenly called my name.

I spun around. "Yes?"

She remained standing by the door, fists held by her sides. "Please be careful," she called out into the cold night air, the short distance between us seeming like thousands of miles. Then she took a step forward, and another, until she was running toward me, colliding into me. "Here," she said, her cheeks wet with tears. She pressed something into my hand, something metallic and warm.

I looked down at the ring, my heart thundering.

"Keep it safe," she said through her tears. "Keep yourself safe."

I slipped the ring onto my pinkie and kissed her one last time, not wanting to let go. "I will."

PART SIX

SURRENDER

1

JULIE

Neal was gone. I'd said my good-byes that Christmas night. He'd made his choice and I'd made mine, and even though the two didn't intersect, I was at peace with that.

Still, it didn't make the separation easier. Each day I still awoke with a gaping hollowness, as if a piece of me were thousands of miles away. Each night I went to bed with a quiet prayer in my heart, hoping that if I never said my worst fear out loud, it might never come to pass.

The only time my mind was ever truly at peace was when I danced. For those precious few moments, I was lost to the music. I wasn't Julie, the woman with all the worries. I was just a feather on the breeze, flitting and soaring wherever the wind saw fit to take me. Dance was my respite, my sanctuary, and along with my son, I was able to forget my worry over Neal for a time.

One sunny Saturday afternoon, while I sat on the bleachers watching Will and his team playing soccer, my eyes wandered down to a young Asian couple in front of me. I looked down at the empty spot beside me, thinking it wasn't that long ago that I had someone to fill it.

I allowed myself the rare luxury of thinking about Neal, because out here, with the sun on my face and the sounds of children's voices, it was hard to imagine anything going wrong in the world. Neal would be fine, he'd be working on computers, setting up e-mails and other monotonous things like that, and would never come to harm.

After the game, I took Will to the frozen yogurt place near our house. We sat by the windows that faced the dance studio across the parking lot. I watched the girls and boys entering the place, wondering how their lives would turn out. Would they go on to dance professionally or was this a temporary thing, a way for them to try various things in order to find their one passion in life?

On the way back to the car, I stopped on the sidewalk and said to Will, "Hey, why don't we check out the dance studio?"

"Sure!"

We walked over and went inside, our ears greeted by hip-hop music. Three girls of about six or seven were dancing in the middle of the dance floor, performing a hip-hop choreography that involved some pop locking.

Will and I stood off to the side of the room, careful to keep from becoming a distraction, until the performance was over.

A woman with a long, flowing red skirt that echoed the hue of her fiery red hair walked over. "Hi. Can I help you?" She glanced down at Will. "Are you looking to start dancing?"

"No," I said before Will could get ideas. "We were just checking it out."

"Well, welcome!" She held out her hand. "My name is Carol and I own this studio."

"I'm Julie," I said, shaking her hand. "And this is my son, Will."

"Feel free to stick around and watch. We're rehearsing for the spring showcase."

"What do you think? Do you want to stay and watch?" I asked

Will, whose attention was on another girl of about six who was across the room. "I guess that means yes." I tugged him sideways and sat him down on a nearby wood bench.

We stayed for the rest of the hour, my attention on the dancing while Will remained rapt by that one pretty girl with the short hair.

"I want to take dance lessons," he said some time later, tugging on the end of my cardigan.

I bit back a smile. "How about after soccer season is over? Deal?"

"Deal," he said with a bright smile, glancing across the room not at all surreptitiously. I figured he had at least a decade before he needed to really fine-tune his skills of subtlety.

I walked over to Carol after the rehearsal was over. "Do you have any adult classes?"

She shook her head, her chandelier earrings clinking. "I wish I did, but I'm shorthanded as it is. My modern dance instructor left before Thanksgiving and I haven't been able to fill her spot."

An involuntary shiver went up my spine as I was reminded of Jason's dream. "Do you need to have a teaching license or anything to be an instructor?"

She was taken aback by my question. "No. Why, are you interested?"

I looked around the room, suddenly filled with hope. "I might be."

We spoke for a few minutes about my qualifications, then she asked if she could see me dance. "Just a quick contemporary."

There was no way I'd refuse to dance when the opportunity presented itself. "Sure. Why not." I kicked off my ballet flats and performed a quick set of stretches. Then I stood in the middle of the room and performed a choreography that I'd been working on the past few weeks. It was a longer piece—probably longer than Carol was ready for—but once I started, I couldn't stop. It was as if liquid melancholy were sliding through my veins, controlling my every movement.

When I was done, Carol's eyes were wide, her mouth slightly agape. "Um," she said, shaking her head.

"What's wrong?" The performance had felt good—had I become so lost in the dance that I'd forgotten about technique and control?

"Honey, I think you're way overqualified. You belong on a stage, not in my little studio," Carol said.

I felt the blush rise up my face. "Thank you."

"If you don't mind my asking, why aren't you in a big city, dancing professionally?"

"Life," I said, flashing Will a smile. "And I don't regret one second of it."

And it was true. Though my life had been anything but easy, I would not have done anything differently. Every decision I'd ever made had led me to this point in time, with this amazing little man in my life.

"Right now I'd really like to try my hand at teaching," I said.

Carol smiled. "Well, I would feel guilty taking advantage of your experience, but if you really would like to try, I won't turn you down."

I started teaching two days later, with an hour-long class on contemporary dance for older kids on Monday and one on ballet for the younger set on Wednesday. It made our already-tight schedule even tighter on those days, but Will and I quickly acclimated to the change. He sat in the corner of the studio and did his homework while I taught the class, and afterward we went home and ate what I'd prepared earlier in the slow cooker.

The first class was a learning experience, but I quickly found what worked and what didn't when it came to children. It wasn't all that difficult, as I had plenty of experience—with both dance and children—to draw from. By the end of that first week, I'd earned a nickname from the older kids.

"Why Miss Lovely?" I asked when it was first said.

"You know, because you're lovely?" one girl said.

I chuckled, feeling warmth on my face. "That's sweet but you can just call me Julie or Miss Keaton."

In the last week of January, Will and I flew out to Denver to attend Henry's police academy graduation. It was a nice change of pace, even if the cold mountain air felt unwelcoming the moment we stepped off the plane.

After the graduation ceremony, we went back to Henry and Elsie's house and cooked up large T-bone steaks and vegetable kabobs, their kitchen a whirlwind of activity.

"This is really good," I told the young couple as I cut up a few bites of the steak for Will, who was having trouble with his knife.

"Right?" Elsie said, almost done with her steak. "I don't normally like eating steak, but this is really good."

"Thank you for making my favorite," Henry said to her, a look of adoration in his eyes. "And thank you for bringing everyone here."

"You're welcome," she said. "I didn't want this day to go by without having family around."

"And how are things with you, Julie?" John asked, sending everyone's attention my way.

"Busy but good. I'm teaching dance at a small studio ten minutes from our house and I'm really enjoying it. It keeps us busy, but Will and I manage."

"That's wonderful," Elodie said. "I honestly don't know how you do it, raising a child on your own."

I shrugged. "I've had years of practice."

"And what about that man you were dating?" she asked. "What was his name? Neal?"

"Harding?" Henry asked. "Yeah, he's a good guy. Met him at Randolph Air Force Base during training."

I glanced at Elsie to see if she'd told her parents about the situation with the letter but she shook her head. "He and I are no longer together," I finally said.

"They broke up," Will piped in. "Neal doesn't pick me up from school anymore."

"Oh, that's a shame," Elodie said, frowning. "You seemed very happy the last time I talked to you on the phone."

"I was, but that was before the letter."

"What letter?"

I glanced at Will and decided he finally needed to hear the truth. "All this time, Neal had Jason's good-bye letter."

Elodie's eyes were bright when she said, "Our Jason?"

I nodded. "Yes. Neal was the guy who cleaned out Jason's room and packed up his belongings. He found the letter but, for some reason, decided to keep it."

Everyone was quiet for a time, chewing on what I'd just said.

"Is that why you and Neal broke up?" Will asked. "Because he didn't give you my dad's letter?"

"Yes. Because he had kept it a secret," I told him gently. "He should have told me right away."

"Did you bring it with you?" Elsie asked.

I nodded. "I figured you'd want to see it."

"May I read it?" Elodie asked. "If you don't mind, that is."

"Of course I don't mind," I said, glad I'd brought the letter with me. "Jason was your son."

After dinner, we retired to the living room and, while Henry told Will a story, I went to the guest room to find the envelope that was tucked safely inside my purse.

"Can I read it, too?" Will asked as he watched Elsie handing the letter over to her mother. John took a seat on the couch beside Elodie, holding her close with one arm while they quietly pored over the last words of their son.

Elodie dabbed at her eyes and John blinked rapidly as they handed the letter back.

"Mom, can I?" Will asked, his little blond eyebrows furrowed, his palm held open.

I stared at Will's hopeful little face and wondered just how much he could take. I'd shielded him from pain, had tried to keep him from learning more about his dad's career in hopes he wouldn't follow in Jason's footsteps. But maybe it was time I stopped sheltering him. More than anything, he needed to know that his dad loved him even before he was born.

So I nodded and handed the letter over. "But there are some bad words."

Will grinned up at me. "Don't worry. I won't say them."

All eyes were on this tiny replica of Jason as he read over his father's words in silence. Every now and then he'd turn to Henry and ask him about a particular word, and Henry would patiently read it to him and try his best to explain.

When he was done, Will set the letter on his lap, deep in thought. "My dad never saw me when I was a baby?" he asked in a little voice.

"You already knew that," I told him. "Remember, he died before you were born?"

Will blinked fast as his little chin trembled. "So he never saw me?"

"No. I'm sorry."

"Does he even know my name?"

I shook my head, my heart breaking into a million pieces. "No, he didn't."

"But . . . how will he recognize me in heaven?"

"Oh, Will." I scooted over on the couch and hugged him to me, muffling the beginnings of his sobs in my chest. We'd been in this same situation so many times before, it was almost second nature to us; Will grieving, never knowing his father, and I bowing over him, hoping to protect him from the pain.

I started when I felt Elsie's arm wrap around my shoulder, and a second later, Elodie came over to offer her comfort. John and Henry, too, seemed closer, watching us with tearful eyes, their hands on our shoulders.

"Don't worry," Elsie said with absolute conviction. "He'll recognize you. There's no way he won't."

It was in that moment, as I looked around at these people who would do anything for my son, I realized I wasn't alone in raising Will anymore. I had a family now.

And I breathed a little sigh of relief.

"I don't get it. If you love him and you're obviously good together, why won't you wait for him?" Elsie asked me the next day on the way to the Cherry Creek Mall for sushi.

"I can't stand to lose someone else," I said. "It's self-preservation."

"I guess I'm the opposite. I tend to just run out there without protection and hope for the best."

I smiled at her. "That's because you're braver than I am."

She sighed through her nose. "You know, love like that doesn't come along every day."

"That's what I'm counting on," I said, causing her to glance at me in surprise. "Can you imagine if our every relationship were all-consuming and passionate? We'd have no control of our emotions and our lives would descend into chaos."

She smiled. "Yes, but it would be beautiful on the way down."

"No, thanks."

"So if you wanted to be in a lukewarm relationship, why not just get back together with Kyle? At least you know he's a good man and will take care of you."

I looked out the window, chewing on her words. What Kyle offered was appealing: a simple, stable relationship. He was offering me security and a tender kind of love. But all that hadn't been enough the first time; would it be enough now?

"Hello?" Elsie asked, looking over. "Earth to Julie."

"Neal has ruined me for all men," I mumbled as she turned into the mall parking lot. "I was perfectly happy without him in my life. Before him, I didn't know how deep a love could go, but I also didn't know how badly a heart can hurt after being betrayed."

Elsie set the car in park and looked over at me. "It's just the nature of love. It will set your heart racing right before it rips it right out of your chest."

"I no longer want any part of that."

Elsie let out a soft chuckle. "That's the thing, though. You have absolutely no choice in the matter."

2

The months sped by. Between work, school, soccer, and dance, Will and I were so busy that we barely had time to kick back and relax. But it was a good kind of busy, the kind that gave me very little chance to think about my life, very little chance to miss those I'd lost.

Neal and I kept our ends of the bargain—he didn't contact me and I stayed well away from news on his unit. Ignoring the coverage on our troops overseas was easy; the difficult part was not knowing what he was doing, if he was okay. I'd asked him not to contact me in hopes that I could pretend he didn't exist, that if I didn't know anything about his life there, I would never have to spend a single second worrying about his safety.

I wished I could say it was working, but the truth was that I could no sooner pretend he didn't exist than I could cut off my own arm. He was there in my thoughts almost every second of the day, his smile always present when I closed my eyes. Each time the phone or the doorbell rang, I expected it to be news of his death. I didn't know how military spouses did this year after year. It seemed to me like you'd just go crazy with worry after a while.

I was better off without him. My brain knew it; someday my heart would, too.

"Hey, wake up!"

I yanked the blanket up over my head with a groan. My chances of sleeping in were apparently slim to none.

"Mom!" Will cried. He tried tugging on the covers, but I held firm. "Wake up! It's your birthday!"

Finally, I groaned and let go, sneezing when the sunlight hit me directly in the face. I sat up, brushing hair away from my face. "It's so early, Will."

"I made you breakfast," he said, proudly setting a tray on my lap.

"Well, thank you," I said, giving him a kiss on the cheek. I looked over the contents of the tray: toast with Nutella, two waffles, a half glass of orange juice, and a tiny vase with several stalks of yellow dandelions in it. "You did this all by yourself?"

"Yup!" he said, beaming. "I toasted the bread and the waffles and put Nutella on the toast all by myself. I spilled some orange juice on the floor but I wiped it up with the sponge."

I nibbled on the toast and then held it out for him. "Thank you, sweetheart. This is the best birthday breakfast ever in the history of the world."

He took a big bite, getting the spread on his cheeks. "I wanted to make you cake, but I didn't know how."

"Well, maybe we can cook some later, then," I said, wiping at his cheeks with my thumbs. He settled in beside me and we turned on the TV, flipping to a cartoon channel.

"I don't want to watch cartoons," he said, reaching for the remote control. "I want to watch something you like."

"Why? I thought you liked *Transformers*."

"Because it's your birthday," he said. "Duh."

I chuckled, tickling his side. "When did you get so ornery?"

"The day I was born," he said through his giggles.

We spent another hour in bed watching reruns of my favorite dance competition show before we went downstairs still in our pajamas and attempted to bake a cake from scratch, with mixed results. The cake itself turned out fine but Will didn't wait long enough before starting to ice the cake and it melted almost immediately.

"Oops," Will said, trying to fix it and making it worse.

I grabbed a tub of vanilla ice cream from the freezer and put it on the counter. "Don't worry. It'll still taste good," I said, putting a scoop of ice cream into two bowls with a generous slice of cake each. "Lunch is served," I said with a flourish of the hand.

Will's mouth dropped open. "We can't eat this for lunch!"

I laughed. "I'm the mom *and* the birthday girl and I say this makes the perfect lunch!" I lifted him off the stool and spun him around.

We froze when the doorbell rang.

"Who could that be?" I asked, setting him down, my heart inexplicably pounding in my chest.

Will took off for the front door before I could recover. "Mom!" he called out. "Mom! Quick!"

I don't know how I made it to the front door in my state of apprehension. But when I reached my son, I found him holding a rectangular box and nothing else.

"The mailman just left this!" Will said, handing me the box.

I looked through the open doorway before closing the door.

"It's from Neal," Will said, setting the box on the floor and starting to rip into the clear tape.

"Hold on, that's my gift." I nudged him out of the way and sat cross-legged beside the box, reading over the sender's APO address to be sure. I ripped open the tape and found another, fancier box inside. The box contained white tissue paper wrapped around a mint-colored dress and a card with a small hand-drawn bird on it.

Julie,

At 4:30 Stacy is coming over to pick up Will for the night, giving you a chance to get ready and make your 5:30 reservation at the Joule Hotel, where something special awaits.

I hope you like it. Happy birthday.

Neal

"What does it say?" Will asked with wide eyes.

I looked over calmly despite the rapid thrumming in my chest. "A surprise."

At four thirty, Will sat at the foot of the stairs with his backpack and sleeping bag by his feet as he stared holes in the door. He jumped up when the doorbell rang.

"Happy birthday!" Stacy said as soon as I opened the door. She threw her arms around me and gave me a tight squeeze. "Are you ready for your birthday surprise?"

I bit my lower lip. I'd tried to keep the hopeful little bubble from getting too inflated all afternoon, but I didn't know how successful I'd been, since I'd pretty much worried my lower lip raw. "What is it, Stacy? I *need* to know what's waiting for me."

Stacy gave me a mysterious look. "I can't tell you. I promised Neal that I wouldn't tell."

"And how are you in contact with him anyway?" I asked, smacking her playfully on the arm. "You never told me that."

She chuckled. "Well, he's been e-mailing me, asking about you. You made him promise not to contact you, so he checks in with me to see how you're doing."

"Why didn't you tell me?"

"Because he asked me not to." She picked up the backpack and slung it over her shoulder. "So anyway, I need to leave you to get all gussied up. Wait—did the dress fit?"

"Yes," I said, and narrowed my eyes. "Was that your doing, too?"

"No, he ordered it. I just told him what size to get."

I hugged her again. "Thank you. You're so amazing. You've been there for me every time I needed you."

"Anything for you, Jules. And don't even act like you don't return the favor. For a single mom, you do your share of babysitting, too."

"Not nearly enough."

She smiled and waved me away. "Just go do your girly things. Epilate, do your hair, put on makeup. Look fab for tonight."

Before she left, I gave her a warm embrace, buoyed by the realization that I was truly blessed. The past thirty years had been rocky, but at the end of the day, I was still privileged enough to have an abundance of love and friendship in my life. And really, that was all I could ask for.

At 5:20 I drove up to the Joule Hotel, deciding that turning thirty was the perfect reason to use the valet service. When I walked inside the hotel lobby, I was immediately thrown back by the casual opulence of the place.

"Now what?" I looked around and, not knowing what else to do, walked up to the reception desk, which sat behind a partial wall of huge metal cogs and gears.

"Hi. I'm not sure where to go. I was told to meet someone here," I said to the young man there.

"What's your name?"

"Julie Keaton."

The clerk smiled, all white teeth and dimples. "Ah, Miss Keaton. You are expected at the top floor, poolside."

I thanked him for not calling me "ma'am" and made my way to the elevators, gripping the strap of my purse and smoothing down the front of my dress. Once the doors opened at the top floor, I found the signs toward the pool and followed them.

"Surprise!"

I walked out onto the open-air pool deck, shocked to find dozens of people crowding around me. Behind them was the pool, glowing blue from underwater lights, and tables flanking its edges set up with an array of food.

Will was first to greet me, throwing his arms around my waist. "Happy birthday, Mom!"

"Did you know about this?" I asked, pinching his nose.

"No. Miss Stacy told me about it later," he said, taking my hand and leading me into the grinning crowd.

I went around, hugging and thanking guests for the wonderful surprise; all were friends and acquaintances I'd made in Dallas. Finally I arrived at Stacy, who laughed before giving me a big hug. "Did you have any idea?" she asked.

"No. This was sneaky," I said, giving her shoulders a shake. "You and Neal arranged this?" I asked, only now noticing the bar set up in one corner, complete with a bartender. Behind him, the city lights of Dallas lit up the skyline. "You went all out."

"Neal paid for everything. All I did was make sure it all went according to plan."

"Nobody has ever thrown me a surprise party before," I said, taking in the gorgeous view of the city. "Thank you."

"You're welcome." Stacy's eyes twinkled as she held me at arm's length, looking over the dress. It was sleeveless and had a gauzy skirt that ended right above my knee and flowed whenever I moved. "That dress looks fabulous. Come on, let's go ring in your thirties."

Later on in the night, Stacy looped her arm in mine and whispered, "Neal has something else for you."

"Okay." With breath held, I followed her toward the interior door.

"Hold on." She ran inside and came back holding something behind her back.

I looked around her, expecting and hoping, when she presented me with a black shoe box.

"Did you buy me shoes?"

She grinned. "I'll leave you to it."

Once alone, I opened the box and found a neat pile of folded papers tied together with a piece of twine. "Oh."

Later, as the party was starting to wind down, I took off my shoes and sat down by the pool, dangling my feet in the water. I stared down at the box in my lap, at odds with myself. My brain was warning me not to tug on that piece of twine, because no doubt, I, too, would come undone. But here in my lap was proof that Neal was alive, that he was okay and thinking of me.

I could give in and read every single letter, or I could put that lid back on and keep it all boxed away, like I'd done for the past few months.

"There you are," Stacy said, sitting down next to me. "You doing okay?"

"Yeah. I'm good."

She nudged my shoulder. "Come on, Jules. You're not exactly a vault of mystery. I can tell you're not enjoying your own birthday party."

I gave her a sad smile, finally dropping the facade.

"So what's wrong?" she asked. Then she whispered, "Is it because you turned thirty?"

I let out a surprised chuckle. "No, it's not that."

"Because I have to tell you, it's not that bad. I don't feel a day over twenty-five."

I set the box aside and looked around at the rest of the party guests. "I guess I was just hoping Neal was here."

Stacy gasped. "You didn't think he was going to show up and surprise you, did you?"

"Yeah. I kind of did."

"That was never in the plan," she said, patting my shoulder. "I'm sorry if I got your hopes up."

"It's not your fault. Really. I don't know why I'd expect him to be here when he's deployed. It's not like they can just come and go whenever it suits them."

She kicked her feet in the water for a few seconds, then said, "You know what, though, for someone who's no longer your boyfriend, Neal sure went to a lot of trouble to make sure you had a good birthday."

"I know. He's too sweet for his own good. That's what I love about him." I took a deep breath. "I think I've made a mistake, Stacy."

"About?"

"I thought breaking up with him would make it easier, and maybe it has in some ways. But it's harder in so many other ways. It drives me crazy that he's free to date anyone he wants to and I can't do anything about it. Hell, I won't even know about it. I don't even know how he's doing, if he's happy. I feel like he's slipping away with every month that passes, and by the time he comes back, I'm afraid he'll be a complete stranger."

Stacy said nothing. She sat beside me and listened, waiting for me to talk through my thoughts.

"And I thought that's what I wanted, until tonight. Until I looked at the group of people around me and realized that his face was the one I wanted to see most."

"Well, you know what they say: admitting the problem is the first step to finding a solution."

"So what's the solution?"

Stacy gave me a look of disbelief. "Julie, you're my friend so I say this with love: stop acting dumb. You already know what you need to do, you're just not brave enough to do it."

I let out a sad chuckle. "You're right. I need to just get over it. It's not like I'm the one whose ass is on the line. I won't be there in the war zone fighting or defending or whatever. All I'll be doing is waiting at home, hoping he's safe," I said. "But in so many ways, to be the one left at home is so much worse."

Stacy touched my hand. "But is he worth waiting for?"

In the quiet of my room later that night, I untied Neal's letters and set them out on my lap. I unfolded every one and arranged them in chronological order by the date at the top of each; by the time I was done, a sea of words lay on the bed before me.

Then I took a deep breath and dove in.

The first letter mainly talked about work, explaining his job and what he did during his many hours of downtime, and sounded detached, as if he were writing to a stranger.

This morning I woke up and I swear, I could smell you, he wrote in the second letter. *I knew it was my memory playing tricks on me, but I breathed you in anyway and pretended I was nuzzling into the back of your neck, holding you against my chest.*

I wrote that first letter after my first day here and then I put it away, never intending to write another. I'd made you a promise and I intended to keep it. But after this morning, after remembering what it was like to wake up with you, I knew I had to do something. Even if I never send these to you, I'm going to keep writing because it gives me some semblance of hope. It tricks my brain into thinking that you're back there, waiting for me.

So wait for me, Julie. I can't wait to come home to you.

With tears prickling at the corners of my eyes, I set the letter aside and got out of bed to turn on my computer, trying to organize my thoughts while it booted up. I wasn't sure how I would put into words what I was feeling, what I'd been feeling since he left, but I knew how I'd close the e-mail:

I'm waiting for you.

I was about to log into my e-mail when a news story caught my eye on the main page.

Convoy attacked on the way to base in Afghanistan.

I closed the window without thinking, my heart skipping a beat. My body broke out into cold chills as I sat staring at the desktop wallpaper, unable to shake the dread that was currently gnawing at my insides.

"It's not about Neal. Neal works on base. He would never be in a convoy," I told myself, feeling slightly better after hearing the words out loud.

It took a few minutes but after I regained my composure, I went back to the website to read the article, to confirm that Neal's unit was not involved.

A U.S. military convoy leaving Bagram Airfield came under enemy fire yesterday on the way to an undisclosed location. An IED took out one Humvee before members of both the Air Force and the Marines were ambushed by the militia with rocket grenades and AK-47s. There were three fatalities and seven injured. Names cannot be released at press time, though we can confirm that members of the 482nd Fighter Wing unit, based out of Homestead, Florida, were among those killed in the attack.

3

I didn't know anything about Neal's reserve unit, but I did know where he flew off to for one weekend every month: Homestead, Florida.

I stood up, pacing the room, fighting back the overwhelming feeling of déjà vu that was rising up in my throat with the nausea. I sat back down and performed searches on the Internet, checking website after website for more information, but no names were reported, no clues as to who had been in that convoy. I didn't even have any idea who to call on base for information, or if that was even allowed.

Then I remembered the business card Neal had given me a while back, from his dad's part-time flying school in San Diego. I ran downstairs, slipping on a few steps in my haste, and rummaged through my purse until I found the card at the very bottom.

I didn't know how I managed to dial through my blurry eyes, but it took three rings before someone picked up. "Hello?" said a deep, rumbly voice.

"Hi. I'm sorry to be calling so late. Is this Patrick Harding?"

"Yes." He paused then said, "Is this Julie?"

I dropped to my knees right there on the cold kitchen floor, the sobs bubbling up in my chest. Patrick had been expecting my call. "Is he . . . Is Neal . . ." I couldn't bring myself to finish the question.

"What have you heard?"

"I only know what they're reporting on the news. I don't know anything about Neal, if that's even his unit, if he's okay . . ." I said, finding myself talking too fast.

He sighed. "That's about all I know, too. I've been calling people all day, but they're not releasing any information right now."

"But was that his unit?"

"Yes."

I choked back a sob. "Okay."

"Julie, if it's any comfort to you, two servicemen in uniform haven't knocked on my door yet to tell me my son's dead." His voice cracked on the last word, revealing his concern and amplifying mine.

I sucked in deep breaths, trying to remember that nothing had been confirmed. As far as we knew, we were freaking out over nothing.

"I know this can't be easy for you," he said. "Try to take it easy. There's no use worrying until we know more."

"You're right," I said, nodding vigorously. "You're right."

"I'm glad you called, Julie. For a while there I thought my son had fallen for someone who didn't love him back," he said.

I breathed hard, feeling as if a knife were embedded in my chest. "I just hope it's not too late."

Despite knowing better, I spent the rest of the night checking for more news on the attack. It was as if I'd been thrust back several years in time, the circumstances seemed so heartbreakingly similar I'd already begun preparing myself for the worst.

"Mom, what's wrong?" Will asked the next morning as we were starting our rushed morning routine.

"Will, just eat your breakfast," I snapped. "We're going to be late again."

"Okay, okay," he said in a huff, shoveling a spoonful of cereal into his mouth. "I just wanted to know why you were so sad."

I set my hands on the sink and hung my head, feeling the air leave my lungs. "I'm sorry." I walked over and sank down at the table across from him. "I've just been worried about . . ." I hesitated, not sure if telling Will about Neal was the right thing. "Just worried about Neal, I guess."

His little eyebrows drew together. "Why? What happened?"

I shook my head. "I don't know. I'm not sure." I didn't tell him about the bad feeling in the pit of my stomach that had lain there, heavy and poisonous, since the night before. I didn't want to breathe my fears out loud, didn't want to give them any more control over me.

Will stood up and walked over to the freezer, rummaging inside for a few seconds. When he came back, he had a fudge Popsicle in his hand. "Here, Mom. I think you need one of these."

I let out a strangled laugh and accepted the Popsicle, taking a large bite off the top. "Thanks," I said, the cold liquid soothing my raw throat.

My head swung around when my cell phone buzzed on the counter. I stared at it for a few moments before Will said, "I'll get it," and handed me the phone.

Without looking at the screen, I answered the call. "Hello?"

"He's alive."

I hung my head and let it out, tears of relief leaking down my face. I set the Popsicle down on a plate and ushered Will in, squeezing him to my side.

"He's hurt pretty bad but he's alive," Patrick said.

"Where is he?"

"He's currently at Landstuhl Medical Center in Germany

undergoing surgery. He sustained shrapnel wounds, from a grenade blast, at the back of his neck and on his leg," he said. "He's out of the woods, but they're not sure they were able to save his spine."

I covered my mouth. "You mean he could be paralyzed?"

"I was told it was a possibility," he said.

"But he's alive." I needed to say it again to make sure it was real.

"Yes."

I sucked in deep breaths, refusing to think about the possibility of Neal losing use of his legs or worse. "Thank you for calling to let me know, Patrick. I really appreciate it."

"You're welcome. I know you're worried about him, too."

After I hung up, I took my first deep breath. "Neal is hurt," I told Will.

"What happened?" he asked, his eyes round.

I told him a sanitized version of the situation, emphasizing that Neal was okay but leaving out the part where his spine might be compromised.

"He's not going to die, is he?" he asked.

I pulled him in for a hug, not knowing what else to do. "No, he's in the hospital but he's stable."

"I don't want him to die like Dad," Will said, his voice muffled by my scrub top.

"I don't want that, either." I pulled away, wishing I could bear all the pain so that he would never have to wear that look of misery ever again. "Hey, let's just focus on what's happening right now, okay? Right now he's okay and getting the best care from the best military hospital."

He sniffed. "Okay."

I picked up the Popsicle and handed it to him. "Here, you can have the rest. I hear they're magic."

Neal was on my mind all day, the image of him lying on a hospital bed stuck in my mind, so much so that it was starting to affect my performance at work. I couldn't concentrate on the task at hand, finding myself staring off into space for a few seconds before remembering what needed to be done.

On my lunch break, I went online to look up information on Landstuhl Regional Medical Center, searching for protocols on visitation. Just as I was about to search for a plane ticket to Germany, my phone rang with Patrick's number.

"He's out of surgery," the older man said with a little more life in his voice. "They are transferring him stateside at the end of the week."

I sat up, my heart thumping wildly. "And his spine?"

"He woke up and was able to move his toes and fingers, so for the time being they are calling the operation a success. They won't know until later if there's any long-term damage."

I closed my eyes and leaned back into the chair, the tightness in my chest beginning to ease.

"But, Julie," Patrick said, breaking through my short-lived relief, "I have to warn you that Neal could be different. Most people who go over there . . . sometimes they're not the same people who come back."

4

I flew up to Walter Reed Medical Center in Maryland early that Sunday morning. I reread Neal's letters on the plane, savoring each word and imagining where he was when he was writing them, so that by the time the plane landed at Reagan National, I was about to burst with anticipation.

Since the medical facility was inside a base, I had to fill out forms at the gate, after which I was escorted inside.

"I'll leave you here, ma'am," said the young soldier with an affable smile. "Please observe visiting hours."

"Thank you." I turned back to the door, feeling light-headed when I put my hand on the handle. I took a few deep breaths then pushed it open.

The room was typical hospital, gray and sterile, with the blinds drawn. But before they even had a chance to adjust to the dimness, my eyes found Neal. As quietly as I could, I closed the door behind me and walked around the curtain, never looking away from the sleeping figure on the bed.

I stopped, overwhelmed by an onslaught of memory. It wasn't so long ago that I'd come to the hospital for someone I loved, had watched him sleep with various machines beeping all around, needles stuck in his little arms. I'd felt helpless then, as I did now, knowing there was nothing I could do to take away the pain.

I moved toward Neal, my body pulled to his as if by gravity, until I was standing beside the bed. He looked like hell warmed over, with scabbed lacerations on the side of his neck and his cheeks, a large bandage covering most of the back of his neck and head.

I reached out and touched his arm, my fingers caressing the soft hair there, finally daring to believe that he was actually back here and that he was alive.

I sucked in a breath when he opened his eyes, blinking slowly, his pupils dilated.

"Water," he said almost inaudibly.

I looked around and found the cup with a straw and held it up to his lips. He took in a few sips with a pained expression on his face. "More?" I asked.

"No," he said, sounding a little less raspy. It was clear from the glazed look in his eyes that he was still heavily sedated. He grabbed my hand, taking me by surprise. "Nurse, I have to tell you, you bear a striking resemblance to a friend of mine."

"Oh?" I asked, deciding to play along. "Tell me about her."

He gave a sleepy smile then closed his eyes. "She's amazing," he whispered. "She's a bird."

I waited for him to say more but his face relaxed and then his breathing came slower, deeper. I grabbed a chair and set it by his side, once again taking his hand in mine, not planning on going anywhere in the foreseeable future.

I sat up with a start when the door opened, realizing I'd fallen asleep with my head on the mattress. I rubbed my eyes and twisted around to find a man in civilian clothes entering the room, his right arm cradled in a wide sling.

"Oh, I'm sorry," he said upon seeing me. "I didn't know you were sleeping. Sorry, I'll come back."

Neal stirred at the noise, letting out a long breath as he opened his eyes. "Julie?" he croaked, his eyebrows drawing together. He glanced up at the visitor then back to me. "Is this real? Is this another trippy dream?"

"No, I'm real," I said, trying a smile. "And he's real, too, as far as I can tell."

Neal's eyes flicked up to the man with the sling. "Horton," he said with a tired smile. "Good to see you up and about, man."

"You, too." The man named Horton shuffled inside as if his entire body ached, and even though it looked like it hurt, he held out his free hand to me. "I'm Chase Horton."

"Nice to meet you. I'm Julie."

"*The* Julie?" Horton asked, his dark eyes growing wide. "Harding was always sneaking away, writing on his pad of paper. Come to find out, he was writing letters and they were all addressed to you."

"Where the hell are we? Are we still in Germany?" Neal asked, pointedly trying to steer the subject.

"Maryland. We're back in country," Horton said.

Neal turned to me. "What are *you* doing here?"

"To visit Horton, of course," I teased, eliciting a tiny lift in the corner of Neal's mouth.

"Is Will with you?" he asked, his eyes flicking around the room.

"No, I left him with Stacy. I wasn't sure what to expect. I didn't want him to freak out in case . . ."

"In case my face looked like raw hamburger?"

I ignored his words and dug around in my purse, taking out the card Will had made. "He asked me to give you this."

Neal reached out and lifted it above his face, reading the note that Will had written the previous night along with the drawings of satellite dishes and their counterparts in space.

"He wanted to know what you did in Afghanistan, so we did a little bit of research based on what you'd written me and that's the best we could come up with."

"It's actually not that far off," Neal said. "We'd make sure the dishes were all pointed in the right direction, make sure the Internet and phone lines worked, set up e-mail accounts, all sorts of boring computer stuff. Occasionally, we'd also go to a new base to set up their communications, which is what we were doing when we hit an IED and were ambushed."

Horton held up the arm in the sling and it was only then I realized there was only a stump covered in gauze where his hand should have been. "I'm lucky to have only lost one limb. The other guys with us were not so lucky."

I turned to Neal. "Were you all in the same unit?"

"No," Neal said. "Some were Marines."

Horton shook his head, sighing. "I haven't had a chance to thank you yet, man."

"Forget about it," Neal said, looking up at the metal grid of the ceiling.

Horton shut his mouth and just nodded.

"What did you do?" I asked. When Neal didn't speak, I turned to Horton for answers. "What did he do?"

"He hasn't told you?" he asked incredulously.

"No."

"It was nothing," Neal said, continuing to glare holes in the ceiling.

"It wasn't fucking nothing," Horton said, clearly agitated. "He saw the rocket coming and shoved me out of the way. Basically, this humble motherfucker saved my life."

My head swiveled around to Neal, but the feeling of awe quickly dissipated as it dawned on me that he, who had confessed he was not afraid to die, had purposefully thrown himself in the way of a rocket grenade.

"You or any of the other guys would have done the same," Neal said.

"No. I think any normal person's reaction would have been to duck." Horton smacked Neal's foot under the sheet, then apologized when Neal grimaced. "Sorry. I forgot it was that leg."

"Should've used you as a shield instead," Neal said with forced levity.

He lifted his stump. "Anyway, man, I'm getting discharged today, but I'll be back in a few weeks to get fitted with a prosthetic and then comes physical therapy and all that bullshit. How about you?"

Neal glanced at me. "I'll be here a while. Docs want to make sure there's no permanent damage to my spine, then I have to undergo physical therapy."

Horton walked over to the other side of the bed and shook Neal's hand, a look of understanding passing between them. "I'll see you later," he said then turned to me. "Nice to meet you, Julie."

"You, too." Once Horton had crossed the room and closed the door behind him, I turned back to Neal. "You threw yourself in front of the rocket?"

"No. Horton's exaggerating. I just pushed him aside."

"Still, you risked your life for him."

"Yes."

I stared at him, trying to make sense of everything. "Neal, you might not care if you die, but I do."

"I care." He took a deep breath and let it out slowly. "You know what went through my mind when that rocket exploded behind me?" he asked, then added with a tiny grin, "Well, apart from hoping that my nuts didn't get blown off."

My lips twitched but I remained, for the most part, angry. "What?"

"I thought, 'Not today.'" He held out his palm and waited until I placed my hand on it. "I thought of you—and Will—and decided I wasn't ready to go. Before I blacked out and hit the ground, I told Death to go fuck himself."

My vision blurred and I swiped at my eyes before he noticed that I was crying. It occurred to me then that it was valor that made him risk his life, not a death wish like I'd thought. "You told me you were ready to die at any given moment."

"I've since changed my mind." His gaze was warm when he lifted his hand up to my cheek.

We were quiet for long moments, just staring at each other, the girl who was afraid of death and the boy who willingly courted it. But despite it all, I loved him and needed him in my life.

I sat on the edge of the bed and leaned down, touching my lips to his. He responded, gently at first, then he brought his hand up to the back of my neck and deepened the kiss. When he tried to sit up, he grunted and made a pained noise.

"You okay? What happened?" I asked, pulling away.

He wrenched his eyes shut and settled back, taking in deep breaths. "I got a little too eager there," he said between his teeth.

"I wanted to thank you for the birthday surprises," I said, running the backs of my fingers against the short stubble on his cheeks.

"You're welcome. How did it go? Did the dress fit?"

I told him about the party, regaling him with a couple of stories—how Naomi had gotten so drunk she almost fell in the pool and how Will had stuck his finger in the cake before I'd even had a chance to blow the candles out.

"I wish I could have been there to see your reaction when you went out onto that balcony," he said, his eyes blazing across my face. "I hope you enjoyed your party."

"I did, but I spent the entire time waiting for you to show up," I confessed. "And it made me realize something."

"What's that?"

"That I was stupid for letting all those things come between us. I kept looking for reasons to push you away because I was afraid of how I felt about you," I said. "I was scared to lose control of my emotions . . . because you do that to me. You have this hold on me, and even months of trying to pretend you don't exist didn't ease it. If anything, it made it worse. And then when I found out you were seriously hurt . . ."

He squeezed my hand. "Hey, I'm still here."

"I'm just glad I'm not too late to tell you that I'll wait for you." I placed a hand on his chest, over his beating heart. "I want to be with you."

His eyes flew across my face, his features impassive.

My heart sank. I didn't know what to expect, but indifference was definitely not something I'd ever anticipated. His letters had made me believe he wanted the same; so why then was he acting like none of this mattered?

"What about Jason's letter?" he finally asked.

I swallowed hard. "I was so angry with you for withholding that letter from me. I'd convinced myself it was because I couldn't trust you, but I think it goes deeper than that." I shook my head. "Just the thought of receiving a letter like that from you . . . it tore me up. I didn't think I could go through it again."

"So . . . you're not afraid anymore?"

"Oh, I'm still scared as hell. I don't think I'll never *not* be afraid for you when you go to a war zone. And I'll always fear that Will will grow up and want to join the military. But I've come to accept that those are all things beyond my control."

His eyes flew across my face, dark brown in the dim hospital room. "If you'd asked me a year ago how I'd feel if I were to die, I'd have told you that I'd go with a smile because I've lived a full life. But that was before I met you, before I realized that there was more to life than travel and money. I always thought my mom was shortchanged because she died so young, but now I know she died with a full heart." He took hold of my hand and pressed it against his chest. "*I'm* the one who's been shortchanging myself all this time, traveling around, watching life happen from a distance."

"So stop and stay," I whispered.

The corners of his mouth tugged up and finally I was able to release the breath I'd been holding. "I think I will."

5

Angela, one of the older students in my Wednesday class, came up to me one afternoon after our class had ended. "Miss Love . . ."

I turned to her with a raised eyebrow. "I thought it was Miss Lovely."

"We shortened it," she said with a sheepish smile. "I can't figure out the part of the choreography where you bend down and stick your leg out."

"Okay, here, let me show you in half time." I took the position and placed one hand on the back of my head and with the other grabbed my stomach as I crouched forward, my knees bending outward. Then I lifted my leg and extended it in front of me along with the corresponding hand, stepping forward then right, swooping my leg back around. "Now you try."

Angela tried the move, and I stood beside her, making adjustments as she went along. I stood back, my chest swelling with pride as she tried three times before finally nailing the move.

"It was the swoop that was giving me the most trouble," she said. "But I think I got it."

"Keep practicing at home. Pretty soon your muscles will remember what to do."

"Okay, I will. Thanks, Miss Love," Angela said, waving before she met up with her mom by the door. I waved good-bye, filled with a sense of satisfaction. So this job wasn't as glamorous as performing on a stage, but I was helping to shape the lives of these kids, fostering the love of dance. And that, in many ways, was more gratifying.

When I was the only one left in the building, I turned off the overhead lights and began to put away anything out of place around the edges of the room, thinking about when I'd get to visit Neal next. Will and I had flown to Maryland a few times to visit him in the hospital as he recuperated from his injuries, cheering him on as he went through the process of physical therapy.

It had been two months since he was admitted to that hospital; the doctors said he'd probably need to stay one month more. For Will and me, who had made room in our house and were ready to start our life with Neal, it felt like forever.

I was deep in thought, lacing up a pair of tap shoes, and didn't notice the door opening. It was only after someone called my name that I finally looked up.

There in the doorway stood Neal, in jeans and a button-down shirt, looking larger than life in the late afternoon light.

"Hi," he said with a crooked grin.

"You're back." I stood frozen in place, my muscles apparently forgetting how to move. I blinked a few times, sure that if I cleared my head, I'd realize he was just a mirage.

"I'm back," he said in his deep, smooth voice as he stepped across the threshold. His hair had grown a little longer and he was clean shaven, but though he appeared put together, his eyes belied the riot of emotions inside. "The hospital released me this morning."

I took in a deep, shuddering breath, then I was crossing the room and colliding with his strong, hard body. I hugged him tight, pressing my face into the crook of his neck and breathing in his cool scent. "I can't believe you're here."

He wrapped his arms around me, pressing his palms flat on my back, and kissed the top of my head. "Me, either."

I turned my face up to his and drew his head down for a kiss that quickly turned into something more, our hands and mouths moving everywhere.

He pulled away, breathing hard. "Are we alone?" he asked, looking around.

"Yes." I reached behind him and flipped the lock on the door then closed all the blinds in the room, cloaking the room in near darkness. "Now we are."

"Will? Carol?"

"Carol's away at a conference and Will is at a birthday party," I said with a smile. "And classes are over for the rest of the day."

Neal walked toward me, a slight limp in his step, and took hold of my hips. "Perfect," he said before pulling me against him and letting me know how happy he was to be back. He bent down and dragged his lips along my exposed jaw, breathing low and raspy against my tingling skin. "It's been torture, seeing you at the hospital but never getting to do more than kiss you."

I closed my eyes and tilted my head back, running my nails along his scalp and feeling the scars at the base of his skull. "The feeling is mutual, I assure you."

"I've had dreams," he ground out. "So many dreams."

"Tell me about them," I whispered, feeling dazed and hypnotized.

"I dream about you under me, moaning as you drag your nails along my back. I dream about bending you over the couch and taking you from behind. I dream about you giving me a lap dance, stripping only for me."

I pulled away.

"It's just a fantasy, Julie. I'm not trying to objectify you," Neal said when I walked off to the other side of the room.

I came back with a chair and set it down at the center of the room. "Sit."

His eyes widened and he came over, towering over me with a question in his eyes.

"I'm going to give you something to really dream about," I said, and pushed him down onto the chair. I walked over to the sound system and put on a song, grinning as the first guitar licks filled the room.

"Nice," he said with a laugh as "Pour Some Sugar on Me" began to play.

I sauntered back to him, kicking off my shoes one at a time, coming to a stop between his legs. I let my hair down, flicking the elastic at his chest, then set my hands on his thighs and performed a dip, flipping my hair back as I dragged my chest along his body and face. "Take your shirt off," I whispered, biting his lobe before straightening up and pivoting around. I bent at the waist and grasped my ankles, sliding my hands up the insides of my legs as I straightened.

Neal threw aside his shirt, hissing when I traced my fingers along his collarbone and shoulders as I walked all the way around him. With a heated look, I reached for the ties on my wraparound shirt, tugging each one loose as his eyes followed my every move. "For the record, I've never done this before."

His lips parted when I pulled away the shirt from my chest to reveal my lacy black bra. "You're so beautiful," he said, his wide chest rising and falling as he reached for me.

I came closer, kicking one leg up over his thigh, then the other, until I sat straddling him, gyrating my hips into his rock-hard erection. He trailed his hands up my back until they reached my bra, his fingers making short work of the hooks. With a smile playing along his mouth, he slid the straps off my shoulders, pressing his lips to my skin before peeling the bra away from my chest.

He gasped audibly, making me laugh out loud at its comic effect. "Excited much?" I asked.

He grinned up at me as he pressed his hands to my shoulder blades. "I've wanted to do this for the longest time," he said before he buried his face between my breasts and shook his head side to side, jiggling my breasts around.

I laughed but it quickly died in my throat when he stopped, his forehead pressed against my collarbone as his hot breath came rapidly. His hands slid around to the front to cup the sides of my breasts, and he turned his face to one side, his tongue dragging along large swaths of my skin until his mouth found my nipple.

I threw my head back and enjoyed the attention he was giving to my breasts, continuing to swivel my hips on his lap. Then his hands dropped to my waist, stilling me.

"You're going to make me come right here with your magic hips," he said, his breath coming out fast.

I dismounted him just as the music changed over to an R&B song with a deep bass beat.

"Do you have a stripping playlist or something?" he asked.

I quirked up one eyebrow. "I've been planning this for a while." I ran my fingers along the sides of my breasts, down my waist, and into the waistband of my black leggings. Then I bent forward so that my breasts were hanging mere inches from his face and slid my pants down my legs, keeping my black thong in place. I tipped forward and pressed a quick kiss on his lips before pulling away, lifting my hands into my hair, sliding my hips up and down like a belly dancer.

As he watched me, his fingers worked on his belt and zipper, lifting his ass up off the chair as he freed his rigid cock. He wrapped his fingers around its base and squeezed. I turned around and shook my ass at him, lifting my hair out of the way as I gave him a sultry look over my shoulder.

He grinned then raised his hand, landing a smack on my ass cheek. I gasped and he did it again on the other cheek, his eyes flashing in excitement.

I raised an eyebrow. "You like that, do you?"

"Ungh, come here," he said a second before he grabbed my thong and pulled me back toward him. He slid a finger along the crease of my ass down to my cleft, hooking his finger into the damp fabric and pulling it aside.

I took hold of his thick shaft and positioned him at my entrance, sliding the swollen head through my folds a few times before slowly lowering onto it. He groaned long and loud when I slid down, sheathing him completely.

I closed my eyes and savored the thickness of him, my insides quivering at the sweet invasion.

He pressed his face into my back, his hands digging into my hips, and gasped, "You feel so good."

I moaned when he began to guide me up and down on his lap, setting my hands on his thighs for support. But as good as this felt, I needed more, needed to see the pleasure and anguish on his face as we made love. So I stood up, feeling a loss when he popped out.

"What . . . where are you going?" he asked in a panic.

I turned around, biting back a smile, and straddled him once again, hooking my feet onto the rungs of the chair. A sigh escaped from my lips when he filled me once again. I wrapped my arms around his shoulders and began to rock my hips back and forth so that my clit was rubbing against him in a delicious way, my gaze never straying from his face.

When I sped up, his mouth fell open and his eyes squeezed shut. To see his normally calm exterior so shaken did strange things to me, and I brought my mouth down on his, kissing him as I moved faster, squeezed harder. All too soon I was coming, quivering around him.

Neal grabbed my hips and slammed me onto his cock two more times before he became rigid, muffling his cries as he came and came, his ass lifting up off the chair.

He bent his head to my chest, his breath cooling my damp skin. I kissed the top of his head, my entire body trembling from the force of having this man in my arms again, thanking all the gods for keeping him safe, for giving me one more chance to get it right.

6

"Sign here," Bob said, leaning over the table to point to the obvious. After Neal scribbled his signature, Bob flipped the page and pointed to another line with the word *signature* written under it. "Sign here again."

After all was said and done, he stood up and shook Neal's hand then shook mine, too, for good measure. He called to someone to bring the car around, then led us out of the glass-walled office. "You're really gonna love this car, Mrs. Harding," he said to me while we waited at the curb.

I opened my mouth to correct him when Neal took hold of my hand and said, "Yep. She definitely will." He grinned down at me, mischief in his eyes, then slid something onto my finger.

With my heart thundering in my chest, I looked down to find my silver ring, a little nicked in places but still whole.

"Someday," Neal whispered. "It doesn't have to be today, but someday."

I swallowed and nodded, gazing up at the handsome man beside me, imagining being his wife.

"There she is," Captain Obvious said when the metallic-blue

Jeep Grand Cherokee rolled around the corner. Neal broke away from me to get the key, smiling as he got into the driver's seat. "She purrs like a kitten," Bob said.

After five more minutes of cheesy lines and handshaking, we were finally on our way in Neal's brand-new vehicle.

"This is fancy," I said, sliding my hand along the black leather seat. "I think I could get used to these heated *and* cooled leather seats."

He smiled over at me. "I think I could get used to seeing you there."

"I meant the driver seat."

He reached over and set his hand on my thigh.

I sat back in the seat and sighed, a content smile on my face. "So where to next?"

"How about we go pick up Will from school?"

"School's not over for another forty-five minutes."

"That's perfect," he said. "It'll give us plenty of time to buy him a booster seat for this car."

"Hey!" Will said when we walked up to the front of his school. He threw his arms around my waist then gave Neal a high five. "Wait a minute, why are you guys both picking me up?" he asked through narrowed eyes.

"I took the afternoon off to help Neal go shopping," I said, taking his hand and leading him back to the car.

He reached out for Neal and linked us all together, swinging our arms as we walked across the parking lot. "What did you buy? Is it something for me?"

Neal laughed. "Not exactly."

We stopped in front of the car; the lights flashed when Neal unlocked it remotely.

Will's eyes were big when he put two and two together. "You bought a Jeep?" he asked Neal.

"Yep. I was getting tired of rental cars and taxis."

"You didn't sell your plane, right?"

"Nope. Still have the Lancair."

"Does this mean you're really going to stick around?" Will asked.

Neal crouched down to face Will. "I have every intention of staying."

"Forever?"

Neal pinched his nose. "For as long as humanly possible."

That night, Will once again pleaded to eat ramen noodles for dinner.

"But it's my favorite!" he said when I told him no.

"I know it's your favorite, but it's not healthy," Neal said from the stove. "Besides, I cooked your second favorite."

"Mac and cheese?" Will asked hopefully.

"Okay, then, your third favorite."

"Spaghetti?"

"Bingo!" Neal set a plate down in front of Will then grated fresh Parmesan on top.

"You ready to eat?" Neal called out to where I sat on the floor, stretching my legs in front of the mirror.

"Almost." When I was done, I got up and joined them at the kitchen table, smiling up gratefully when Neal set a plate in front of me. "Thank you."

He kissed the top of my head then sat down at his seat.

"Should we move the stuff back to the actual living room so we can have a formal dining room for a change?" I asked as Neal shredded cheese on both of our plates.

He shook his head without hesitation. “Why? You love having your own little dance studio.”

I shrugged and turned my attention back to the food before me. I swirled my fork around then brought it up to my mouth, groaning in surprise when the flavors hit my taste buds. “Oh, my God, this is so good,” I said after I’d swallowed the first bite. I looked down at my plate. “This is not the Prego in the pantry.”

He shook his head, the skin around his eyes crinkling. “It’s my mom’s recipe.”

I took another bite. “It’s delicious.”

He set his fork down, studying me. “You would have liked her,” he said. “And she probably would’ve disliked you.”

“What?!”

“At first,” he said, laughing and holding his palms up. “Only at first. She didn’t think anyone was good enough for her son.”

I pursed my lips and glanced at Will. “I guess I can understand that.”

“But you would have won her over. She’d have been grateful that you took pity on her little wandering son and gave him a place to call home.”

“I’m grateful to her, too,” I said with a smile. “For this recipe. And for giving birth to you.”

After we put Will to bed, Neal and I checked the doors and turned off all the lights then went upstairs to our room.

He took off his clothes and stood beside me at the bathroom sink in only his gray boxer briefs, his muscular body on full display. He’d been living with us for two weeks, and still the sight of him like this, standing nearly naked beside me in front of the mirror, never failed to steal the breath from my lungs.

“You’re staring,” Neal said with one cocky eyebrow raised.

"I'm just wondering if it's actually possible to have a ten-pack," I teased.

With his toothbrush in his mouth, he flexed, allowing me to count each raised, delineated muscle. "Eight," I said, shaking my head. "You're a slacker."

His mouth stretched out into a foamy smile. "I need to do more exercises that include the plank position, then."

I palmed his butt and squeezed. "Perhaps that can be arranged later," I said on the way out. "Hey, have you seen my iPad?" I asked before leaving the bathroom.

"In the office," he mumbled around the toothbrush.

I went down the hall to what had once been the guest bedroom, but since Neal needed a quiet place to work, we'd pushed the bed against the wall to make room for a desk and chair. Sometimes we'd find Will up there, drawing on his notebook with the smartpen, claiming to be "working," but mostly it was a place for Neal to find solace when the reality of what had happened in Afghanistan hit him, when he needed to sit by himself for a little while and sift through his thoughts.

I found my iPad on the table, like Neal had said. When I picked it up, I noticed Will's notebook with the smartpen lying on top, blinking red for record. I pressed the little stop button on the side, making a mental note to remind Will about conserving battery. Curiosity got the best of me and I pressed the back button to listen to his last recorded message, holding the pen up to my ear.

A computer chair creaked, the sound it made when someone sat on it. From the long length of silence, with only paper rustling and the pen scratching discernibly, it became clear Will hadn't meant to be recording.

Then Will started mumbling, that thing he'd described as talking to his guardian angel. "Did I tell you I have a big game on Saturday?" he asked. "My team's going to play this other team who's really, really good. They've won two games in a row. But I'm pretty sure we'll kick their butts because I've been practicing my soccer drills. I even score goals all the time now. Neal tells me to just keep practicing so I can get better."

He paused. "I like Neal. He loves me and my mom a lot. And he has his own plane. And he has a scar on his stomach just like mine. Mommy was scared for him when he got hurt, but I knew you would watch over him like you watch over me. I knew you wouldn't let him die."

He stopped talking when the door squeaked open and Neal spoke. "Hey, bud, who are you talking to?"

"My dad," Will said in the same matter-of-fact tone he'd used with me.

Neal's voice sounded closer. "Oh, yeah? What were you telling him?"

"About things," Will replied. "Do you think he can actually hear me?"

"I bet he can," Neal said without hesitation. "And I'm pretty sure he's got a big smile on his face because he's so proud of you."

"How do you know?"

"I'm not your dad and *I'm* proud of you. Can you imagine how your own dad feels?"

"Do you think your mom is proud of you?"

"I hope so," Neal said, and cleared his throat. "At the very least, I think she'll be happy that I have you guys."

"Are you going to marry my mom?"

"Uh . . ." Neal was quiet for a second, then, "I don't think she's ready for it yet. I just moved in, so we're still trying to figure things out."

"Don't you want to marry her?"

"I do, I really do. One day, bud, I'm going to drop down on one knee and ask her, and she'll say yes. But not yet."

"After you get better?"

There was a long pause, then Neal said, "What do you mean?"

"Sometimes you're really quiet and you don't smile. Remember, this morning I was telling you a joke and you didn't even laugh."

"Yeah. I'm sorry. Sometimes I get really sad when I think about what happened over there. It doesn't mean I stopped listening to you or paying attention. It just takes a little while for me to stop being sad," Neal said in a soft voice.

"You can think about something that makes you happy."

"I do," Neal said with a smile in his voice. "I think about you and your mom."

Will snorted. "Lame," he said a moment before bursting into delighted laughter.

Neal gave a short clap. "Well, I've got to start cooking and you have to do homework. Meet you downstairs in a few minutes?"

"Okay." The door creaked shut and the pen scratching across paper started up again. He was quiet for a long moment then said softly, "Neal told me before that you were up in heaven, looking down at me. Is that true? Can you see me when I'm playing Legos or when I don't eat my peas? Or when I hurt myself and want to cry but I don't because I want to be tough like you?" Then in a wavery voice, he whispered, "Dad, are you happy?"

In the background, my voice could be heard shouting up the stairs, reminding Will to start his homework.

"I have to go and do homework," Will said on a sigh. "But is it okay if I call Neal 'Dad,' too?"

I turned off the pen when the recording ended and it was only when I was setting it back down that I noticed the drawings in his notebook. Will had drawn kids kicking a soccer ball, a car with JEEP written across it, a woman standing on her toes with her arms outstretched, a man flying a prop plane. Up at the top corner of the lined page was a cloud and peeking around it was a face, smiling, watching it all take place.

With a tightness in my chest, I crept into Will's room and kissed his sleepy head, wishing more than anything that he'd known his father. "He's happy, Will," I whispered, hoping he'd hear me in the dream world. "Knowing how you turned out, I don't know how he couldn't be."

Back in the master bedroom, I found Neal on the bed, lying on his stomach.

"Did you find it?" he asked, his voice muffled by the pillow.

I undressed and crawled into bed, stretching along the entire length of his body. I touched a finger to his shoulder and felt the raised white scars that lay scattered across his arm and back, then pressed my lips to the puckered patch of skin on the base of his skull where hair no longer grew. "Yes, I definitely did."

He shivered when my lips traveled downward, to the bird with outstretched wings. I laid my head on the expanse of skin between his shoulder blades and breathed him in, savoring his warmth against my cheek. "I could stay here all night."

He gave an appreciative moan, the sound rumbling through his back.

"Do you feel at home here?"

He rolled to the side, throwing me onto my back, and before I knew it, he was hovering over me, studying me with a dark expression on his face. "I feel at home with you," he said, his voice husky with emotion.

I wound my arm around the back of his head and pulled him down, our lips parting for a kiss that spoke volumes about love and passion. And later, when he slid home and touched the deepest part of me, I realized that Neal and I were more than an optical illusion, that once in a great while, the ocean finds a way to create a wave so immense, so powerful, that it can rise up and kiss the sky.

EPILOGUE

"Let me see that sweet little baby!" Elodie said, rushing us at the door of their house in Monterey.

"Me?" Will asked, pointing to himself.

"No, she means me," Neal said behind him, eliciting chuckles all around.

Elodie smiled at the group gathered at her stoop. "You're all wonderful, really, but I was talking about Lucy."

Neal and I stepped aside to let Henry through, who had a near-one-year-old cradled in one arm. "She fell asleep in the car," he said in a hushed voice.

"I'm surprised she didn't wake up when we took her out of the car seat," Elsie said, hugging her mom then setting down the various diaper bags and baby items on the floor.

"Well, look who's all here!" John's voice boomed throughout the house as he came toward us with open arms; we all quickly turned to him with fingers up to our lips.

"Henry, are you ever going to let me hold my granddaughter?" Elodie asked with a teasing grin as we all migrated to the family room.

Elsie chuckled. "Good luck with that."

Henry smiled over at his wife then down at the sweet little bundle in his arms. After a few moments he gently—if a little reluctantly—handed her over to her grandmother. "I didn't want to wake her. She didn't sleep much on the plane," he said.

John looked around the room. "It's good to see everyone again in one place," he said, looking very pleased. "Henry, how's the beat?"

His son-in-law shrugged, well aware of everyone's curious gaze. "It's fine, sir. Doing better."

"I imagine having a baby adds to the stress."

"It's the opposite, actually," Henry said. "Elsie and Lucy are my glue. No matter what I go through out there, coming home to them at the end of my shift keeps me together."

Elsie leaned over and kissed his cheek, her face aglow as she stared up at her husband.

"And you, Neal," John said, turning to the man sitting beside me. "Any deployments on the horizon?"

He shook his head. "No, sir. We're not in the bucket. Right now we're in the training part of the cycle."

"I thought for sure, with your injuries, that you could have gotten out with disability," Elsie said.

Neal glanced at me before saying, "I could have. But I didn't want out just yet."

It had taken me a while to understand Neal's commitment to the military, but I finally got it: sometimes when you find something you really love, you hold on for as long as you can, no matter the cost.

John nodded. "And your other job?"

"That is going pretty well," Neal replied.

"Three giant technology companies are currently in a bidding war on a program he's been working on all year," I said.

Neal's shoulders lifted in a casual shrug. "But I can't really talk about it with the nondisclosure agreements."

Elsie went over to an antique steamer trunk in the corner of the family room and pulled out a long red box. "Anyone up for a game of Scrabble?"

"You know I am," John said, getting to his feet. "It's been a while since I kicked your butt."

"Oh, can I play?" Will asked, jumping up. "But I don't know how."

"Sure," Elsie said, leading the way to the kitchen table, which her dad had already cleared for the game.

Henry swooped in from behind and lifted Will up over his shoulder. "I'll help you out," he said as Will laughed. "You are getting way too heavy."

"Soon I'll be as big as you!" Will cried, and I sat there, watching them leave, knowing it was only a matter of time before that was true.

Later, as we got dressed in what used to be Elsie's old room but was now a guest room, I said to Neal, "Do you ever think about being a dad?"

He raised an eyebrow as he put on his Air Force wings cuff links. "I know Will is not my biological son, but I already feel like a dad."

"I mean, having a kid with your own DNA."

He smiled. "Are you trying to tell me something?"

I turned away, pretending I needed his help zipping up my dress. "No. I was just wondering if you've ever thought about it."

He clasped my dress together then pressed a soft kiss to the base of my neck. "Julie, I'm very happy with what I have right now. You, me, and Will."

"So you never think about having a baby with me?" I asked, turning to face him.

"Why does this sound like a trick question?" he asked with eyebrows drawn. "Aren't you, uh, sterilized?"

"There are ways. In vitro being one of them."

There was a long silence that followed, when we were both lost in our thoughts as we finished getting ready.

Neal was first to break the silence. "Do you? I mean, will you want a baby later on?" he asked, sitting on the edge of the bed.

"I don't. But if you wanted to, I'd be open to it."

He gathered me close between his legs, looking up at me. "Julie, I don't need a baby as proof that what we have is real, that we're a real family. I have you and Will, and that's more than enough."

I nodded, brushing my fingers across the back of his neck, and bent down to touch my lips to his. "So you're really fine with everything? Living with us in Dallas?"

"Are you?"

I paused, staring down at the handsome man before me in his formal uniform, thinking about the past year that we'd lived together. "Yes. I couldn't ask for more."

Elodie and John's thirty-fifth wedding anniversary party was held in the grand ballroom in Herrmann Hall, at the Naval Postgraduate School. It had once been a resort hotel visited by the likes of Charlie Chaplin and Jean Harlow but was now owned by the U.S. Navy.

Service members and civilians alike attended the formal party, many of them retired officers who had once held powerful positions in the military and who wore their many accomplishments proudly on their chests. Neal looked gallant in his mess dress—the military's version of a formal suit—and I couldn't have been prouder to stand by his side.

All night people came up to him, asking about the Purple Heart pinned on his jacket, and all night he tried to deflect the attention by talking about anything *but* that heart-shaped medal.

"Poor Neal," Elsie said when I sat down at the table where she was feeding Lucy some mashed carrots. "He doesn't seem to enjoy all the attention, does he?"

We looked across the room at Neal talking to two men—one with an eagle insignia on his suit and one with enlisted stripes. "Who is he talking to?" I asked.

"I'm not sure who they are, but one is a full-bird colonel and the other is a chief master sergeant, the highest enlisted rank." She wiped at Lucy's chin with a cloth napkin. "No wonder he's nervous. Those guys are pretty influential."

I watched Neal talk, taking note of the stiffness of his back. "He just doesn't like talking about the attack, so of course that's all everyone wants to talk about."

"Did he suffer from PTSD when he came back?"

"I don't know. Maybe," I said. "He seems the same, but sometimes you can tell he's in a dark place when he gives monosyllabic answers. During those times, he kind of hides away—either works in the office for several hours or works on his plane—and when he comes back, he's back to normal. It doesn't happen quite as often these days, though." I looked at her. "Was Henry the same way?"

She gave a sad smile. "Not exactly. He used to keep it inside, too, but then it ate away at his confidence until he started to crumble." She blinked a few times. "But he's really trying. God, the year before we had Lucy was . . ."

I touched her hand, remembering the state she'd been in when she came to our door unexpectedly the year before, pregnant and hysterical. "It's okay now," I said. "You two went through hell, and now look at you, stronger than ever."

Elsie looked across the room at her husband, who was talking animatedly with a few people. "Just call me Orpheus, saving my love from Hades."

"Hey, we do whatever it takes to protect those we love. That's our very own warrior ethos."

Elsie smiled, her eyes bright with understanding. "Hoorah."

I woke up early the next morning to a hand on my breast, my nipple pinched between two fingers.

"Wake up," a husky voice whispered by my ear.

I rolled away and burrowed under the blanket. "It's too early."

"Wake up, Julie, or I'll be forced to deploy my secret weapon," he said with amusement in his voice. When I didn't respond, he nudged at me from behind with said secret weapon.

"That torpedo was already deployed last night," I grumbled.

He chuckled and nipped at my shoulder. "Twice, if I remember correctly," he said. "But that's not what I'm talking about."

"Then what?"

"This," he said and tickled my sides, making me squirm around the bed, trying to keep from waking the entire house with my laughter.

"Stop! Okay, I give up!" I cried, throwing my hands up. "I'm awake."

He pulled away with a grin on his face and slid a palm up my exposed stomach and into the thin fabric of my shirt. "The secret weapon saves the day."

I looked up at him, brushing hair away from my face. "Why are you waking me so early, anyway? It's not even light out yet."

He slid his hand up through the collar of my shirt and pinched my chin, tilting my head up to give me a quick kiss. "I figured we could watch the sun rise then go for a run," he said against my lips. "Like old times."

My body tingled at the memory and I lifted my head to kiss him again. "Only if you can keep up."

Carmel Beach was chilly that early in the morning, even with our fleece sweatshirts on. Still, we stood together at the edge of the waves and waited for the sun to bathe the world with light. Neal wrapped an arm around my shoulder and I hugged his side as brilliant colors erupted around us, the intense pinks and purples making way for the peach-colored hues as the sun began its ascent in the sky.

Neal cradled my face in his hands and kissed me, his lips soft as they parted mine, his tongue gentle and probing as it dipped inside. I stood on my toes and deepened the kiss, my body coming alive, reacting to him with urgency and need.

After long moments, he pulled away and gazed down at me with a furrowed brow, breathing hard. But just when I thought he was going to tell me some earth-shattering news, perhaps that he was getting deployed again, his face brightened. "Race you," he said and took off.

It took me a second to recover before I ran after him, my competitive instinct surging. After I caught up to him we jogged for almost a mile down the beach, our footsteps light on the sand, the wind blowing around us. When I closed my eyes for a few seconds it felt like I was truly flying.

We stopped when we came across enormous dark lines on the sand and a man with a small rake. Neal and I stood at the edge of the marked area, trying to catch our breath while the man dragged his rake, creating a giant, intricate sand drawing.

"Come on. We can see it better up there," Neal said, starting toward a tall dune covered in rocks and plants.

I followed him up, finding it difficult to gain traction on the sandy slope. Neal held his hand out and pulled me up, helping to dust off my sandy running capris.

I turned to look at the drawing on the sand, blown away by the elaborate design the man—the artist, really—was carving onto the beach. He had drawn hundreds of interlocked feathers, some big, some small, all intricate and beautiful.

"I've never seen anything like it," I said as the artist completed the final feather and moved closer to the water, where he scratched out some letters on the sand where every wave threatened to wash them away. "What's he writing?"

I shielded my eyes from the sun and watched closely as the man wrote a *J*, then a *U*, *L*, *I*, and *E* in quick succession before they were carried off to sea.

My heart stuttered.

M-A-R-R-Y

I held my breath.

M-E

"So, will you?" Neal whispered by my ear, coming up behind me and sliding his arms around my waist. "Marry me?"

He lifted his left hand up to the sun, fingers spread out, a delicate diamond ring sitting on the end of his ring finger.

I stared at the princess-cut diamond sparkling in the morning light, then took hold of the strong hand that was offering it and pressed it against my heart. I didn't say anything; I simply closed my eyes and felt peace washing over me.

"I love you, Julie Grace Keaton. You're the calm in my heart and the air in my lungs and I will need you always."

I spun around in his arms, sure that my face was glowing. "Yes," I whispered without doubt or reservation, feeling like a tiny sun was lighting me up from the inside. "I will."